This book is due for return on or before the last date shown
above; it may, subject to the book not being reserved by
another reader, be renewed by personal application, post, or
telephone, quoting this date and details of the book.

HAMPSHIRE COUNTY COUNCIL
County Library

100%
recycled paper.

Fred Secombe

GOODBYE
CURATE

Fount

An Imprint of HarperCollins*Publishers*

Fount Paperbacks is an imprint of
HarperCollins*Religious*
Part of HarperCollins*Publishers*
77-85 Fulham Palace Road, London W6 8JB

First published in Great Britain by
Michael Joseph Ltd in 1992
This edition published in 1993 by Fount Paperbacks
3 5 7 9 10 8 6 4 2

Copyright © 1992 Fred Secombe

Fred Secombe asserts the moral right to be
identified as the author of this work

A catalogue record for this book
is available from the British Library

ISBN 0 00 627685 7

Printed and bound in Great Britain by
HarperCollins Manufacturing, Glasgow

1

'It's pointless going to the furniture stores, all they have to offer is 1946 utility rubbish. It will fall apart in no time. Auction rooms, here we come!'

Eleanor, my bride-to-be in six weeks' time, surveyed the newly-papered and -painted front room of number 11 Bevan's Row, our future home. Bevan's Row was a street of terraced houses built to accommodate the miners of Pontywen in the 1880s.

'Whatever you say, love. I'm an innocent abroad in these matters.'

'That is an understatement, Frederick. I'm sure you think a Welsh dresser is someone who prepares salads in Aberystwyth. Anyway, what about a visit to the auction rooms in Cardiff tomorrow?'

'If the Vicar will let me switch my day off, that will be fine.'

'I'm sure he will when you tell him the reason.'

My Vicar, Father John Whittaker, had not been long in Pontywen but had succeeded in alienating most of the congregation with his High Church inclinations. However, he was a social climber and was impressed by the fact that his Curate was about to marry a lady doctor, who was the daughter of a doctor.

Our conversation was interrupted by a knock on the door followed by the hesitant entry of Llew, one of the two odd-job men employed by Mr Lloyd Evans, solicitor and landlord, to make the house habitable. For many years it had been occupied by an eccentric spinster who had turned it into a hovel and a refuge for stray cats.

'Morning, both. I 'ope you like the job we've done on this room.'

'Excellent.' said Eleanor. 'I'm sure the rest of your work will be just as good.'

'Wot I was coming to ask was wot colours do you want in the front bedroom? Mr Evans says 'e can't afford to paper it.'

'Oh, does he? You'd better hold your horses until I've had a word with him.'

Our future landlord was a friend of my future father-in-law. Moreover, he was somewhat in awe of the little dynamo I was about to marry.

'Righto, Miss. We'll get on with the bit of rewiring we've got to do.'

He closed the door and bellowed to his mate who was upstairs.

''Arry 'ave you got your auger up there?'

'Can't 'ear you,' came the muffled reply.

'Your auger. 'Ave you got your auger.'

''Old on. I'm coming downstairs.'

'What in heaven's name is his auger?' I enquired of Eleanor. 'I thought an auger was a soothsayer.'

'You're in the big outside world now, Secombe,' she replied. 'The auger Llew is talking about is a bore, like most of the soothsayers you studied in your Latin prose. It's an instrument used for making holes in things and it happens to have an "e" for its penultimate letter instead of a "u".'

'Here endeth the second lesson. Before we get to the third, when are you going to see Mr Lloyd Evans?'

'I do believe you are a wee bit peeved, my dear. In answer to your question, *we* are going to see him now. There's no time like the present.'

We moved into the hall and almost collided with Llew and Harry who were in earnest conversation. Llew was small and desiccated while Harry was big and fat. Inevitably we had christened them Laurel & Hardy, but unlike the cinema duo, the little one was the dominant one.

'Excuse me, Miss. I 'ope you don't mind me asking,' said Llew, 'but could you see Mr Lloyd Evans as soon as possible? We want to finish 'ere by next week because we've got some work to do for the dilapidated Board.'

'Don't worry,' said Eleanor, 'we're off to see him now.'

'What's the dilapidated Board?' she asked once we were outside the house.

'I'm glad it's my turn for the third lesson,' I replied pompously. 'The Board of Dilapidations is the Church's committee for the maintenance and repair of all vicarages and rectories.'

Peals of laughter greeted my explanation.

'What a comment on your Church houses. They must be in a continual state of disrepair – a never ending series of number 11 Bevan's Row.'

Half an hour later we were seated in the office of Mr Lloyd Evans, an elderly widower and the only solicitor in Pontywen.

'To what do I owe the pleasure?' said the white-haired old man.

'I don't think you'll call it a pleasure, Uncle Frank. We'd like you to dig deeper into your pocket, please, and paper the front bedroom. Heaven knows what lies behind the faded, nondescript flowery stuff covering those walls. There could be all kinds of bugs and crevices. You wouldn't like your favourite little girl to be sleeping in a room like that, would you?'

Uncle Frank scratched his chin. His parsimony and his regard for Eleanor were in conflict. The furrowed brow was painful to behold. After an eternity of contemplation, there came a deep sigh which seemed to rack his whole being.

'All right, you win but don't expect any more favours. I haven't a bottomless pocket.'

'Come off it, Uncle. What about all these postwar divorces building up? Anyway, thank you very much indeed.'

She went over to the old man and kissed him gently on the forehead.

'That's what you would call an expensive peck. Remember, I can't afford any more of those.'

So saying, he rose to his feet and ushered us out of his office.

As Eleanor forecast, the Vicar was quite amenable to the change in my day off.

'Certainly, Fred. Have tomorrow off by all means. You can't live in an empty house. It gets most uncomfortable sitting on the floor all the time.' It was one of his rare attempts at humour.

'By the way,' he went on. 'I have decided to take a fortnight off before your wedding. Next Sunday evening, straight after service, I shall be off to Tenby to stay with relatives. I feel I need a break after all the turmoil of the past months. Needless to say, I want you to take charge of the parish and of your fellow Curate.'

My fellow Curate was Charles Wentworth-Baxter, an ecclesiastical misfit 'born to trouble as the sparks fly upwards'.

'I'm sure I can cope with the parish but Charles will be a different proposition. However, I'll do my best.'

When I arrived at my lodgings, 13 Mountain View, my landlady Mrs Richards, an elderly Mrs Malaprop, greeted me with the news that I had a caller waiting for me in my room.

'It's that Vicar of Abergwynlais. You know, the one with the high voice and the roaming nose.'

The Reverend Arthur Bowen's Roman proboscis was the one fascinating feature of a chinless face. He was in his early seventies, tall and thin, supported by long legs which looked like stilts in trousers. Abergwynlais was a mining village which had been his incumbency for thirty years or more.

He was noted for his indolence. It was said that on one occasion a relative of an old lady, a member of the congregation who had been bed-bound for several years, came to the Vicarage to inform him that she was at death's door. Apparently the Vicar had not paid a visit for the whole of the time she had been confined to the house. He arrived at the old lady's bedside and said, 'I'm sorry I haven't been to see you before but I've had the flu.'

When I entered my room, he rose from my armchair and advanced on me with his arm outstretched.

'How are you, Mr Secombe,' he squeaked. 'I hear from John Whittaker that you are getting married.'

His cold, bony handshake was unnerving. I felt as if I had caught hold of a bunch of keys.

'I am indeed, Vicar, in six weeks' time.'

'Well, that's why I am here. I am retiring in a few months' time. I have laboured long enough in the Lord's vineyard. I think the hour has come for me to lay down my arms.'

He went on to explain that by laying down his arms in the Lord's vineyard, he had furniture I might like to buy. Moving to a smaller house necessitated a big reduction in his goods and chattels.

'Perhaps you and your young lady would care to come and see.'

'It's very kind of you, Vicar. Would it be convenient if we came to see you tomorrow? We are thinking of going to the auction rooms in Cardiff but before doing that it would be a good idea to come to you first.'

'By all means, young man. When would you be arriving?'

'Shall we say about ten-thirty?'

As soon as he had left, I went into Mrs Richards's kitchen where she was about to cook our meat ration: a few slices of liver, one rasher of bacon each, with onions, unrationed. A pan of potatoes was boiling away merrily on the gas stove.

'Do you mind if I dash out and phone Eleanor? I won't be long. I'll tell you why when I come back.'

The old lady pushed aside a straggly white hair which had invaded her forehead.

'Don't be too long, Mr Secombe. As you can see, I'm ready for the getting off, as Miss Jacobs would say.'

Miss Jacobs was the local illegal bookmaker, and a friend of Mrs Richards.

Eleanor was most enthusiastic. 'If he has plenty to offer there may be no need to go down to Cardiff,' she said.

We arrived at Abergwynlais Vicarage prompt at ten-thirty. The car bounced over the primitive track which served as a drive. Overgrown rhododendron bushes impinged on the narrow passageway.

'Not very promising,' forecast my fiancée.

An aged black and white spaniel ambled towards us from the side of the house and indulged in a couple of wheezy barks. It was just as well that he did so because the door bell was not working.

As I was about to press the button for the third time, the Reverend Arthur Bowen opened the door.

'I thought I heard the dog bark. Good house dog. Is this the young lady? Pleased to meet you, my dear. Come on in.'

The hall was painted in the Great Western colours, dark yellow and chocolate, possibly through the good offices of the local stationmaster. The walls were unadorned by pictures. We were ushered into the sitting room where the windows overlooked a lawn of tall waving grass.

'Sit down and make yourselves comfortable. I'll bring my wife to meet you. She's making a cup of tea for us in the kitchen.'

As soon as he had gone, I said, 'I think we are wasting our time here. Sorry about that, love.'

'Nothing of the sort,' retorted Eleanor. 'The furniture in this room is good stuff. It's leather. None of your rexine. This settee is well sprung. So are the armchairs by the look of them.'

Our conversation was cut short by the entry of the lady of the house bearing a tray full of the best china. She was short and plump, rosy-cheeked and grey-haired. Mrs Bowen was very light on her feet and hummed indecipherable tunes quietly as she moved. The Bowens were an oddly assorted pair. A choreographer once told me that people can be divided into balls and pins. In that case the Vicar was a bodkin and his wife a bouncy ball.

When we left the house, we had bought bedroom furniture, a dining-room table and chairs and a couple of leather armchairs from the study. During the afternoon in Cardiff, we bought carpets and a leather settee to match the armchairs. All these purchases were made with Eleanor's cheques, much to my embarrassment.

'I've heard of a kept woman but never of a kept man,' I said as we were driving back from Cardiff.

'Come off it, Fred. Marriage is a joint enterprise. Your turn will come when you're a Vicar. You will be supplying the house and your income will double. So let's have no more of this argy bargy.'

She said it so firmly that I dropped the subject never to raise it again. However, I was determined that I should become a Vicar as soon as possible, if only to escape from a house with no bathroom and an outside lavatory. To Eleanor it was an adventure. She informed me that she knew a curate and his wife in similar circumstances who used to dress for dinner each evening after sharing the tin bath. 'Admittedly she was upper crust,' she added. 'She felt she had to maintain her standards even when slumming it.'

'Slumming it' was my future mother-in-law's term for our occupation of 11 Bevan's Row. Mrs Davies, the daughter of a barrister, had been educated in an expensive private school in Cardiff and regarded her time in the Valleys as an incarceration. Physically, Eleanor was 'the splitting image' of her mother, as Mrs Richards described her. That was where the resemblance ended. Eleanor loved the Valleys people and had a keen sense of humour – a quality conspicuously lacking in her mother.

Next morning, halfway through reading the second lesson at matins, I was stricken with an acute bout of toothache. I sped through the last ten verses of St Luke, Chapter 11, at an unseemly rate. The Vicar looked up from his Bible, startled by the acceleration. My normal practice was to make a meal of each reading, savouring the best verses.

By the time Father Whittaker had finished the prayers, I was in agony. As we stood up to go into the vestry he said, 'What's wrong, Fred?'

'Toothache, Vicar. Ramping, violent toothache.'

'Isn't it ludicrous that one tiny thread of a nerve can convulse the whole body with pain?' he mused.

I was in no mood to philosophize.

'If you don't mind, Vicar, I shall have to forgo coffee in the Vicarage this morning and pay a visit to the dentist instead.'

'You are very wise. I should go forthwith if I were you.'

I went forthwith.

The appropriately named Mr Pullen was the only dentist resident in Pontywen. There was a peripatetic practitioner who came on Thursdays to the front room of a house near the Vicarage. He was reputed to be more competent than Mr Pullen. However, as it was Tuesday, I could not wait until then to have my pain relieved.

Mr Pullen's surgery was some distance from the parish church. Every step jarred as I climbed halfway up the hillside to reach it. The brass plate outside the door was in need of cleaning. It was difficult to distinguish his name and impossible to read his qualifications.

I pressed the button of the door bell. There was no reply. I pressed it again. This time a voice from within shouted, 'Mr Pullen, there's someone at the door!' Eventually the door opened to reveal a tall, thin grey-haired, red-faced man, wearing a grubby white jacket and holding a lighted cigarette in a shaking right hand. It was too late and too urgent to turn back. The die was cast.

'Good morning, Father,' he said in a voice hoarsened by a plethora of packets of Players. 'What can I do for you?'

I was wearing my cassock. Evidently he thought I was collecting for the Church or on some errand of mercy.

'You can take a tooth out for me, please. As soon as possible.'

'It's that bad, is it?'

'I'm afraid it is. The pain is unbearable.'

'Come on in then. I've got a patient in the waiting-room. He's had his injection and I'm waiting for his gum to go numb. I was in my surgery. That's why I didn't hear the bell.'

I was taken into the front room where, sitting on one of the half-dozen dining chairs, was the patient. White-faced, wearing a scarf tucked inside his waistcoat, he sat on the edge of his chair, like a prisoner in Death Row, waiting for his execution.

'Can you feel anything when you touch your cheek?' enquired the dentist of the unhappy man.

'Just a bit.'

'We'd better wait a few more minutes.' Mr Pullen drew heavily on his cigarette and puffed out a cloud of smoke before retiring into his surgery.

I sat down opposite the injected one. He stared at the floor as if mesmerized by the pattern on the oil cloth. A couple of dog-eared editions of *Punch* adorned a rickety table. With my face pounding with pain I was in no mood to be amused. The 'few more minutes' lengthened into ten, according to my watch.

Suddenly there was a blast of loud music from inside the surgery. It was a brass band record of 'The Entry of the Gladiators'. Mr Pullen emerged and beckoned my fellow patient to come inside. He rose reluctantly, his head still bowed. The door was closed and I took over the examination of the oil cloth, holding my right cheek.

'The Entry of the Gladiators' ran its course and was followed by a rendition of 'Colonel Bogey'. As the last notes died away, a pathetic figure was ushered from the surgery, obviously intent to get through the front door as quickly as possible.

'Would you care to come in, Father?' said Mr Pullen.

It was the most unwelcome invitation I have ever received.

'Take a pew, shall we say?' The dentist indicated the chair with a bland wave of the hand.

No pew could be as uncomfortable as this one, I thought, as I sat in the contraption.

'Relax and put your head back. Open your mouth. Now where is your offending tooth?'

I pointed to the source of my pain.

He peered at the molar for a while.

'Yes, it is nasty, isn't it? Well, it will soon be out. I'm going to give you an injection. Before long that will take all feeling away from your gum. Then we'll whip out the offender and you'll be as right as rain.'

With my legs outstretched, I laid back and examined the ceiling which had not been decorated for some time and was suffering from the effects of subsidence.

Completely unsuspecting, I was attacked from behind by nicotined fingers manipulating a needle which punctured my gum in three or four places.

'In a minute or two your toothache will disappear and ten minutes later the blighter will be out. Your troubles will be over. Believe me.'

I would have believed him more readily if his hand had not been shaking so much. As it was, I sat in the front room, examining the oil cloth as closely as the previous victim had done. Soon my right cheek parted company from the rest of my face and was lost in the splendid isolation of numbness. I tried to convince myself that anything was better than that rampant toothache. It was a vain attempt.

To my horror the band began to play again and the surgery door opened to reveal the entry of the gladiator.

'Ready now, Father,' he said. 'Back in the pew. I hope you don't mind the music. It helps me in my work, you see.'

I did not see but I was in no position to question his motivation.

'That's right. Now head right back, open wide.'

He attacked me from behind again, this time with his pincers. His hand twisted and turned in my mouth. There was a sound of a crack. He pulled out three-quarters of a tooth.

'Blast! Sorry, Father. I'm afraid this back tooth was rotten. Hold on and I'll get the rest out.'

There was no other option for me but to hold on.

He went to the side table and spent an age rummaging through the assortment of instruments lying there.

'Here we are!' he proclaimed – brandishing what looked like a scalpel. 'Excuse me while I change the record.'

The next minute to the accompaniment of 'Colonel Bogey', he was probing my gum and digging out the remnants.

'Spit into the bowl,' he ordered.

A plentiful stream of blood flowed into the receptacle.

'I think that's everything out now. Swill your mouth out.' He gave me a glass of water, every mouthful of which was still coloured after a number of expectorations.

'It will bleed for a bit but that will soon stop.'

'How much do I owe you?' I mumbled through my numbness.

'I don't charge the clergy. One profession to another. Perhaps you will bury me for nothing.'

'If I'm still around,' I managed to reply.

The band's last notes died away as I left the surgery, with my handkerchief firmly held to my mouth.

By the time I reached my digs my handkerchief was saturated in blood. Mrs Richards stared in disbelief at the pathetic creature who entered her kitchen, ashen and bloody mouthed.

'Mr Secombe, what have you been doing? You look as if you've been in a fight with Joe Lewis.'

'Wrong man. Somebody far worse. Mr Pullen. I'm going upstairs to recover.'

Before she could say any more I dashed upstairs and into my bedroom to cope with the gradual disappearance of the numbness. As the effect of the injection wore off I found myself confronted with such pain that I began to bang my head against the wall in frustration. It was far worse than the toothache which drove me to the dentist. I wished I could die and end it all.

In the midst of my agony there was a tap on the door.

'It's me, Eleanor,' the voice announced. No words can describe the relief I felt. Mafeking was never like this.

'Come in, love,' I managed to say.

When she saw me, she came and put her arms around me as I sat on the edge of my bed.

'You poor lamb. What on earth made you go to Pullen? He's got more blood on his hands than Sweeney Todd.'

'Desperation. I couldn't wait till Thursday for the other dentist.'

'Open your mouth and let's see what he's done to you.'

She examined the cavity.

'Fair amount of butchery but nothing drastic,' she pronounced. 'I'll get back to the surgery and bring some cotton wool and painkillers. Don't move. Eleanor will soon return.'

'What brought you here?' I asked. 'A message from heaven or a request from Mrs Richards?'

'Neither. A comparatively empty surgery and a desire to see my fiancé.'

Ten minutes later, she was back with a wad of cotton wool and a bottle of aspirins. She plugged the gap in my gum and gave me two pills.

'Now then,' she said. 'Try and get some sleep. I'll be round at seven o'clock this evening.'

Slowly the pain eased and, exhausted by the traumas of the morning, I fell asleep.

I was awakened with a knock on the door by Mrs Richards. She came in with a tray bearing a bowl of soup.

'It's one o'clock, Mr Secombe. I thought you'd like something easy for you to eat, but flourishing. The butcher gave me some bones this morning for boiling. How's your face?'

'Very sore but all that dreadful pain has gone.'

'What a good thing you've got a lady doctor as your bride-that-will-be.'

'Tell me, Mrs Richards, does Mr Pullen always put gramophone records on while he's taking people's teeth out?'

'Oh, yes! He do put them on to drown all the noise from his customers when he's pulling out their teeth. He's very heavy-handed. Well, that's what they do say.'

'Amen,' I replied. 'He's made an impression on me that I shall never forget. I always thought that music was intended to soothe the savage breast not encourage it to butcher.'

2

It took five days for my swollen face to subside – just enough time for my elevation to stand-in Vicar, for the duration of Father Whittaker's holiday.

'I have asked Mrs Lilywhite to make a record of all telephone calls. She will let you know if there is any urgent matter that needs your attention. In any case, call in at the Vicarage every morning after matins. There are two weddings next Saturday but none the following Saturday. No baptisms.'

With these instructions the Vicar drove off into the Sunday evening sunshine, leaving behind the polluted air of Pontywen for the welcome ozone of Tenby.

Mrs Lilywhite was the housekeeper at the Vicarage. Short, rosy-cheeked, amply-bosomed, grey-haired, she was as careless of her person as she was of the house. Father Whittaker was a bachelor and housekeepers were not in plentiful supply. As a hostage to fortune he had no alternative but to ignore her slovenliness. At least he was well-fed and there was someone at the Vicarage to answer the door or the phone in his absence. She had one other great asset. Mrs Lilywhite never gossiped.

As far as my colleagues and I were concerned, we were only too grateful that the lady at the Vicarage was not the Vicar's wife. We had suffered at the hands of the late Vicar's consort to such an extent that Mrs Lilywhite with her amiability appeared to be heaven-sent.

On Monday morning I called for Charles Wentworth-Baxter at his digs which were over Pontywen's one green-grocery shop run by Moelwyn and Myfanwy Howells. Myfanwy answered the door. Tall, thin, with red hair which was losing its battle with an invasion of grey, Mrs Howells had a pleasant and ready smile.

'Come on in,' she said. 'He's almost ready, I think. At least he's out of the bathroom. Not that he spends much time in there.'

Charles was not over-attentive to his appearance but under Myfanwy's encouragement he had progressed some-what in his personal care. When he came to Pontywen first, he was more like a vagrant than a Curate.

Minutes passed as Myfanwy and I chatted about the Gilbert & Sullivan society I had formed and in which she was a prominent member, playing the part of Ruth in our performance of *The Pirates of Penzance*. I looked at my watch. It was five past nine and matins was due to begin at nine o'clock.

'Do you mind if I go to his room and eject him forcibly,' I asked Myfanwy.

'By all means,' she replied, 'and use the maximum of force.'

I went upstairs, two at a time, and banged on his door.

'Get a move on,' I shouted.

The door opened to reveal a bare-footed, but otherwise fully-dressed Curate, more asleep than awake.

'What's the hurry?' he croaked. 'While the cat's away the mice will play.'

'This is one mouse who won't play. Tomorrow morning you'll be ready when I call.'

'OK bossy boots. Wait till I find my socks and I'll be with you.'

A quarter of an hour later we were saying matins in the parish church. A fit of giggles engulfed us both as Charles tried to cope with the name of one of Saul's sons, Mephibosh-eth. I managed to control myself eventually but my colleague erupted every so often throughout the rest of the service. It was small wonder that Eleanor had nicknamed him Peter Pan.

We made our way to the Vicarage to check if there had been any phone calls. Mrs Lilywhite was outside the back of the house, carrying a basket of her Monday-morning washing.

'Why I bother to put them out, I don't know. If it isn't the coal dust it's the smuts from the engines.'

She deposited the basket by the line-post and invited us into the Vicar's study.

'Mr Matthews the undertaker rang half-past eight this morning, would you believe it? There's a funeral on Friday, three o'clock. He's seeing Full-Back Jones about the grave. It's a re-opening.'

'That will please Full-Back,' I said. 'Not so far to dig down.'

'About three feet at the most,' added Charles, 'the way he digs a full-depth grave.'

'Anyway,' went on the housekeeper, 'the name is Eliza Jenkins aged eighty-two, number 17 Thomas Street. Service in the house and straight to the graveside.'

'Put like that,' I commented, 'it sounds as if they are in a hurry to get rid of the poor old soul. Well, you or me, Charles?'

'You, Fred,' came the instant reply. 'You're better at funerals and weddings than I am. By the way, do you mind if I take Saturday off instead of Thursday? I want to go to Newport.'

'That means you get out of the two weddings as well. You weren't born yesterday. In that case you can do the hospital visiting this week and take the Mothers' Union service on Thursday.'

His face dropped, to the amusement of Mrs Lilywhite who had been an interested listener.

'Fair's fair, Charles,' she said. 'You are hardly over-worked.'

'It's not the hospital visiting that I mind. It's the Mothers' Union service. All those nattering old girls. They should call it the Grandmothers' Union. Then that lukewarm cup of tea and a Marie biscuit afterwards in the church hall. Ugh!'

'Is there anything about our work that you really like, Charles?' I asked.

Before he could reply, the telephone rang. The house-keeper moved smartly to the Vicar's desk to answer the call. 'It's for you, Fred. Your young lady.'

'I guessed you might be there,' came my fiancée's voice. 'This reminds me. We must have the phone put in Bevan's Row. I'll have priority as a doctor, but that's not the point of this call. Dr Hughes has told me that the only day I can have off this week is Thursday. Do you think that you could have the same day and we can go down to Swansea to meet your family? It's about time, isn't it?'

'God moves in a mysterious way, His wonders to peform,' I said.

'What on earth do you mean?'

'Charles has just agreed to take the Mothers' Union ser-vice on Thursday. So the way is clear. I'll write to my parents when I get back to my digs. They'll be delighted to meet you at last. See you tonight. T.T.F.N.'

'S.W.A.L.K. to you,' she replied.

'If you don't mind me asking,' said my colleague. 'What does T.T.F.N. stand for?'

'Even I know that,' Mrs Lilywhite looked scornfully at him. 'Ta-Ta-For-Now – from ITMA: It's That Man Again. You know, Tommy Handley. Don't tell me you haven't heard him on the wireless.'

'Of course I've heard him. I'm just puzzled by the initials.' Charles looked annoyed. The thought of having to take the Mothers' Union service was still causing him pain.

From the Vicarage I went to number 17 Thomas Street to call on the relatives of the late Eliza Jenkins. Thomas Street was one of the more respectable streets in Pontywen where the housewives competed with each other for the best scrubbed doorstep and where Venetian blinds were a *sine qua non*. The Venetian blind at number 17 was down and the front-door step defied any visitor to set foot on it. I felt loath to sully the surface of the gleaming brass knocker by handling it.

I decided that a gentle rap on the knocker would be appropriate for the house of mourning. It brought no response. I tried again with a short sharp shock of a knock.

Inside a door opened and a female voice said, 'All right, don't knock the door down.'

I braced myself for the confrontation which was delayed by the rattling of bolts and chains more appropriate to the opening of a high security prison than a house in Pontywen.

Eventually a diminutive white-haired lady appeared, dressed in black. Pince-nez spectacles were perched on her beaky nose. She held herself upright, all five foot of her.

'You must be from the church. Come on in, young man.' Her attitude and voice indicated a retired schoolteacher.

She led me into the front room where I was ordered to sit in a chintz-covered armchair. On the mantelpiece was an ancient silver-framed photograph of a young lady in cap and gown, proof positive of my assumption.

'I'm sorry to hear of your bereavement. What relation was Mrs Jenkins?'

'Don't be sorry, Mr – er?'

'Secombe.'

'Don't be sorry, Mr Secombe. She had been bed-ridden for some years now. It was a merciful release from her sufferings. I am her sister. She was widowed in the First World War and I have lived with her ever since. As her only sister and unmarried, I felt it was the sensible thing to do. I was teaching by then and earning enough to buy the house eventually.'

'Where did you teach? Locally?'

'I taught in Pontywen Grammar School all my working life. English. These were my tools.' With a sweep of her hand she indicated a large bookcase filled to capacity. 'I retired in 1942.'

'In that case you might know my fiancée, Eleanor Davies.'

'Indeed I do. A very intelligent but determined young lady. I had hoped she would take a degree in English. She chose medicine instead. I am sure she will excel in that. You are a lucky man, Mr Secombe.'

'I know I am, Miss – er –?'

'It is my turn now. My name is not an uncommon one like yours. I am Hannah Jones. My parents were Baptist and inevitably decided on an Old Testament name for their daughter. I am afraid I am no Hannah in the Biblical sense. I have been an agnostic since my university days and what has happened over the past six years or so has convinced me that I have been right to hold that view. Perhaps an agnostic should not use the word convinced. To put it in a nut-shell, two wars in my lifetime have drawn me to the conclusion that if there is a God, He has made a mess of the world He has created.'

'Miss Jones, all I can say in answer to your conclusion is that if the people of this country had not been so convinced that their cause was a just one, the world in which you live today would have been intolerable, even for an agnostic.'

'Touché, young man. All I can say is that Eleanor is a lucky girl to have you as her fiancé.'

'About the funeral arrangements, Miss Jones. I understand that you want a short service here in the house and then straight to the churchyard for the interment.'

'That is correct. My sister, like myself, has not been a churchgoer. We discussed funeral arrangements some time ago. Eliza knew that her end was near and told me not to ask the Baptists to do the service. There would be those dreadful extempore prayers and insincere eulogies from a minister who never knew my sister. At least the language of the Book of Common Prayer would be dignified.'

'I shall do my best to fall in with her wishes. I promise you that there will be no extempore prayers and that the language of the Book of Common Prayer, plus that of the authorized version, will be used.'

'Thank you, Mr Secombe. Apart from myself and a few family friends, there will be no others at the burial. It will not be one of those gentlemen-only funerals at the graveside. Mr Matthews, the undertaker, will supply the bearers and we shall come to the churchyard, such as we are, male and female.'

'I shall be here at five to three on Friday, Miss Jones. It has been a pleasure meeting you, even if it is under such sad circumstances.'

'The pleasure is reciprocated. You will be welcome to come back to the house afterwards for a glass of sherry and a sandwich.'

As I left the house I could hear the bolts and chains being put back into place. Walking back to my digs, I tried to remember if I had split my infinitives. Such was the effect Miss Hannah Jones had on me.

When I told Mrs Richards where I had been, she was not surprised at my reaction.

'She was an old battle axer in Pontywen Grammar. All the girls were afraid of her. Mind, she's very clever. She went to the Universal College in Cardiff. They do say she used to be a bit lovey dovey with Dr Hughes till his wife found out. That soon put a stopper on the goings on.'

'I would never have thought she was capable of that, nor Dr Hughes, come to think of it.'

'That was donkey's ages ago. They were both quite different then. Hannah Jones was very up to date. She used to smoke cigarettes in those holders and wear those short dresses that the flapping girls used to have on. Dr Hughes played tennis with her in some games club in Cardiff. He had a little black moustache and had his hair parted in the middle with a lot of that grease on it.'

'After what you have said, Mrs Richards, I had better keep an eye on Eleanor.'

'You're joking, Mr Secombe. Dr Hughes has got two of his feet in the grave these days. It won't be long before your young lady will be on her own to do the doctoring, believe me.'

Leaving me with that sobering thought, she went into the kitchen to prepare our Monday lunch, bubble and squeak, composed of the leftovers from the previous day, with potatoes and swedes thrown into the frying pan. It was predictable but palatable, as were all her meals.

Halfway through lunch there was a loud knock on the front door.

'You stay and finish your dinner. People coming when they know you must be in the middle of your food. They ought to be more considerable.'

I could hear a conversation going on at the door, with a man's gruff voice predominating. Eventually he was shown into my room and my landlady returned to the table.

'There's a Curate wants to see you. He's got a red face and his hair's cut short like a prisoner. He says for you to carry on with your eating and he'll wait for you.'

'That's kind of him,' I said. As I ate, I racked my brains in a search for his identity. By my last mouthful, light dawned. With a gruff voice and such an appearance it could only be Maldwyn Evans, commonly known in college days as Mal. It was.

'Sorry to disturb your lunch, boy. It's all a bit urgent.'

'What's urgent, Mal?'

'We've revived the clergy cricket team and we've fixed a match with the St Deiniol's Diocese at Cardiff Arms Park on Wednesday. We're two short. I know you used to play a bit in College and what about that Wentworth whatever his name is? Does he play?'

'He says he used to play for the school team.'

'Right then. Got transport?'

'I'm afraid not.'

'Albert Thomas, the Vicar of Penyglais, has got room for two in his car. Pick you both up half-past twelve on Wednesday.'

'Hold on, Mal. I haven't played cricket for a couple of years and I have no idea what Charles is like. To play on a County Cricket Ground you've got to be good.'

'It's Clergy Cricket, Fred, not County Cricket. Don't worry. Do your best. See you Wednesday.'

'Pick us up at Howells the Greengrocers,' I shouted as he went down the steps.

Trying to talk to Mal was an impossibility. He was a whirlwind of a man in speech and action. As a cricketer he was a fearsome bowler who terrifed the wicket keeper as much as the batsman. Neither would know where the ball would hurtle next. One visiting umpire who accused him of throwing instead of bowling ended up more terrified by Mal's reaction than the wicket keeper and the batsman.

Charles was quite excited when I called round to pass on the invitation. His eyes developed a dreamy far away look at the thought of playing in Cardiff Arms Park.

'You realize you'll have to play in flannels,' I said.

His face dropped.

'Can't I play in my greys?'

'Of course not – on a county cricket ground! You'll have to borrow some.'

There was a moment's silence.

'Bertie Owen!' I exclaimed. 'He's always bragging about his prowess as a cricketer for Pontywen in prewar times. I bet he still has his flannels.'

Bertie was the churchwarden at St Padarn's, the daughter church which was in my charge. He was as unpredictable as Mal's bowling and much more dangerous. In the course of the short time I had known him, he had been responsible for the burning of the Vicarage garage and the late Vicar's car, for a fiasco of a Sunday-school outing and for blacking out the first Christmas Midnight Mass in Pontywen. None of these things had been done by intent. He was simply a magnet to disasters.

Later that day Charles and I paid him a visit at his home in Highfield Avenue. He was in his back garden, watering his peas and beans.

'To what do I owe the pleasure, gentlemen?' Bertie's face split, ear to ear, with a typical grin.

'Bertie I have been telling Charles that you used to play cricket for Pontywen before the war.'

His chest expanded as much as face had done.

'Opening bat and change bowler for twenty years. I'm past it now, though.'

Charles coughed. 'Er, have you still got your whites?'

The churchwarden stared at him.

'Yes, they're upstairs in the bottom drawer of the wardrobe.'

'Do you think I could possibly – er – borrow them?'

Bertie's eyes opened wider.

'What for?'

Fred and I have been asked to play for the Diocesan Clergy team on Wednesday. He's got flannels and I haven't. We're playing at Cardiff Arms Park.'

By now Bertie's eyebrows were almost in contact with his hairline.

'Cardiff Arms Park?'

'Honest,' I said.

'Of course you can borrow them but don't you think you need some practice? I've got a couple of cricket balls here somewhere as well as my old bat. There's no time like the present. What about half an hour or so behind St Padarn's. Nobody will see us there.'

'No more than that, Bertie. I'm meeting Eleanor in an hour's time.'

Ten minutes later, with Charles clutching a pair of mothballed flannels and me holding a well-oiled cricket bat, Bertie drove us down to the tin church. There was a patch of waste land behind St Padarn's ready for the day when a permanent church would be built. It had been ready for the last forty years.

'Now then,' said Bertie. 'What are you – bowlers or batsmen?'

'I've done a bit of both. My grandfather bowled against W. G. Grace once,' I boasted.

'Let's see you bowl to me then.'

Bertie took the bat and threw me the ball. He patted the ground as he crouched over the bat, waiting for my delivery. In his mind he was back at the crease on Pontywen Welfare Ground. I swung my arm. The ball pitched innocuously on the bare ground. Our expert opening bat treated it with the contempt it deserved – straight through the east window of St Padarn's.

'Glass stopped play. I think we'd better clear up the mess inside and leave the cricket to Cardiff Arms Park.'

'Sorry, Mr Secombe. I had intended a straight drive.'

Bertie's expression belied his words. He seemed delighted that he could still clout a cricket ball.

Charles looked quite relieved that he was not to be put to the test. I feared for him on Wednesday, not to mention myself.

By the time we had swept up the glass inside the church plus the shattered remains of the china vase given by Mrs Collier, the organist's wife, two months earlier, it was time for me to meet Eleanor at my digs.

'There was a lot of force behind that ball to break a window and a vase,' Bertie beamed at the recollection of his drive.

'There will be a lot of force behind Mrs Collier's words when she discovers what has happened to her mother's memorial.'

With that remark I left for number 13 Mount Pleasant View, leaving Charles and Bertie searching for a piece of cardboard to cover the gaping hole in the east window.

Eleanor was very subdued when she arrived at my digs. As the wedding day drew nearer she had become more and more animated. This was quite out of character.

'What on earth is the matter?' I inquired.

She seemed near to tears.

'My mother; she's utterly and completely impossible.'

I took her in my arms and she began to weep uncontrollably. Even when the tears had gone, her body was racked with sobs. It was some minutes before she could speak.

'Don't worry, my dear. It's just that she caught me at my most vulnerable.'

'Why your most vulnerable?'

'My female condition. You wouldn't understand, because you will never experience it. Anyway, not for the first time, she more or less suggested that I was marrying beneath my status. We had an almighty row. The one good thing to come of it is the fact that she realizes now any more talk of that nature and she will be losing her daughter for good.'

'What a pity my name isn't Wentworth-Baxter,' I said, 'but come to think of it, Secombe is a much more upmarket name than Davies. Perhaps I can invent some distinguished ancestors like Sir Marmaduke Secombe, Knight Crusader, or the Right Reverend Septimus Secombe, Bishop of the Outer Hebrides.'

She began to giggle.

'I promise you, Eleanor my love, that despite my humble beginnings, I shall do my best to make your mother feel that you are in very good hands even if my blood is not quite as blue as she would wish it.'

'Since my father was born and bred in a miner's cottage, I don't think she is in a position to criticize her daughter's choice of a partner.'

'Let's forget your mother for the rest of this evening,' I said. 'Come and sit on my lap in my armchair, my little one, and I'll tell you a nice juicy story.'

She pulled away from me and stood erect, all five feet two inches of her, in mock fury, her lovely dark eyes fixed on me.

'What do you mean – little one? You're only five foot seven yourself.'

'What I mean, Eleanor my love, is that I have a titbit of gossip which will interest you.'

'Carry on then,' she said and kissed me lightly on my cheek.

'That's exactly what it is – a carry on. This morning I had to pay a visit to a house of mourning. There I met a Miss Hannah Jones the sister of the deceased.'

'Say no more,' replied my fiancée. 'Old Hannah, the dragon of Pontywen Grammar.'

'She said you were very intelligent but determined. I can vouch for that.'

'I was determined that she was not going to dictate my future – any more than my mother has tried to do.'

'Let's not get back to square one. The point is that Mrs Richards has just informed me of a past liaison between your aging partner, Dr Hughes and the aforesaid Hannah Jones.'

She began to laugh. As a look of total bewilderment settled on my face her laughter increased.

'What's the joke?' I asked testily.

'The joke, my lovely innocent Fred, is that the past liaison is *not* past. It still continues, sub rosa. If Mrs Hughes died tomorrow, there would be wedding bells within a month.'

3

I had arranged to be picked up at the Howells' greengrocery shop in the square, partly because it would be easier to find for our chauffeur and partly because Charles suffered from a chronic tendency to be late for appointments.

It was a quarter-past twelve when I arrived at the shop. Myfanwy Howells led me into the back room and supplied me with a cup of tea while I waited for my colleague to appear from upstairs. At twenty-five past twelve a vision in white appeared. He was clad in Bertie Owen's flannels which were several sizes too large for him and were tucked up at the waist where an ancient college tie was substituted for a belt. On his feet were a pair of filthy gym shoes. A Persil-clean shirt, washed and ironed by Myfanwy, covered his scrawny torso.

'You are not coming like that, Charles,' I expostulated. 'You are supposed to have that outfit in a case. There are such things as changing-rooms – especially at Cardiff Arms Park.'

'What did I tell you?' exploded Myfanwy.

He retreated to his bedroom to escape any further verbal barrage.

Precisely at half-past twelve the clang of the doorbell in the shop announced the arrival of Albert Thomas, Vicar of Penyglais. He was a large teddy bear of a parson, with a face mottled by a penchant for aqua vitae.

'A cup of tea?' inquired Myfanwy.

'No thanks. I've had some before I came out,' replied the Vicar, emitting an odour which came from north of the border rather than from across the Indian Ocean. 'Are we all ready then?'

'Almost,' I said. 'Charles has just gone to his bedroom to change into his canonicals.'

He looked quizzically at me, and was about to reply when Charles came hurtling downstairs in clerical dress, case in hand, and his hair looking as if it had been caught in a whirlwind.

'All set,' he announced.

The Vicar of Penyglais stared at him in wonderment, unable to connect the image before him with Cardiff Arms Park.

'I think we're on a hiding to nothing today,' he said lugubriously as he put our cases into the boot of his old Wolseley. 'They've got David Jenkins playing for them. He had a few games for the Glamorgan Seconds in the twenties.'

'Perhaps he's got arthritis since then,' I suggested.

'I don't care if he's got arthritis and housemaid's knee, he'll still make rings round us,' he replied with a meaningful jerk of the head in the direction of Charles.

It was a protracted journey to Cardiff Arms Park, caused by road works and a clapped-out engine in the Wolseley which refused to respond to the blandishments of the Vicar.

'Come on, you can do better than this,' he said to it at least a dozen times. The engine appeared to be deaf.

We arrived at the famous ground at twenty-five past two. The match was due to begin five minutes later. Fortunately for us, our skipper Gareth Davies, had won the toss and decided to bat, since five of his side had not arrived, including Mal Evans, the demon bowler.

'Thank God!' he said fervently. 'Only two more to come. Still, they are the ones who matter.'

'There's nothing like inspiring confidence in the three who have just arrived,' replied Albert Thomas.

'What I mean is,' grunted Gareth Davies, Rector of Treginnis, 'I wanted Trevor and Mal to open, Trevor to stonewall and Mal to swing the bat and destroy their morale at the very beginning.'

'That's if he connects. It depends on the grace of God rather than any technique.' Evidently Albert had a low opinion of Mal as a batsman, based on past experience of the absence of grace.

We had the privilege of using the Glamorgan dressing room. I was surprised to see such spartan surroundings, but as we sat on the wooden bench the surprise became lost in the awe I felt at sharing the same seat as heroes of my boyhood.

Gareth Davies came in with the score book as we were changing. 'Albert,' he commanded, 'get the pads on. You open with George Williams.' Then he turned towards Charles and myself. 'You two will bat last. You, Secombe, tenth and your fellow Curate, eleventh.'

'His name is Charles and I'm Fred,' I said.

'Let's hope you are not both proper Charlies,' came his reply.

As I watched my hapless colleague struggle to convert his tie into his belt, I could see what he meant.

It was a sunny afternoon and as we sat outside on the pavilion seat, the ground looked a perfect picture. Our opponents were already out on the field, bowling the ball at each other and attempting catches in between the bowling. They were very vociferous, having called in at a number of hostelries on their way to Cardiff. This might have accounted for the large number of missed catches.

There was some trouble about umpiring. St Deiniols had brought an umpire with them as well as a scorer. He was Ivor Howells, Rector of Llandyfrig, a large, red-faced country parson with thick, pebbled spectacles.

'I doubt whether he goes anywhere without a white stick,' said Albert Thomas as he buckled on his pads.

Our umpire had telephoned Gareth Davies at the eleventh

hour to say that he was unavailable because of an emergency in the parish. Our scorer was Canon Llewellyn Pritchard, an elderly gentlemen who walked with the aid of a walking-stick and was unable to stand to umpire.

'I'll go out and umpire,' announced our captain. 'Perhaps somebody will turn up later on who can do the job. My main worry is when Mal and Trevor are coming. Albert, you do the stonewalling and George, play yourself in, open up.'

The remaining six of our team clapped as Albert and George made their way down the hallowed steps, behind the makeshift umpire who was engulfed in a white coat intended for a giant.

'Gosh, it's a long walk to get to the wicket. I'll be tired out by the time I get there.' Charles sounded terrified at the thought of playing on such a large ground.

'It will seem an even longer walk on your way back,' I replied, 'especially if you've been out there for just a few seconds.'

He winced at the thought.

George Williams was a short, stubby man in his forties with spectacles and whose teeth seemed to be at war with each other. His protruding jaw, combined with his teeth, gave him a vicious appearance. However, he was a sheep in wolf's clothing, a gentle, amiable parish priest, loved by his people in Aberonwy.

After taking guard from his captain-cum-umpire, George crouched and patted the pitch nervously as he waited for the first delivery.

It was bowled by a burly young Curate who had set his mark some twenty paces or so distant. He hustled up to the wicket and clean bowled George who had his bat upraised as if in surrender.

'No ball!' shouted Gareth simultaneously with the clatter of the stumps.

'That was a late call.' shouted the distraught bowler in an even louder voice.

As he walked back to his mark, he shook his head several times. Red-faced with anger and puffing out his cheeks he charged up to the wicket for a second time.

This next delivery was a wild one, yards away from the batsman and everyone else. It ran down to the boundary with the speed of lightning.

Gareth signalled four runs with an extravagant gesture and with a grin on his face which infuriated the young bowler even further. By the end of the over he had given away ten runs. George had only connected with the ball once and that was with his shoulder, not his bat.

At this juncture, a noisy car engine heralded the approach of Mal Evans and Trevor Harris. Mal's car had broken down en route and the AA patrolman had taken an hour to arrive. Mal's temper was at boiling point – I feared for the St Deiniol's team when their turn to bat arrived.

Meanwhile, out on the field, a tall, thin, distinguished, white-haired gentleman had taken the ball for the next over. He spent some time arranging his field while Albert and George enjoyed a short chat in the middle of the pitch. Preliminaries over, Albert returned to his crease and took guard. This was a lengthy operation as the St Deiniol's umpire seemed incapable of providing the necessary information required by the batsman.

Eventually David Jenkins, ex Glamorgan Seconds, took four leisurely steps and bowled a leg spin beauty to Albert, who knew not whence it came nor whither it went. His off stump tilted backwards. So far, in the innings, bat and ball had not met each other.

As Albert made his long trek back to the pavilion, Trevor Harris buckled on his pads in desperate haste. Trevor a small Humpty Dumpty with a fresh complexion, finished his preparations just in time to take the bat from Albert as he entered the dressing room.

'Played back instead of forward,' explained the victim.

'What he means,' I whispered to Charles, 'is that he missed the ball.'

'Well, we can't do any worse than that, thank heavens,' said my colleague.

To my amazement, Trevor weathered the next five balls of the Jenkins over, using his bat instead of his anatomy. He scored no runs but he survived, majestically, if that can be said of someone who looked like a balloon on two legs.

At the other end, George Williams began patting the pitch again, as he waited for the next thunderbolt from the St Deiniol's express. He was patting the pitch so vigorously that he must have excavated a small pit by now.

Down came the first ball which appeared to be making for George's Adam's apple. He fell backwards in his anxiety to escape mortal injury and collapsed on all three stumps, his spectacles dangling from his right ear.

The fast bowler stood astride the pitch like Hercules and surveyed the wreck at the other side.

'How's that?' he asked.

'Out,' said Gareth, 'but any more dangerous bowling like that and I'll ask your captain to take you off.'

George picked himself up, adjusted his spectacles and walked off slowly, still shaken by the experience.

'Right, if it's a fight they want, they've got it.' With these words, Mal Evans strode out of the pavilion. He met the incoming batsman before he reached the boundary, grabbed the bat and the gloves and went to the crease like a gladiator ready for battle.

'I hope that bloke doesn't bowl at me,' Charles confided. His terror was increasing by the minute.

The first ball that Mal received was driven to the boundary with a wild swing of the bat.

'There you are, Charles,' I said. 'Just swing your bat and the runs will come.'

Mal and Trevor stayed together for half an hour. Trevor played a watchful innings with a straight bat against David Jenkins at the one end while Mal, by the grace of God, flailed away at everything the young Curate bowled at him and made the runs.

When the score was fifty for two, Trevor Harris missed a ball which was going wide but was given out lbw by the St Deiniol's umpire. The next batsman suffered the same fate two balls later.

Gareth came off the pitch exchanging his umpire's coat with Albert Thomas.

'I told Fred their umpire looked as if he used a white stick before we started. Now I know he must use one,' said Albert.

The next over the fast bowler was taken off. His twenty-yard run had exhausted him and Mal Evans had exasperated him. Charles breathed a sigh of relief.

By the time the eighth wicket had fallen and my moment of glory had arrived, we had 102 runs on the score sheet.

'You'd better get your pads on straight away,' I said to Charles as I left.

'Watch it,' warned Gareth Davies as he handed me the bat and gloves. 'I think they are going to bring on that hothead of a Curate to finish off the tail.'

'Thank you very much,' I murmured.

Sure enough, when I began the long trek to the wicket, in the far distance, I could see Tarzan limbering up as if thirsting for blood. My heart and my stomach collided as I contemplated being 'finished off'. It took an eternity to reach the crease.

'Centre,' I called to Albert Thomas in quavery tones.

'That's middle and leg,' he announced as I put my bat down.

'Fine, leave it there,' I said. I knew that by the time the fearsome bowler delivered the ball, he would have all three wickets visible to him.

The fielders clustered around me, waiting for the kill. I had an acute attack of claustrophobia and nervous indigestion combined. I decided to keep my eyes trained on the ground till the last second.

It was the noise of the pounding hoofs that made me look up. There he was, snarling alongside Albert. His arm came over. I moved away, almost colliding with the short leg. The ball flew over the wickets to the keeper who stopped the ball with his rib cage.

'Come on!' shouted Dave Lewis at the other end. I needed no further invitation. By the time the bruised wicket keeper had retrieved the ball, I was home, safe and sound in Albert's company.

'I'm not moving from here till the end of the over.' I told Albert. Dave managed two fours off the edge of his bat but with the last ball of the over was clean bowled by a ball which sent his off stump flying. I sent a prayer of thanks for deliverance while I waited for Charles to appear. At least I was safe at my end.

Down the pavilion steps came my terrified colleague and began his journey to the wicket. He walked like Groucho Marx, his long body bent and supported by his two short legs. As he drew near to the fielders, they burst into laughter. I knew Charles cut a comical figure with his gait but it was not such as to cause raucous laughter. When he reached the wicket, I could see the reason. He had put his pads on, upside down.

David Jenkins was brought on at the other end to bowl to me. The St Deiniol's umpire bent low over the stumps, his nose an inch away from the bails to give me my guard.

'Middle and leg,' I called.

He peered down the wicket through his thick spectacles.

'That's about it,' he said.

I decided I would not make Albert's mistake of playing back to the leg spinner. I would advance to meet the ball as it hit the ground. The bowler twiddled the ball with his fingers and bowled. By some miracle I connected with the ball which flew off the edge of my bat and through the two slips.

Charles stood still, staring.

'Come on, run!' I shouted.

We both ran, looking at where the ball had gone. It was a nasty collision, which resulted in the two of us lying flat out on the pitch, while the St Deiniol's side were so convulsed with laughter that they almost forgot to run one of us out. Eventually it was the wicket keeper who removed the bails at his end.

As we arrived in the pavilion, Gareth Davies said, 'As I thought, you are both proper Charlies.' At least the farcical ending provided by the two of us had taken most of the tension out of the game for the time being.

Tea and sandwiches were provided by Mrs Gareth Davies and Mrs George Williams. These two large, jolly ladies presided over the proceedings with an aplomb acquired through years of experience with the Mothers' Union. Half-way through the refreshments, there was flurry of excitement when Albert Thomas who had been on a visit to the gents arrived with the news that the Bishop's car had just arrived in the car park.

The Bishop was a tall, thin, white-haired intellectual who had been cloistered in a college until he had been let loose into the diocese. He was a kind soul; completely unworldly in every sense of the word.

'Here's our answer to the umpire situation,' said Gareth Davies quietly to George Williams. 'I'd rather have him at one end than two of theirs at both ends.'

'I don't think he knows what a cricket pitch is,' replied George.

'If it comes to that,' whispered Gareth, 'neither does their umpire.'

The Right Reverend James Wilkinson could be seen through the pavilion windows a few minutes later, per-ambulating around the field, hands behind his back and his face lifted towards the sky, apparently in communion with the infinite.

'I think you've had your umpiring,' George said to Gareth. 'He's come for a spot of meditation, not for the match.'

'Don't be so sure; look he's coming towards the pavilion.' Gareth swallowed the last bit of his cucumber sandwich and made towards the door. A few moments later he could be seen in earnest conversion with the Bishop at the foot of the pavilion steps.

It was not long before the two of them entered the pavilion. The smile on Gareth's face indicated that he had succeeded in his quest.

'Good afternoon, gentlemen,' said the Bishop. 'Please stay sitting. I hope you're having an enjoyable game. I trust the second half will be as enjoyable because I'm afraid I have been dragooned into umpiring.'

The dignitary was ushered into a chair and offered a cup of tea by the captain's wife. He refused politely on the grounds that he had come straight from a committee meeting where he had been plied with several cups of tea.

A few minutes later Gareth arose and banged on the table. 'My lord, fellows, welcome to Cardiff Arms Park. We are grateful for the privilege of playing on this famous ground. ("Hear! hear") I'd like to thank the authorities and of course our ladies for giving us such a splendid tea. ("Hear! Hear!") Well, the game is poised at an interesting stage. May the best team win.'

There followed some banging on the table.

In these matches the game was always 'poised at an interesting stage' at tea time, even if one side was all out for ten and the other side was nine for no wicket.

The captain of St Deiniol's got to his feet, to the accompaniment of banging on the table from his fellow cricketers. He was Herbert Smith, Vicar of Aberclwyd, in a remote rural parish in mid Wales, an expert bee-keeper who supplemented his stipend with the sale of his honey – and with bed and breakfast for tourists.

'My lord, friends, thank you, Gareth for your kind words and thank you to the ladies for this excellent tea. Let's hope we have an enjoyable second half to the match. Diolch a'n fawr.'

'This is the cricket ground,' whispered Albert Thomas to me, 'not the rugby ground. That's the other side of the pavilion.'

Ten minutes later a self-conscious Bishop accompanied the short-sighted Rector of Llandyfrig down the steps and out on to the field to umpire the second innings.

Mal Evans was flexing his muscles for the fray. Trevor Harris was keeping wicket. It seemed that Gareth was to be the other opening bowler, 'Right arm, medium paced. Used to be fast but inaccurate. Not much better with his direction now.' That was Albert's assessment, as we walked together to do battle. 'I expect they'll put you long stop,' he added to Charles. 'So, what with Mal Evans and him, you're going to be busy.'

My fellow Curate paled at the thought.

Albert's prognostication was correct. 'Charlie,' ordered the captain, 'you go long stop. How far can you throw?'

'Not very far,' stammered Charles.

'In that case, don't go down to the boundary. Field further in. Secombe you to mid off. Concentrate, keep your eyes on the ball.'

When the field was placed finally, Mal Evans prepared to gallop to the wicket. Herbert Smith was the opener facing our spearhead attack. He had played against Mal in a previous match and knew what to expect. As Mal approached the shoulder of the St Deiniol's umpire, Herbert pulled away from the wicket with his bat upraised. Mal continued halfway down the pitch, ball in hand, with his brakes failing to stop his legs.

'Sorry,' said Herbert. 'Something got in my eye.'

Mal seemed about to tell him that he would have the ball there instead next time when he realized that his Bishop was standing at square leg. He swallowed deeply and stamped back to his mark.

His first ball was a flier which went past the wicket keeper and hit the ground a few yards away from Charles who leapt over the ball as it came towards him.

'You're supposed to stop it not dodge it,' yelled Gareth Davies.

I suppose Charles must have given away twenty runs or so

before they decided to move him to deep square leg. The score was mounting rapidly in extras to such an extent that the thirty-three for no wicket included only four runs off the bat. It was a repeat of the first innings.

Mal Evans was in a state of high dudgeon, especially when Gareth decided to replace him with George Williams, our team's off-spin bowler. It proved to be a shrewd move. In no time at all they were forty-five for three.

It was at this stage that David Jenkins came to the wicket. He had his shirt collar turned up in the manner of J. C. Clay the famous Glamorgan spin bowler. In some ways, with his tall thin figure and his lean features, he resembled him. His walk to the wicket was unhurried and his attitude oozed confidence.

Runs came freely from his bat. His timing was impeccable and his driving graceful. His only weakness was his legs. They were no longer youthful and impeded his progress between the wickets. Our only hope was to run him out.

Fortunately the rest of the St Deiniol's team were well out of his class. Five more wickets fell but because of David Jenkins's battling they were now ninety-two for eight, and the great man had the bowling. Another four followed off Gareth's bowling, yet another four. Five more runs and victory would be theirs.

With the last ball of his over, our captain managed to deliver a ball which the star could only return down the pitch. The ninth wicket batsman faced Mel Evans who had returned to the attack. A fast rising ball caught him on his shoulder and dropped on to his wicket. The last man in arrived among tense excitement. By closing his eyes and holding his bat as a shield he managed an easy single.

Four to win. David Jenkins looked around the field, as if deciding where he would make the wining hit. The Bishop was at the umpire's end, unmoved, still in communion with the infinite, while all around him were in a fever of excitement.

Down came Mal, breathing fire and slaughter. The ball hit the batsman a painful blow in the solar plexus.

'How's that?' appealed Mal.

The Bishop raised his finger and the match was over.

'That ball would never have hit the wicket in a month of Sundays,' Albert Thomas said to me as we walked off. 'It was far too high.'

'Perhaps,' I replied, 'he was like a boxing referee stopping the contest to save the man further injury.'

Back in the pavilion the atmosphere between St Deiniol's and ourselves was very strained. Our opponents were afraid to criticize the Bishop who had stayed behind to see them off. However their captain did say as he shook hands with the Bishop, 'We must get our Bishop to umpire the next match.'

'What a good idea,' said our diocesan. 'With the bishop at either end you would certainly see fair play.'

4

At nine o'clock next morning Eleanor was outside my digs, blowing the horn in her Morris Minor and all set to meet my parents in Swansea. Mrs Richards stood on the steps to wave us goodbye.

'Have a nice day,' she said. 'It will be lovely for your intended young lady to have an acquaintance with your father and mother.'

When we reached Swansea, we drove through the devastated heart of the town.

'It makes you want to cry,' commented my fiancée.

'Much more so if you are a native,' I replied. 'I remember walking through that particular pile of rubble on the way home from school. It was an arcade with a fascinating mixture of businesses. The phrenologist's window always attracted me with its large picture of a brain divided into its localized functions. A few of the boys in school were taken to have their bumps read.'

'That's one good thing the German bombs did in that case, putting the phrenologist out of business. It's the kind of science more suited to the stone age. I bet your mother didn't take you there.'

'She had far too much sense in her brain for that. You'll be able to judge for yourself in a few minutes.'

Soon we were in the pleasant road in Glanmor where my family had come to live in rented accommodation, after we had been 'blitzed' in our council house in the docks district.

My father was a commercial traveller whose recent appointment as a Crosse & Blackwell's representative gave him more prestige and more money. Carol, my nineteen-year-old sister, helped with the family finances by working as a telephone operator. My brother Harry, a lance-bombardier in the Royal Artillery, was due to be 'demobbed' from Italy anytime. He had spent the last year in the army entertaining his fellow soldiers, hoping to play to a wider audience as a civilian.

My mother met us at the door and straightaway kissed Eleanor. There was an instant bond between them. I was devoted to my mother. Small, grey-haired and not so plump as she was during my school days, she was a warm, smiling matriarch who ruled her domain by kindness combined with firmness. Over the past ten years she had been plagued by illness. She had undergone an operation to remove a kidney which left her wearing a heavy surgical corset for the rest of her life. In addition to that burden she had to cope with a heart condition which necessitated a daily intake of tablets. Yet she never complained.

In no time at all she and Eleanor were discussing her operation. My mother was a great talker and my fiancée was a willing audience. Had Mam been born in a later generation, I am sure she would have been a district nurse or perhaps even a doctor. When I was a boy she was in demand in our street as a consultant on childish ailments, as a midwife's unpaid help and as an expert at laying out a corpse. To find that her son was to marry a doctor was a joy to her.

Eleanor had brought with her material and a pattern for the bridesmaid's dress my sister was to wear for the wedding. After the two women had concluded a discussion on the outfit, I suggested that Eleanor might like to visit the lovely Gower peninsula which was on Swansea's doorstep, while my mother prepared the family meal.

'Before you do that, you must have a cup of tea and a piece of cake,' Mam insisted. She had baked her 'cut and come again' speciality, a fruit cake which was irresistible. An hour later we left Hazel Road to head west to the seaside.

As we drove along Mumbles Road the sun was high in an unclouded sky, the tide was halfway in and the sea was blue.

'Do you know,' I boasted, 'that people say Swansea Bay is second only to Naples?'

'For what?' retorted my beloved. 'Size or magnificence? It can't be magnificence. Look at those chimneys belting smoke in the distance and the oil tanks, not to mention the docks.'

'Let's say that once upon a time the bay was not only vast but magnificent. The Industrial Revolution has a lot to answer for. Come to think of it, Pontywen was once a charming little village in a luscious green valley and look at it now. Anyway, a few miles further on and you will see a sequence of lovely little bays untouched by industry.'

As we parked the car in Oxwich Bay sometime later, Eleanor looked around her.

'Secombe,' she said, 'I must admit that this is delightful. Let's go for a walk.'

The beach stretched for miles. We skirted the tide as it lapped gently along the strip of sand it had failed to engulf. Seagulls and oyster catchers filled the air with their cries. A small dog barked at a seagull he was chasing. The bird teased the hound by waiting till the last second to get off the ground.

Hand in hand we ambled to the furthermost point and then sat on the sand dunes before returning. In the distance a line of ships were steaming their way out of the Bristol Channel.

'Not so long ago they would have been in convoy with their naval escorts. I've seen them many a time setting out on their journey. I used to wonder how many would reach their destination. They were terrible times.'

'Gone, never to return, I hope,' replied Eleanor. 'Speaking of which, isn't it time we returned? Otherwise your mother will have a very poor opinion of her future daughter-in-law who came down to Swansea to meet her and then spent most of the time down in Gower, watching the ships go by.'

By the time we reached home my father had arrived, cutting short his calls for that day. Five feet-five inches tall, stockily built, he was the ideal commercial traveller, a cheerful extrovert, conscientious, able to make friends of grocers whom he supplied with goods. Apparently he had had to rush to catch the train at Pantyffynon, an exploit which he described in detail.

'I'm sure Eleanor doesn't want to hear about Pantyffynon,' my mother said. 'Go and show her your pride and joy while I get the table laid.'

My father's 'pride and joy' was the little greenhouse in the back garden. Horticulture had never been one of his strong points. The small patch of grass in front of our council house was knee-high most of the time we lived there. I remember my grandfather telling my mother when he came to visit us that he had been attacked by a tiger which had escaped from our 'jungle'. However, on finding that the diminutive greenhouse was part of our rented property, my father developed a love affair with it, spending much of his spare time there.

All he had to show that afternoon were some spindly tomato plants he had put in the week before and some liquid manure which he had manufactured from sheep droppings he had collected. He proceeded to make up for the visual lack of prowess by giving an account of the amount of tomatoes he had grown last year, with an approximate indication of the size of the biggest. Eleanor looked suitably impressed. She could have mentioned that her father had a greenhouse at least four times the size of ours.

Soon we were joined by my sister, a pretty, vivacious, brunette who came from the telephone exchange with a tale of a caller who complained, 'Please, miss, there's no diary in this "kyeosk".' She and Eleanor indulged in talk about the wedding attire until we were called to the table by my mother. Evidently she had used up the week's meat coupons on the small shoulder of lamb which adorned the table. My father carved and enquired of Eleanor if she had conducted such an operation on human beings.

Before she could reply, my mother launched into a severe reprimand, 'Don't embarrass the girl. In any case, it's not the kind of talk to indulge in when we're about to eat.'

'I'm not easily embarrassed,' said my fiancée. 'In any case, the answer is no. I have never cut slices off any of my patients. Surgery is not one of my skills.'

'She's not that kind of person, Dad. She never wants her pound of flesh.'

'With a remark like that, Fred,' commented my sister, 'it's time to drop the subject.'

Instead the conversation switched to Gilbert & Sullivan during the meal. My parents were disappointed that they had not been able to see the performance of 'The Pirates of Penzance' by the Church Society I had formed in Pontywen. The journey to my parish would have been impossible to make in a day and there was nowhere where they could stay for the night.

'Never mind,' said Eleanor, 'next year you will be able to stay with us.'

'What a privilege to be able to spend the night with the leading man and the leading lady.'

'You really are a big head, Frederick,' retorted my loved one.

'Hear! hear!' my mother exclaimed. 'You put him in his place, my dear. I have had to do that on times. I remember when I went to meet him at the station after his first term in college, something happened with his luggage. "Oh, damn!" he said. "So that's what they teach you up there, is it?" I said to him. He didn't swear anymore after that.'

'I've done a lot of amateur dramatics and concert party stuff,' my father said. 'Comic monologues and sketches. I've got a part in the local dramatic society's play but that's all spoken. I'd like to do something like Gilbert and Sullivan.'

'That wouldn't be much use,' replied my mother. 'You always shut your eyes when you sing and in any case it's always off key.'

'Don't be so hard on him, Mam,' intervened my sister. 'He's all right in "The monks of St Bernard's".'

'What's "The monks of St Bernards"?' Eleanor asked.

'It's the Secombe song which we used to sing at every Christmas party down at my grandparents. There would be about thirty or more Secombes there and it was the family anthem – very rude and very funny but not suggestive.'

'That's enough of that, Carol,' my mother said. 'I don't know what Eleanor will think of us what with your father's carving question and now "The monks of St Bernard's".'

'I think you're a great family and I'm glad I'm going to join you. After the stuffy conversation we have at our dinner table this is like a breath of fresh air.'

My mother beamed.

It was a very happy ride back to Pontywen. We sang most of the 'Pirates of Penzance', solos and choruses, with a few hymns thrown in for good measure, including two repeats of 'Cwm Rhondda'.

'I can see by the look on your face.' remarked Mrs Richards, 'that you've had a really salubrious time. I thought they'd like Eleanor and vice versus.'

'You are dead right, Mrs Richards,' I replied. 'We've had a wonderful day. She has become part of the family already.'

Charles Wentworth-Baxter was equally anxious next morning to know how the day had gone in Swansea. When I went into rhapsodies about the visit, he said. 'I'm glad about that. It makes up for the miserable afternoon I had with the Mothers' Union.'

'Why, was it more miserable than usual?' I asked.

'When I got there, Miss Phillips informed me that the speaker had been taken ill. Would I give a talk instead? Imagine me.'

I could, I said.

'Well, I rummaged round in my brain,' he went on. 'OK don't look at me like that, as if there was nothing there to find. Anyway I thought I would give them a potted version of a book I've just finished reading for the third time.'

'What book was that?'

'Jane Austen's *Emma*. It's one of the best novels in English literature and it's about a woman whose life, despite her many faults, has a happy ending. I thought they would be interested. They weren't. After the first few minutes they started talking to each other. So much so that I lost the thread of the story and it just finished nowhere. I've never been so glad as when Miss Phillips announced that tea was ready and the whole ghastly thing was over.'

'You must admit, Charles, that Jane Austen's *Emma* and St Mary's Pontywen Mothers' Union don't go together.'

'Why not? Women are women the world over and it's a classic, woman's story.'

'There is a slight difference between the aristocratic world of Emma in the early nineteenth century and the mining valleys of South Wales.'

'Perhaps it was the way I told it,' said my crestfallen colleague.

'I doubt if Jane Austen would have done any better if she had told it herself,' I assured him. 'What's more, if you had a miserable afternoon yesterday, I shall be having a miserable morning today. I have to take the funeral arranged by Mr Matthews.'

Miserable it was not. I turned up at the house of mourning, wondering whether Dr Hughes would be one of the few present. The mourners were imbibing in the front room and among them was Eleanor's senior partner.

'Ah! Mr Secombe,' he exclaimed, 'have a little something "for your stomach's sake" as St Paul put it. Dry or sweet?'

He poured me a glass of dry sherry.

'I'm here as a friend of the family,' he explained. 'I've known them for very many years. Splendid people.'

Miss Hannah Jones came in from the middle room, neatly

dressed in black and carrying a large Bible which she placed on the table.

'Good morning, young man,' she said, as if addressing one of her pupils. 'Would you mind reading your lesson from our family Bible. It was used at the funerals of my parents and, perhaps, at those of their parents. Isn't it a lovely sunny morning? My sister could not have had a more congenial day for her farewell.'

She introduced me to Mr Elias Griffiths, 'my former head-master', and his wife, to Councillor and Mrs Moses Evans, 'old friends', and to Mr and Mrs Gwyn Tobias, 'neigh-bours'. 'Dr Evans, you know, of course.'

Conversation continued at a sherry party level, as if there were no corpse involved or a service to follow. The arrival of the hearse and the two limousines outside cast a shadow over the proceedings.

The undertaker and the bearers were ushered upstairs. In the meanwhile, I began the service in the front room with the reading from St Paul's First Epistle to the Corinthians, Chapter 15, verses 20 to the end, beginning with the awe-inspiring words 'Now is Christ risen from the dead and become the first fruits of them that slept.'

By the time I had come to the prayers, Mr Matthews and his employees were carrying the coffin into the hearse.

'Thank you,' said Miss Hannah Jones as I finished my ministrations. 'My sister would have appreciated that.'

Mr Matthews knocked at the front-room door. Looking at his list, he announced 'The Reverend Secombe, Miss Hannah Jones and Dr Evans in the first coach. Councillor and Mrs Moses Evans and Mr and Mrs Gwyn Tobias in the second.'

I sat in the front seat of the first limousine, with Miss Hannah Jones and Dr Evans sharing the seat in the back. He appeared to be holding her hand.

When we arrived at the churchyard, I donned my surplice and stole ready for the procession to the graveside. Miss Jones, dry-eyed and apparently unmoved by the occasion, engaged in conversation with the other seven mourners. The undertaker summoned his four bearers who lifted the coffin from the hearse in professional style and we made our way to the burial plot, as I recited the sentences from the Book of Common Prayer.

By now I had been caught up in the unreality of the situation. I felt as if I were engaged in some kind of a charade. 'Almighty God,' I prayed, 'with whom do live the spirits of them that depart hence in the Lord, and with whom the souls of the faithful, after they are delivered from the burden of the flesh, are in joy and felicity.'

This is all gobbledygook to these people, I said to myself. They cannot wait to get it all over to return to the sherry and the sandwiches. Full-back Jones winked at me as I passed him on my way back to the funeral car. That wink from the gravedigger summed up the travesty.

'You will stay for some refreshments,' said Miss Hannah Jones as I shook hands with her after the service.

'Please accept my apologies,' I replied. 'I'm afraid I have to get back.'

'What a pity! I was hoping to have the further pleasure of your acquaintance. Perhaps another time.'

'I'll call and see you again in the near future.'

Little did I know how near the future would be.

That afternoon I decided to visit Idris and Gwen Shoemaker. Idris 'the Milk' and his wife had become dear friends of mine since I arrived in Pontywen. During my first week in the parish they invited me to a fish and chip supper at their little terraced house. Since then, Friday-night fish and chips with them had become a regular date in my social diary. However, over the past few weeks, my Friday evenings had been spent with Eleanor in preparing our first home in Bevan's Row – or, to put it more exactly, attending on Eleanor as she did the preparing. Tonight was going to be no exception.

Gwen opened the door to me.

'What a nice surprise!' she said. 'Idris will be pleased.

He's having his forty winks. It's a wonder you didn't hear his snores in the street.'

She led me down the passage and into the middle room where Idris was outstretched in the armchair by the fireside, a newspaper draped over his legs and his head sunk deep into his chest. A loud snore greeted us as Gwen opened the door.

'Idris, stir yourself! We've got a visitor.'

The little milkman sat up, as if jerked on a string. His paper fell to the floor. He stared as if seeing 'through a glass darkly'.

'Mr Secombe!' he croaked. 'A bit early for fish and chips. Lovely to see you, boy. Sit down and stop making the place look untidy.'

'You're soon awake,' commented Gwen.

I sat down opposite him. There was a roaring fire in the grate.

Summer or winter there was always a roaring fire. It was small wonder that Idris fell asleep so quickly in his armchair.

'I've been thinking,' he said. 'What about an outing or a dinner for the G. and S.? Keep them together till we start again in the autumn.'

He had been an excellent Sergeant of the Police in 'The Pirates of Penzance' and his son Percy had been a great success as the little policeman at the end of the line. Reluctant to join the company at the beginning, Idris was now its most enthusiastic member.

'Good idea, Idris, but don't ask me to organize it. I've more than enough on my plate at the moment. Since you thought of the idea you had better take charge. Wait until after the wedding and then I'll call a meeting.'

'Fine, Mr Secombe. I don't mind doing the organizing, if you say so. Better me than Bertie Owen offering his services. E'd end up with booking an outing and a dinner on the same day, knowing 'im.'

Later in the evening as Eleanor was putting up the curtains

in the front room in Bevan's Row, I told her about the proposed function.

'I'm all for it,' she said. 'As Idris says, it's a means of keeping them together. Now that we're talking about G. and S., life is going to be very hectic next winter – I shall be busier than ever once this National Health service gets under way. We'll have to see to our own meals. There'll be no Mrs Richards to cook yours. It may be that I shall have to withdraw my valuable services as leading lady.'

'In that case, I shall have to follow suit. Get somebody else to do the production and Trevor can take over as tenor lead.'

'Come off it, Fred. I am not *making* any decisions at this stage, neither are you. It's something we shall have to bear in mind. At the moment, the only thing that matters is a very important event just round the corner.'

She kissed me lightly on the lips and went back to arranging the curtains.

When we came back to my 'digs', Eleanor came in for a cup of tea before returning home. Mrs Richards met us at the door with a parcel.

'It's that Miss Jones. The one whose sister's funeral you were the official at this morning. She said there's a letter inside.'

I took the parcel into my room. While I was tearing the brown paper covering from a large cardboard box, Eleanor proceeded to tease me about the remarks I had made earlier over the uncaring attitude of her former schoolteacher and the rest of the mourners that morning.

'You should have given it back, not opened it, if you feel so strongly about her attitude.'

'Hold on, let's see what's inside,' I said.

I removed the rest of the paper and opened the lid of the box. Inside was a cut glass sherry decanter.

Eleanor indulged in a whistle of appreciation.

'Do you realize, Secombe, that is Waterford glass? It's a very expensive present.'

While she was admiring the unexpected gift, I read the letter which accompanied it:

Dear Mr Secombe,

First I must thank you for the dignity and the sincerity of your ministrations this morning. The Authorized Version and the Prayer Book combined with your reading to provide a fitting end to a life which had seen more than its fair share of suffering.

It might have seemed to you that the absence of any emotion on my part indicated a stony heart. I can assure you that this is not the case. My sister had wished to die long ago but it was not to be. Although I do not share your convictions about an after life I rejoice that her tribulations are over.

Dr Hughes informed me this morning that you and Eleanor are to be married in a fortnight's time. I had no idea that the happy day was so near. Will you please accept this wedding present with my best wishes for your future happiness.

Yours sincerely,

I handed the letter to Eleanor. When she finished it, she took my face into her two hands.

'Fred, my love, I think you have been put in your place. Judge not, than you be not judged. Old Hannah may be the third member of an eternal triangle with the emphasis on "eternal", or shall we say twenty years at least, but she has much more compassion that you think. In any case, if you knew Mrs Hughes, you would understand why she and my partner need each other.'

'Every day I learn,' I replied. 'I am beginning to realize that I shall never stop learning. It's a hard lesson to take in. When I was eighteen I went up to London to represent my school at the Empire Youth Rally to celebrate the Coronation in 1937. On the final night Stanley Baldwin spoke to us in the Albert Hall. It was his last speech as Prime Minister. One sentence has remained with me ever since. 'Dogmatism is the prerogative of youth.' I can only assume that as I grow older, I shall grow wiser.'

'Amen,' said Eleanor. 'PS. Shall we go together tomorrow evening and thank her for the present?'

'Amen to that also,' I sealed the compact with a kiss.

5

I was kneeling down in the Vicar's stall in the parish church, enjoying the peace and tranquillity. I had finished reading morning prayer. Since Charles had chosen Saturday as his day off, I was able to indulge in a warm bath of mental torpor and went to sleep on my knees.

Suddenly there was a tap on my shoulder. I awoke with a start, like the child Samuel when the Lord broke the stillness of the shrine.

'Mr Secombe, can I have a word with you in the vestry?' It was not the voice of the Lord but that of PC Will Davies, otherwise known as 'Will Book and Pencil'.

I followed his big hulk into the vestry.

'Sit down, Constable,' I motioned him into a chair while I sat behind the Vicar's desk, enjoying the seat of authority.

'Well, it's like this. You may have some trouble at your twelve o'clock wedding this morning. We have reason to believe that a member of the bride's family will try to stop the marriage when you ask if there's any impediment.'

'Is there any impediment?'

'None at all. There's been some bad feeling between the two families, including a bit of fighting but the two youngsters want to get married despite all that. We'll have two of the boys from the CID there in plain clothes just in case anything happens. They'll make themselves known to you before the service. Don't worry in any case.'

'Thank you. I'll try not to.'

'Right, I'll be going then. By the way, if anybody gets up, they'll whip him or her away quickly for breach of the peace. Then you can carry on with the service. I don't think there'll be any trouble anyway. Morning.'

So saying he heaved himself out of the chair and plodded into the chancel. I could hear his heavy footsteps echoing down the nave. My heart was thumping in unison.

I opened the safe and took out the marriage registers. There were two weddings scheduled for the morning, one at eleven and one at twelve. The Vicar had filled in the details of both weddings neatly.

The bridegroom at the twelve o'clock wedding was named as Iorwerth Evan Jenkins, aged eighteen; occupation miner; address 24 Gelli Street. The bride was recorded as Shirley Ann Griffiths, aged eighteen – occupation, machinist; address, 26 Gelli Street. Neighbours. Both fathers were miners but evidently not comrades in arms.

It was a delightful May morning when I left the church. As I walked back to Mount Pleasant View, I kept thinking of a line from a Stanley Holloway monologue about the Battle of Hastings. 'It was a beautiful day for a battle.'

Mrs Richards did not know either family.

'That's a rough place, Gelli Street. When the Strike was on you couldn't walk down it. Children had no shoes or stockings on their feet. There had always been conflagration there, always.'

I arrived at the church at half-past ten to prepare for the first wedding. Already there were a handful of people outside the church doors. Ten minutes later Mr Greenfield the organist appeared in the vestry with the list of hymns for the two weddings. It was the usual diet of 'Love Divine' and 'The Lord's my Shepherd' for both occasions.

'Once upon a time,' said the organist, 'we used to have the marriage hymns set in Ancient and Modern. "The voice that breathed o'er, Eden", for example.'

'I can understand why they don't want that hymn nowadays. If you have a sense of humour, you could never sing it.'

'Why, Mr Secombe?'

'It contains that dreadful verse which begins 'Be present, awful father, to give away this bride'!

'Does it indeed? Well it's a nice tune, despite that.'

Soon he was at the organ, using the tremolo stop ad nauseam in his favourite voluntary, 'Moonlight and Roses'.

The bridegroom and his best man entered the vestry. They were two fresh-faced young soldiers from the South Wales Borderers Regiment, exuding good spirits, in more ways than one.

'Good morning, Reverend,' said the bridegroom. 'Lovely day, isn't it? This is my best man, Philip. He's a Londoner, but he can't help that.'

'Watch it, Dai O,' warned Philip. 'I'll see you in the playground after.'

The church was full of wedding guests, filling the air with excited chatter and drowning the tentative music supplied by Mr Greenfield. Having placed the bridegroom and the best man in their appropriate positions at the chancel steps, I went down to the back of the church to meet the bride and lead her down the aisle. She was a pretty little blonde, in full bridal array, on the arm of her proud father, whose occupation in the marriage register was given as 'colliery winder'.

It was a very happy service, overflowing with good will and with excellent congregational singing of the hymns. The signing of the register took place in the midst of cheerful banter. I was asked to stand outside the church door in the sunshine for a group photograph. Such was the bonhomie that I forgot for the moment the menace of the twelve o'clock wedding.

I went back into the church, gathered up the hymn books and prayer books and placed them on the table by the door in readiness for the next service, if they were needed. Perhaps both families will be more concerned with glowering at each other across the aisle than singing from a hymn book, I thought.

A few minutes later there was a tap on the vestry door and two young men entered. One of them, a diminutive figure in a suit which appeared to be too big for him, sported a black eye. He looked panic stricken. His friend introduced himself to me as Llew, the best man.

'Iorrie 'ad a bit of an accident last night,' he explained, 'and 'e's still a bit dazed.'

Iorrie nodded.

'Shall I pay you now?' asked Llew. 'Save time later, won't it?'

'If you want to,' I said.

'Get it all over a bit quicker at the end,' Llew fished into his inside pocket and handed me an envelope.

'Do you want to stay here in the vestry or go into the front pew in the church?' I enquired.

The bridegroom shook his head violently. I interpreted this as a sign that he preferred the safety of the vestry.

At five to twelve I decided that the time had come to escort the two of them into the nave of the church. In contrast to the noisy hubbub of the first wedding there was a deafening silence. There were about twenty or so guests either side of the aisle with a few more huddled at the back near the door. Mr Greenfield must have exhausted his repertoire at the organ. He was examining some copies of music on the organ stool. The atmosphere was fraught with menace in the nave.

I placed the bridegroom in his correct position at the foot of the chancel steps with his best man on his right hand side. Iorwerth Evan Jenkins stared fixedly ahead, as if expecting a bullet in his back at any moment.

There were so many hostile glances exchanged as I walked down the aisle that I felt as if I had made a path between a shower of arrows.

When I reached the church door, two large men approached me. They had carnations in their buttonholes and each had a camera slung over his shoulders. The taller of the two came up to me and said, out of the corner of his mouth, 'Don't worry, Mr Secombe, we're the CID. We've got it all in hand.'

At this moment the bride arrived, attended by two brides-maids whose facial expressions indicated they were about to witness an execution. Although it was a warm, sunny morning, young Shirley was shivering with apprehension. Her father, Caradoc Griffiths, miner, had the look of a mourner about him. His thick black moustache drooped at the ends.

I signalled to Mr Greenfield to begin the Wedding March. One by one the congregation arose. As I walked slowly down the aisle, I felt as if I was being followed by a coffin rather than a bride.

When I turned round to begin the service, I faced a sullen congregation. Which one of these, I wondered, is to be the disruptive element. They all looked qualified for such action.

'Hymn number 520, "Love Divine all loves excelling",' I announced. I gave a hymn book to the bridegroom to share with the bride. They managed a wan smile at each other. The bride's father looked solidly ahead.

No one attempted to sing. It was unnerving. I sang all six verses as a solo. The hymn ended and I had to begin the service. My mouth was dry. My heart beats were accelerating again at an uncomfortable pace. I read through the preface at an unseemly speed. Then came the critical moment.

'Therefore if any man can show any just cause, why they may not lawfully be joined together let him now speak or else hereafter forever hold his peace.'

Normally at this point I would pause and look around the congregation. Not today. I went straight into the charge to the bride and groom. 'I require and charge you both . . .' The flash point had come and gone. There had been no dramatic interruption. I could feel the sweat trickling down my back.

The rest of the service proceeded without incident and without the participation of the congregation. Apparently they did not know the words of the Lord's Prayer and they could not be bothered to read the responses. I rendered another solo in 'The King of Love'. A few minutes later and the silence in church was continued in the vestry. I asked both fathers to witness the ceremony. They were like boxers. Each went back to his respective corner after they had signed the register. There was no exchange of partners among the parents for the parade down the aisle. The one redeeming feature of the wedding was the obvious love the bride and groom had for each other.

As I went down to the back of the church to close the doors, the two CID men came up to me. 'Well, Mr Secombe,' said one of them, 'no trouble after all. Still, you can never tell with family feuds.'

'It was like having the Montagues and the Capulets in church,' I commented.

'Who are they?' asked the other detective.

'Don't be so ignorant,' his companion said. 'They're in one of Shakespeare's plays. *Macbeth*, I think.'

'*Romeo and Juliet*,' I corrected.

'I knew it was something like that. Come on, Hugh, time to get back.'

When I went across to the Vicarage to deliver the marriage fee into the safe keeping of Mrs Lilywhite, ready for Father Whittaker's return, the housekeeper asked me in.

'I'm glad you've called,' she said. 'I was going to come down to your lodgings if you hadn't called..'

'Father wants you to phone him in Tenby. He said it's urgent. I've got the number for you on his desk.'

I went into the study which reeked with the smell of polish in Canon Llewelyn's time. Now the only odour was that of fried onions wafted in from the kitchen. The dust on the top of the desk would have made Mrs Llewellyn die of shame.

It took a few minutes for the local exchange to put me in touch with Tenby. While that was happening, I tried to think what merited the urgent call. The Vicar was not due back until the following Saturday.

When eventually I made contact with my superior, he hastened to assure me that there was nothing traumatic to report.

'I was in such a hurry to get away last Sunday that I forgot to remind you that there are three baptisms tomorrow afternoon in the Parish Church. One of the mothers wants to be churched by the way. I hope you haven't arranged any baptisms in St Padarn's at the same time.'

'Fortunately, Vicar, I haven't.'

'Good. Otherwise Wentworth-Baxter would have to do them and I wouldn't wish that on any child. By the way, would you mind calling at the homes of the parents sometime today? I usually pay a visit to them the week before. Is all well?'

'Apart from a strange wedding this morning, there is nothing unusual to report. I'll tell you about the wedding when you come back.'

'You certainly must. Thank you about the baptisms. See you next Saturday. Oh, you will find all the details of the baptisms in the top right-hand drawer of the desk. Goodbye.'

I opened the drawer and extracted the three immaculately completed forms at the top of the pile of papers. They were a strange duo, the Vicar and his housekeeper. He was neatness personified and she was careless of her person as well as negligent in the house.

I had arranged to meet Eleanor at our future home in Bevan's Row that afternoon. As she said when we met there, 'This is going to be the bane of our married life, having to cope with the unexpected. So we may as well start getting used to it now. Off you go. See you later.'

The first address was 'The Hawthorns', Ashburnam Close in the Upper market end of Pontywen. There were half a dozen Mock Tudor detached houses cocooned in a cul-de-sac, each with its tree-lined drive plus garage.

A brand new Jaguar was parked outside for all the neighbours to see. I edged my way past the gleaming showpiece and pressed the button at the side of the door. A middle-aged lady appeared, clad in tweeds, more like a squiress than a Valleys housewife.

'I'm the Curate of Pontywen and I've called about the baptism arranged for tomorrow of Deborah Jane Morris.'

It was evident that she regarded me as a minion.

'Well, I'm Mrs Nicholls. My daughter fixed the ceremony with the Vicar some weeks ago and we have arranged a baptismal party. Has there been any hitch?'

'None at all. The Vicar is away on a short holiday. He has asked me to take the service and to check on the three baptisms involved.'

'So there are two other baptisms and Father Whittaker will not be there. We understood that he would be officiating and that my grandchild's christening would be the only one.'

'I'm afraid that I shall be the officiant and that there will be two other baptismal parties present. If it's any comfort to you, I have baptised many babies – and so far satisfactorily to all concerned.'

She raised her eyebrows and fluttered her eyelashes.

'Don't misunderstand me, Mr – er –'

'Secombe,' I said.

'Mr Secombe. I am sure that you are quite capable of taking the service. It's simply that we had Father Whittaker's name as the officiant on all the invitations we sent out. Furthermore we assumed that my granddaughter's christening would not be one of a number.'

'Is it possible for me to have a word with your daughter?'

'She has gone down to Cardiff to pick up the christening cake. I'll tell her that you have called.'

With those words I was dismissed and went on my way to my second port of call, 14 Sebastopol Street. Evidently the Crimean War had made a big impression on the builders in Pontywen. Inkerman and Balaclava were also commemorated in the terraced cottages of the town. Sebastopol Street looked as dated as the Crimean War. Every house needed a coat of paint and the stonework was encrusted with the grime of heavy industry.

Number 14's front-window curtains were partly off the hooks and were in need of cleaning. I banged on the discoloured brass knocker. A baby's crying wailed from the middle room and a woman's voice screamed, 'Stop fighting you two or I'll break your bloody necks.' I braced myself for the confrontation.

A lady in her thirties flung open the door. She was wearing a dirty pinafore and little else behind it. It was a warm May afternoon. The sight of a clergyman on her doorstep transformed her in an instant from a virago into a quietly spoken model of respectability.

'Oh, you're from the church?'

'Yes, Mrs Williams. Your daughter, Ava Joan, is due to be baptised tomorrow.'

'That's right and I want to be churched as well. My mother always says that you've got to be cleansed before you go out and about.'

'It's not cleansing, Mrs Williams. It's just you giving thanks for the birth of your child.'

'Is it? Well, I never knew that before. Anyway my mother was done every time there was a christening and so 'ave I been with my other two.'

'Could you possibly come a bit earlier than three o'clock tomorrow? I'd like to have you churched before the baptisms.'

At this stage pandemonium broke out in the middle room. Her self control broke.

'Will you two stop fighting!'

Her voice would have done credit to a sergeant major.

Again there was instant modulation.

'Excuse me, but I'll 'ave to see to them in there. I'll be there early tomorrow.'

The door was closed and from inside came an indication that Mrs Williams was about to break the necks of the two miscreants.

My third visit was to number 22 Station Road, one of the more respectable streets in Pontywen. Venetian blinds with lace curtains behind adorned the front window. The door knocker gleamed. The lady of the house appeared to be in her early forties, neatly dressed in blouse and skirt.

'Mrs Thomas, I've called about the christening of your son Thomas William tomorrow.'

'Come on in, Mr Secombe. I've not met you before but I have been at St Mary's when you have taken the service.'

I was shown into the front room where the rexine armchairs and the settee sported lace covers on the armrests. On the mantelpiece between two china dogs were photographs of a wedding and of a soldier in battledress, with sergeant's stripes.

'Would you like a cup of tea? It won't take a minute.'

While she was out of the room, I took the opportunity to examine the photographs.

Mrs Thomas came back into the room with an embroidered cloth to set on a side table.

'That's our wedding photograph taken outside St Mary's in 1936 and that's my husband just before he went to Singapore. Tom was in a Japanese prisoner-of-war camp. I didn't hear anything for more than two years. We all thought he was dead. Well, not exactly, I had a feeling deep down that perhaps he was alive. Then I had a card in his own handwriting. It was the most wonderful moment in my life. That is until he came home last year and I fell for a baby, our first. What's more he's a boy. So he's got his father's name. As it says in the Bible, my cup is running over. Talking of which, I must get you a cup of tea.'

I had never seen such radiance in a face as there was in that of Elspeth Thomas.

'We've arranged a family party for tomorrow, grandparents on both sides and loads of aunties, uncles, cousins – everybody. Sorry, Mr Secombe, I forgot to ask – milk and sugar?'

She continued to talk, non-stop, through the light refreshments and until I left the house, with my head in a whirl. When I arrived back at Bevan's Row, Eleanor was busy with her sewing-machine on the kitchen table.

'The curtains for the bedroom,' she announced. 'Then that's the lot. You look in a daze, dear boy.'

'I've been talked into insensibility by a very happy woman who has just had her first child at the age of forty-two. Before that I had to contend with someone who wished to be "cleansed" from the sin of having a baby and before that I was interviewed by a duchess with a new Jaguar in Ashburnam Close.'

'Who was that, for heaven's sake?'

'A Mrs Nicholls who objects to her grandchild being baptized by a curate and to other children being "done" at the same time.'

'You know who that is, Frederick. Her husband is Ernest Nicholls, the managing director of the steelworks. Her daughter, a snotty young lady, has appeared in the *Tatler*. She's married to an officer in the Welsh Guards. I think he's a captain.'

'In that case it's going to be a very interesting afternoon tomorrow – what you would call a genuine social mix.'

I arrived at the parish church the following afternoon at two-thirty p.m., to find some early comers outside the main door. It was obvious that they were part of the Ashburnam Close party by their accents, their clothes and their general attitude.

'Which part of the church is reserved for the Morris christening?' demanded a dowager clad in the kind of dress and hat worn by the late Queen Mary in the thirties.

'You may sit where you like,' I replied.

'But surely it is advisable that each baptismal party be together.'

'On the basis of first come, first served, I would suggest that you begin to occupy the front seats on the south side opposite the font, leaving the front pew available for the parents and godparents.'

Soon five pews were full, leaving the front one occupied by the three godparents.

At a quarter to three, Mr and Mrs Tom Thomas and Tom Junior arrived with godparents and friends. They occupied the front pew on the north side of the aisle. Mr Thomas's lean face still showed the effect of his imprisonment by the Japanese.

Five minutes later there was a hullabaloo outside and the Williams contingent erupted into the church. It sounded as if some of them had spent a few hours in the Working men's Club as a warm up for the occasion. Mrs Williams was carrying the baby, wrapped in a shawl around her, Welsh fashion. She came up to me as I stood in the aisle handing out cards containing the baptismal service.

'Sorry I'm late,' she said. 'Do you mind if I'm done after the christenings are over. I don't fancy doing it in front of that crowd.'

'As you please,' I replied, only too relieved.

At three o'clock Captain and Mrs Morris plus baby and Mr and Mrs Ernest Nicholls had not arrived. The laughter and banter at the back of the church grew louder to the disgust of the society element up front in the south aisle who turned round and glared. Meanwhile the two obstreperous brothers of the Williams baby were running amok in the side aisles, despite noisy remonstrations from their mother.

After waiting another ten minutes, I was about to go ahead with the service without the Morrises, when they made a ceremonial entrance at the back of the church to muted cheers from the Sebastopol Street crowd who had already begun to sing 'Why are we waiting?' *sotto voce*.

The Captain was in uniform and his wife was dressed in a style worthy of the *Tatler*. She carried the baby who was robed in an elaborate christening gown, as she would a bouquet. Behind them stalked Mr and Mrs Ernest Nicholls, glowering at the two little boys who impeded their progress down the aisle.

I waited on the chancel step for the noise to die down. The two boys were dragged into a pew by someone whom I assumed to be their father.

'Will you please follow the service on the card provided and would the parents and godparents please come to the front and stand at the chancel step.'

There was something akin to a rugby scrum at the back of the church as the Williams party sorted themselves out. Eventually they arrived at the front. In the meanwhile the Ashburnam Close section rose to their feet, looking around at the others who were still seated, as if pitying their ignorance.

'Will you all be seated, except, of course, for the parents and godparents?'

Very self-consciously, they sat down.

'Have these children been already baptised or no?' I asked, according to the opening words of the service. It must be the most pointless sentence in the Book of Common Prayer. Why should parents bring children for baptism when they have been already baptised?

The Morrises and the Thomases, with their godparents, said firmly 'No'. The Williamses shook their heads. As the sonorous centuries-old language echoed around the church, Ava Joan Williams, held by a teenage girl, began to wail. Mrs Williams produced a dummy from thin air and thrust it into the infant's mouth.

Ava Joan's crying aroused Deborah Jane from her slumbers in her sumptuous christening gown. She began to show her vocal prowess on a scale several decibels more powerful than her neighbour. A lady in her forties, in picture hat and silks attempted to silence the child by gently rocking her. Father, moustachioed and erect, stared in front, in the best traditions of the Welsh Guards. Mother, red faced, stared at the floor. Ex-Sergeant Thomas and his wife looked at each other in smug satisfaction as their offspring slept soundly in the arms of his elderly grandmother.

The Godparents made their promises against the background of Deborah Jane's continuous wailing and Ava

Joan's young Godmother fighting a losing battle to control a remarkably agile young baby, dropping her service card in the process.

'I'll 'old it for you to read, Marlene,' said Mrs Williams. There did not seem to be much point in the exercise since Marlene's literacy was not of the highest order.

'All this I steadfastly believe,' was a sentence which left her in bemused silence while the others repeated it. She did manage to say 'I will' as the last of the promises was made.

I decided to baptize Deborah Jane first, in the hope that perhaps someone would take the noisy infant out once her baptism was completed. The transfer of the baby into my arms, proved to be a complicated process since her elaborate gown became entangled with the sleeve of my surplice. All this time the crying was incessant. When I poured the cold water on the child's forehead, the decibel count multiplied to earsplitting intensity.

After I had received the child 'into the congregation of

Christ's flock' and given her the sign of the cross, I bent over to kiss her on the forehead. As I did so, she chose that moment to regurgitate her feed. The sour milk bespattered my brow and trickled down my cheek. Her crying ceased.

'There,' said Mrs Williams, 'the poor little bu-er-bundle had the wind, that's all.'

Deborah Jane's mother gave her a withering look. As I wiped my face with my handkerchief, I said a silent prayer of thanks for the restored stillness in the shrine.

Now I was faced with a struggle with the energetic Ava Joan. Marlene handed over her charge with a sigh of relief. 'Name this child,' I said. There was no answer. 'Tell the Curate the baby's name, Marlene,' instructed Mrs Williams.

'Ava Joan,' she whispered.

'Ava Joan, I baptize thee', I pronounced 'in the name of the Father', the first drop of water on her face made her shoot up in my arms, 'and of the Son', I brought her down from my shoulder and applied the water, 'and of the Holy Ghost.' This time she stiffened her legs and pushed against me, almost disappearing into the font.

By the time I had received her into the Church and made the sign of the cross on her forehead, I felt exhausted. 'You can give 'er to me now, Marlene,' said Mrs Williams. 'You've done your little bit.' The young Godmother gave back her Godchild to its mother with alacrity, only too pleased to be free from her burden.

The baptism of Thomas William Thomas was conducted without incident as he slept soundly throughout, to the evident pride of his parents.

'Never mind,' said Mrs Williams to Mrs Morris in the vestry at the end of the service, 'she've cried the devil out of her.'

Mrs Morris eyed her icily for the second time and stalked out of the vestry to rejoin her party who were admiring the now peaceful Deborah.

'What about me being churched then?' asked Mrs Williams.

6

'We've got to get Will Book and Pencil to sort this out.'
Bertie Owen, Charlie Hughes, his elderly fellow church-
warden and myself were in the St Padarn's vestry after
Evensong, Charlie's deaf-aid battery had run down.

'What's that you say, Bertie?' he inquired.

'I said we've got to get Will Book and Pencil to sort this
business out,' bellowed Bertie.

'All right, there's no need to shout for all the world to
know. We've got to keep it quiet, you dull bugger. Anyway,
the last thing we want to do is to bring the police in. Think
of the scandal.'

'I think Charlie's quite right,' I said. 'This is something
we must do ourselves. We shall have to think of a way to
prevent it happening again.'

'In that case, leave it to me. I'll put my thinking-cap on.'

'I didn't know you had one, Bertie. No, it must be a
strategy we devise between us, preferably before we leave
this vestry. It's our problem and we must solve it ourselves.'

The problem confronting us concerned pilfering from the
collection plate. There had been complaints from some
members of the congregation that the list of money received
from their numbered envelopes did not tally with their contributions. Furthermore, that evening I had put a ten-shilling
note on the alms dish. It was given to me as a thanksgiving by an invalid, an elderly lady, after I had taken her

Communion at her home. When I returned to the vestry some time later, the note had vanished from the alms dish.

'The first thing: from now on,' I said, 'the alms dish must remain on the altar until the time comes to count the collection. Leaving the money on the vestry table for ten minutes or so before counting is asking for trouble. What is unpleasant is the fact that it puts everybody in the choir under suspicion or anybody else who comes into the vestry.'

'I think that's the only thing to do, Mr Secombe. Mind, it may not be somebody from the choir. The sidesmen come in and out as well,' said Charlie.

'It wouldn't be any one of my sidesmen, Charlie. I know them all. Could be a choirboy, perhaps.'

'Bertie, suspicion rests upon everybody, including your sidesmen. In any case it is no use surmising.'

'Don't you think we ought to set a trap, like putting marked coins in the collection? Or perhaps I could keep a watch, hiding in a corner or something?'

Bertie's thinking-cap had come into operation. Already he could see himself as Sherlock Holmes.

'For the time being, I suggest that all we do is to make sure that the alms dish is not left unattended in the vestry. If there is further pilfering then we must track the person down.'

'As you wish, Mr Secombe, but I shall certainly be keeping an eye open.'

'You do that, Bertie.'

There the discussion ended and I made my way to Bevan's Row to meet Eleanor. Every spare moment she was down at our future home, like a bird preparing its nest. The curtains were up, the furniture in place. There were still the carpets to come for the front room and the bedroom. Otherwise the house was ready for occupation.

When I arrived I found her in conversation with Mrs Williams, a garrulous old woman who lived next door with her one and only son, a miner. I met her first on the day when I discovered Miss Bradshaw, the previous occupant of our house, unconscious on the floor in the middle room. At that time she was clad in a filthy old mackintosh and sporting a man's flat cap. Her face was covered in coal dust. She had been shovelling her son's quota of coal nuts in a wheelbarrow.

Now she was dressed in her Sunday best, having returned from chapel.

'There's nice to see you again, Mr Secombe. I've been telling the doctor how thrilled we are to have you as neighbours. Baptist I am. Never miss a Sunday but we're all one, aren't we? I expect you know Mr Protheroe, our pastor, BA, BD. Very good preacher.'

I have met him once or twice, Mrs Williams, at funerals. Perhaps one of these days I'll meet him on a more congenial occasion.'

'Oh, he's wonderful at funerals. He gave my husband a beautiful send off. He had everybody in tears, even the organist. One of the best funerals they've ever had at Bethel, they say. He died of the dust, doctor. No compensation. Acute bronchitis they said. Now I'm worried for my son. He hasn't started coughing yet. So that's something.'

'Perhaps he will not get pneumonoconiosis, Mrs Williams. Some of the men seem to avoid any trace of it. I hope so for his sake. It's a very distressing complaint. Well, we must go and see what's next to be done in the house.

With these words, Eleanor turned quickly and with her key poised, opened the door in a trice. Once inside, she said, 'That was a narrow escape. I could see she was ready to give a graphic description of her husband's condition. Before long I expect I shall be treated to another monologue, not to mention you.'

'I'm afraid that's going to be a constant hazard, my love. However, if I can make as quick an exit each time as you this evening, I shall cope nicely.'

'Let's sit down on our leather settee and share the flask of coffee I've brought. You can tell me about the christenings this afternoon.'

I launched into an account of the baptisms, with special reference to the incessant wailing of the Morris baby. She burst into peals of laughter.

'The Morrises and Nichols must have wished the earth to swallow them up, especially since they were in the company of the lower classes. I can't think why Father Whittaker hadn't arranged a special event for them.'

'Neither can I. He is such a snob.'

'Perhaps you slipped up with the times of the baptisms.'

I don't think so. If I have, I shall know it when he returns from Tenby.'

As we drank our coffee, I mentioned the mystery of the missing ten-shilling note.

'I think we shan't have any more trouble like that. We are going to leave the alms dish on the altar until they are ready to count the money in the vestry. That should cure it. I hope it does because next Sunday is the Whitsun collection for the Curate and I don't want to lose any of those precious takings.'

'In that case I shall be in St Padarn's next Sunday and I shall boost your income with a pound note not a ten-shilling one.'

'You lady bountiful.'

I kissed her warmly.

'Thank you,' she said. 'Save the rest for a fortnight's time. You can have as many kisses as you want then, not counting those I want. Speaking of which, as it were, I must get the car serviced for our trip to Cornwall.'

We had arranged to spend our wedding night in a hotel in Bristol and then to drive to our hotel in Newquay to stay for ten days.

'I think we ought to have a short service of intercession for the Morris Minor before we set out as well as the garage service. It will need both.'

'My poor old car needs a vote of confidence, Secombe. It has served me well and must continue to do so for the next couple of years. So please don't knock it.'

'Only playing, Miss. Honest.'

'I'll forgive you this once and that's it. Now come and help me measure the space for the carpet in this room.'

On returning to my digs I was surprised to find my colleague's bicycle parked outside. Since it was past ten o'clock I scented trouble. Before I could open the door, Charles flung it open.

'Am I glad to see you,' he breathed. 'I've been waiting here for the past hour or so.'

'I've been down at Bevan's Row with Eleanor, measuring up the room for the carpet. What's the matter?'

He preceded me into my room and closed the door behind me as if we were about to be attacked by some hostile force.

'It's Jones, Blaenycwm.'

'What's the matter with Jones, Blaenycwm?'

'He told me after Evensong that they're going to petition the Vicar to have me out of Llanhyfryd. He said they've made a list of complaints about me: that I'm late for service; that I only preach for a few minutes and they can't understand what I'm preaching anyway; and that I don't visit anybody out there and so on.'

Evan Jones, Vicar's warden at Llanhyfryd parish church, which was linked with Pontywen, was a mischief-maker who had attempted to cause trouble for me during the interregnum before Father Whittaker became Vicar. He added injury to insult when his dog bit me on my visit to his farm.

'Now, calm down, Charles. Let's have a cup of tea and look at all this in perspective.'

I went into the middle room where my landlady was ensconced, half asleep, in her rocking chair.

'It's all right, Mrs Richards. I'm just going to make a cup of tea for Charles and me.'

'You'll do no such thing. You go back and look after that young man. He needs your help. He's all strung up like a wasp in a jam jar.'

When I went back to my room, my colleague was pacing about the room.

'For heaven's sake, sit down, man. Mrs Richards is going to bring us some tea in a minute.'

'What am I going to do, Fred? I'm not in the Vicar's good books as it is.'

'First of all, sit down.'

He sat, at my word of command.

I sat opposite him in my armchair.

'Don't you remember that he tried to get me on the wrong foot with the Rural Dean before the Vicar came? I dealt with him then and you can deal with him now, but you must keep your cool. Now then, how often have you been late for service?'

'Well, the congregation are never there on time, for a start. They're all farmers or farm labourers, as you know, and if the milking takes longer than expected or something like that, they'll come in halfway through the service. Old Jones himself is sometimes late. So I don't see what he has got to shout about.'

'You haven't answered my question, Charles. How often have you been late for service?'

'It's not easy when you're cycling, especially if the wind's against you. So sometimes I have been a little late but never more than ten minutes or so.'

'That's ten minutes or so too much. As for your preaching they haven't any right to talk about that. I know what you are like as far as visiting is concerned – abysmal. The only thing we can do is to put a stop to this petition before they bring it to the Vicar. That means a confrontation with Evan Jones. Without him there would be no petition.'

There was a knock on the door and Mrs Richards came in with a pot of tea and a plate of biscuits.

'Help yourselves,' she said. 'I'm going to bed. You're looking a bit better now, Mr Wedgewood. Have a cup of tea and you'll be as right as the rain. Goodnight both.'

'She evidently thinks you are fragile, Mr Wedgewood, my old china.'

He began to laugh.

As we drank our tea, I told him about the christenings and the mystery of the missing money at St Padarn's. The tension began to drain from his face. Then came the inevitable.

'Do you think you could have a word with him, Fred? You know what I'm like.'

'It's your problem, Charles. He will probably tell me to mind my own business and he would be right.'

'Please, Fred.'

'Let me think it over. There must be something we can do.'

He left my digs much less desperate than when he arrived.

When Eleanor and I met next evening, shortly after her surgery stint, I told her about Charles's predicament.

'You're in luck, Secombe. Mrs Blodwen Jones is now a patient of mine and is housebound with badly ulcerated legs. The new treatment I am giving her is beginning to clear up her trouble. She is under the impression that I am a miracle worker. I am due to see her tomorrow afternoon. You come with me in my derided Morris Minor. You will avoid having your legs attacked by Evan Jones's dog and since you are soon to be my husband you can apply some psychological pressure on the old man. He is overjoyed to see his wife improving with the prospect of good cooked meals back again in the offing. He won't offend you if it means offending me.'

'Eleanor my love, you're brilliant.'

'I think every parson should marry a doctor. With one proviso.'

'What is that, pray?'

'She must be like you.'

'There's only one me.'

'In that case, I'm just thankful that this parson is going to marry this doctor.'

I gave her a bear hug.

'Would you mind leaving my ribs intact? Otherwise I

shall be in no fit condition to drive you to Blaenycwm Farm tomorrow.'

It was a lovely afternoon when we drove out into the countryside. The hedgerows were adorned with wild flowers and the fields were a fresh green.

'I wonder whether I'll have a country parish,' I mused.

'If you do, my dear, it will have to be near Pontywen for a number of years at least.'

'That is not impossible. There are quite a number of doddery rural rectors or vicars in this deanery, near to Pontywen.'

'And I'm sure there will be quite a number of rural parishes who would be only too pleased to have a young, go-ahead parson to replace their doddery dotard.'

'We shall see. In the meanwhile I have to contend with someone who is no doddery dotard. I don't think Evan Jones will ever dodder even if he does stutter.'

As we approached the farmyard, I could see the dog who had made a meal of my leg sunning himself outside the farm. The gate was closed. At the sight of the car the hound began to bark and to move towards the gate.

'It's a good thing you are with me, love. This time you can render immediate first aid.' So saying I was about to open the car door when the farmer came hurrying out of the house. He shouted at the dog and it slunk into the barn. The next minute he was opening the gate. He looked at Eleanor and smiled. Then he saw me. The smile vanished.

'G-good afternoon, D-Doctor. She's w-waiting for you. D-Didn't expect to s-see you, Mr S-Secombe. C-Coming for the ride?'

His rosy-cheeked face displayed no pleasure at my appearance.

'I'm not coming for the ride, Mr Jones. I'd like to have a little chat with you while my fiancée is attending to Mrs Jones.'

The furrows in his forehead deepened.

'Oh! Well, c-come on in, D-Doctor and you Mr S-Secombe as well.'

He led us into the farmhouse. His hobnail boots clattered on the stone floor of the hall.

'She's downstairs today, D-Doctor!'

He opened the door of the parlour and a musty smell emerged as if the room had been used but little and had no contact with fresh air. Seated in a chintz-covered armchair, with her swollen legs swathed in bandages and stretched out across a stool, was Blodwen Jones. She had her husband's ruddy complexion but was as plump as he was thin. Mrs Jones was a pleasant, homely person with a ready smile.

Her face lit up at the sight of Eleanor.

'Doctor, how lovely to see you and what a nice surprise to see you, Mr Secombe. It won't be long now for you two, will it?'

'A fortnight's time, Mrs Jones; it's that near. Glad to hear your legs are improving. I'll leave you with your – er – physician while I have a word with your husband.'

'C-Come on in the kitchen, M-Mr S-Secombe,' said the farmer.

The kitchen was a large one, with an Aga cooking range, a big Welsh dresser laden with china and a table with a scrubbed uncovered top, big enough to accommodate eight persons. A grandfather clock ticked away in a corner. Like the hall, the kitchen had a stone floor.

'T-Take a seat Reverend. W-Would you l-like some c-cider?'

The omens are propitious, I thought. To be offered a drink by Evan Jones was an unusual event.

'I'd love some, thank you, Mr Jones.'

He disappeared into the larder and emerged with a large stone jar. He took two tankards from the dresser and filled them to the brim.

'It's home-m-made from our own orchard.'

I took a mouthful from my tankard. It was delightfully cool on a warm summer afternoon and it was very strong.

'N-Now then, w-what do you w-want to s-see me about?'

I gulped down some more of the welcome liquid.

'I hope you don't think I am interfering, Mr Jones, but I'd like a word with you about Charles Wentworth-Baxter.'

His face hardened.

'Apparently, you are about to organize a petition to have him removed from Llanhyfryd.'

He nodded his head vigorously.

'He came to me on Sunday evening in a very upset state. As you know, the Vicar is away on holiday. Otherwise he would have gone straight to him.' At this stage I offered up a short prayer for forgiveness for a decided untruth. 'So the only other person he could turn to was me. Mr Jones, he is doing his best. I know he is no preacher and I know that he is not always on time. It's quite a cycle ride to Llanhyfryd, with more than a few hills to climb. As for his not visiting, well, the Vicar gives him a lot to do in Pontywen during the week. Charles is a very good, kind person, even if he is sometimes scatterbrained. He doesn't know that I have come to see you.' That was true because I had not told him at matins. 'I think it would be a good idea for Llanhyfryd as well as for Charles if you dropped the idea.'

The old man stared past me at the wall opposite him. There was a long pause during which the grandfather clock ticked with the rhythm of a heartbeat. He shifted his gaze towards me.

'M-Mr Secombe, if you knew w-what it is l-like to s-sit and l-listen to that m-man S-Sunday after S-Sunday, you would understand h-how we all feel. All right, I won't g-go ahead with the p-petition. Perhaps you can t-tell him to p-pull his socks up b-before he gets into d-deep trouble.'

Eleanor, my sweet, I thought, You have done it once again.

'Mr Jones, I can't tell you how much I appreciate your thoughtfulness. I'm sure that Charles will make every effort to improve in his ministry at Llanhyfryd. Maybe it required the fright you gave him to pull his socks up, as you say, and to be a better Curate for the parish. If you can encourage him from now on, it should help him to do so.'

Evan Jones looked at me quizzically, undecided about his response, as well as my motive.

'All I can say is that he is p-paid to look after us and that if he c-can't do it, then it's his f-funeral. Anyway, for the t-time being, that's it. I w-won't do anything about it.'

'Mr Jones, you won't regret this. Thank you.'

He poured me another tankard of cider.

'You haven't s-seen my f-farm. C-come and have a l-look. B-bring your d-drink with you.'

We went out through the back door of the kitchen. Hens clucked around us. The hound which had bitten me came towards us and sniffed me.

'This is D-Dell. He's the one who b-bit you. Now he knows you are with me, he'll be no t-trouble.'

'Hello, Dell,' I said tentatively. He wagged his tail. I ventured to pat him on the back. He did not bite me. By the time I had emptied the tankard, I felt I could have dealt with the wild beasts at Ephesus, like St Paul. This was something I could not have done on my previous visit to Blaenycym, as I informed Evan Jones at the time.

On our return to the farmhouse, my head was spinning. Eleanor was standing in the doorway of the parlour with her doctor's bag in her hand, ready to depart.

'Well, Mr Jones, your wife is much better. Next week she will be able to get up and about.'

The farmer indulged in one more of his rare smiles.

'Thank you, D-Doctor. Mr S-Secombe and me have had a g-good chat. So all is w-well.'

Once we were off in the car, my beloved turned to me and said.

'Frederick, you are tight.'

'Isn't it a glorious feeling, my dear? And lucky old Charles is delivered from the lion's mouth, thanks to you.

'You've been drinking scrumpy.'

'So that's what it is. I remember my brother telling me that when he was on his motor bike as a despatch rider in the army, he called in at a farm because he was thirsty. He drank pints of the stuff and ended up on a charge because he kept roaring around the camp on the vehicle, claiming to be a professional motor bike champion.'

'I'll tell you one thing, my love. I'm sure he woke up with a raging headache next morning and the same thing will happen to you tomorrow.'

She was right, as usual. When Mrs Richards called me on Wednesday morning, I was convinced that there was a gang of little men with hammers attacking my head with gusto. The bedroom was rotating round me at speed and my stomach felt as if it had been spending the night in Evan Jones's butter churn.

When I came down to breakfast, Mrs Richards expressed alarm at my condition. 'You look as white as a clean sheet. I don't think you are right to go to service this morning.'

'It will pass,' I replied. 'To tell the truth, I drank too much of the Blaenycwm brand of scrumpy. In a few hours' time I'll be as right as rain. In any case, I have to pass on the good news to Charles. I hope he appreciates the sacrifice of my health for his sake.'

He did. He was beside himself with the news of his unexpected reprieve.

'Fred, you're a genius.'

'I am no such thing. It's Eleanor you have to thank. Without her you would have been destined for a torrid weekend with our employer and possibly the chop. My contribution was a somewhat coloured defence of your saintliness for which the Lord has stricken me. From now on, Charles, you are on your own. If there is no improvement in your ministry in Llanhyfryd, believe me, that petition will be a reality.'

'Thank Eleanor for me and thank you for what you have done. I promise you I shall be much more diligent after all this. I promise you, too, that I shall be the best best man you've ever had.'

'Excuse me, Charles. I have never had a best man before and I do not contemplate having a succession of them in the future. All I ask is that you will produce the ring when the time comes.'

'It will be as safe as houses with me.'

'I trust that will not come under the heading of famous last words.'

'How could you say such a thing?' he said.

7

It was a sunburnt and almost jovial Father Whittaker who returned from Tenby on Saturday afternoon. Charles and I were there to meet him at the Vicarage. He had requested our presence on the postcards he had sent us.

'Let's have a coffee and an update,' he said as he unloaded his suitcases from the car. 'I hope you and Eleanor have weather like this for your honeymoon.'

Once in his study he sat behind his desk and surveyed his two minions, savouring his return to power.

'Anything to report?' he asked, addressing me and ignoring Charles.

'Quite a number of things,' I replied. I told him about the wedding and the threatened interruption of the proceedings. He did not appear to be surprised.

'Typical of that street. How did the baptisms go?'

I took a deep breath.

'Quite well. There was a large contingent for the Morris baby's christening. Mrs Nicholls seemed to think that you had arranged a one-off ceremony for them.'

'Not at all. I told Mrs Morris when she came to see me that her baby's baptism was the only one so far. No more than that.'

I breathed again normally.

'These so-called captains of industry. They are not like the country squires, like Sir David Jones Williams, for example, or even the professional classes with their academic backgrounds. Most of them have risen to the top from the shop floor by treading on anybody who got in their way and by their exploitation of the workers. Nicholls is in that category.'

Evidently the Vicar's snobbery was more selective than I thought. Perhaps he did not know that Sir David's baronetcy had come to him via his ancestors who were much more ruthless in their exploitation of the workers than Mr Nicholls.

'There is one other thing, Vicar. I am afraid there has been some pilfering from the alms dish at St Padarn's. A ten-shilling note I had been given by Miss Aitken when I gave her communion at home had disappeared from the plate when they came to count the collection. I think we shall prevent any more thefts by leaving the alms dish on the altar until it is taken away for counting in the vestry.'

'Good thinking, Fred. And how about you, Wentworth-Baxter? How are things at Llanhyfryd?'

'Nothing to report,' said Charles uncomfortably.

'Oh, by the way, Vicar,' I intervened quickly, 'the first week you were away I buried a Mrs Eliza Jenkins from Thomas Street. Her sister, Miss Hannah Jones, a retired schoolteacher, arranged the funeral. She knew Eleanor at Pontywen County and has given us a delightful wedding present, a piece of Waterford glass.'

'Very kind,' said the Vicar. At this stage in the conversation Mrs Lilywhite entered with the coffee and ended the inquisition.

There was a large congregation at St Padarn's for the Whit Sunday Family Communion Service the next morning.

'Good box office,' commented Idris the Milk in the vestry before the service. 'They want to give you a good wedding present. I see Dr Davies in the church to keep an eye on the takings. Once you get married, Mr Secombe, you'll find it will be always the same.'

Bertie Owen paraded up and down the aisle, supervising the sidesmen who were finding seats for the latecomers.

When the first hymn was announced, I followed the choir into a full church. 'Come, Holy Ghost our souls inspire,' we sang. It was a most moving experience, uplifting and humbling for me. Humbling because I had not expected so many to be there, not only to worship but to show their support for me.

During the sermon, Bertie did his usual ticktack act to indicate that he reckoned there were 170 communicants, not far short of the number at Easter. From the pulpit I could see Eleanor at the back of the church. To my surprise she was seated beside Miss Hannah Jones, the non-believer.

The long offertory hymn, 'The Church's One Foundation', had barely enough verses to enable the sidesmen to take the collection. One by one they put their collection plates on the alms dish. I looked for Eleanor's pound note; it was not on any of the plates which were laden with silver only. My heart sank.

It took a great effort of will to concentrate on the consecration prayer and the administration of the communion. At the back of my mind all the time was the thought that one of those kneeling at the altar rails was a thief.

When the service was over, I went round to the back of the church to shake hands with the worshippers. Throughout the hand-shaking I endeavoured to keep an eye on the alms dish on the altar. As they filtered out of church, I could see Eleanor at the back of the queue with Miss Hannah Jones. We had been to thank her for her wedding present and she had told me she might come to church one day. I had thought that was a pie-crust promise. Now the crust was intact and she was in St Padarn's.

'How wonderful to see you,' I said. 'Did you enjoy the service?'

'Very much so,' she replied. 'Now that I have put my foot in the water and found it pleasantly warm, perhaps I shall come again.'

I took Eleanor's hand and held on to it. 'Can you spare a few minutes?' I asked. 'It's urgent.'

'Let me drive Miss Jones back to Thomas Street and I'll be back in a tick.'

She was true to her word.

'What's urgent, love? Don't make it a long explanation because I have told my mother I shall help her to prepare our Sunday lunch.'

'To put it in a nutshell, who took your collection?'

'What a strange question! It was that rather smart dark haired youngish man with a grey suit and a yellow rose in his button hole.'

'Thank you, my dear. He not only took the collection. He took your pound note.'

As I walked back to the vestry, I decided I would say nothing to Bertie Owen and Charlie Hughes. Instead I would tackle the problem myself that very morning.

The man in question was Tony Luxton, whose father was a member of the choir. Old man Luxton, a retired miner, was a keen gardener, an expert rose-grower who sported one of his specimens every Sunday during the summer. Evidently he had provided his son with the button hole.

Tony Luxton worked in the steelworks in nearby Caeravon. He was married to Emily Luxton, a large friendly lady. They had two teenage daughters who were much sought after by the local young Romeos. I had been entertained to supper with them on more than one occasion. It was a warm, friendly household. I was convinced that Emily would know nothing about her husband's misdemeanours. She had a lovely open face and a generous nature.

The sidesmen were collecting the hymn books and prayer books from the pews. Some of the ladies from the choir were gossiping in the chancel and at the back of the church there were little groups of members of the congregation who were loth to leave, it seemed. It was a happy scene, so happy that I began to question whether the pound note had been taken by Tony. Perhaps it had fallen from the plate and was on the floor somewhere.

I put my cassock and surplice away in the vestry and went back out in the church. There was no sign of a pound note anywhere on the floor. By now the sidesmen were preparing to leave. I steeled myself for the confrontation and approached the suspect as he was about to disappear.

'Tony. Can I have a word with you?'

The colour drained from his face.

'Of course, Mr Secombe.'

I led him to a pew halfway down the aisle which gave us comparative seclusion.

'I don't know how to put this,' I began. 'Money has been missing from the alms dish over the past few months. We were thinking of getting the police to make investigations but decided against it. This morning my fiancée put a pound note on your collection plate. By the time you had arrived at the altar, it had vanished. Perhaps you can clear up the mystery.'

'Are you accusing me of being a thief?'

'I have done no such thing, Tony. I have asked you if you can explain what happened to that pound note. I would much rather find the answer to the riddle myself than have the police brought in to sort it out.'

There was a long, painful silence throughout which he closed his eyes and bowed his head. Suddenly he sat bolt upright.

'All right, Mr Secombe,' he said, addressing the altar rather than me. 'I have been taking money and here's the pound note.' He put his hand into his trouser pocket and produced the money.

'Thank you, Tony. Last week there was a ten-shilling note given me by Miss Aitken as a thanksgiving for her communion. She is a housebound old-age-pensioner and that money meant a big sacrifice for her. Apart from that, there are also the offertory envelopes which disappeared. How are you going to pay back all you have taken? Why have you been doing it anyway? Does Emily know?'

He looked at me.

'You know Emily. Of course she doesn't know. She'd never be able to lift up her head again, if she did.'

'Then why have you been so stupid as to take this money?'

'It's the horses.'

'Don't tell me that Miss Jacobs got you into this mess.'

Miss Jacobs was the local illegal bookie who attended the parish church regularly and who was a friend of my landlady.

'No, of course not. I go to a man in Caeravon. Some of my "butties" at the works have been betting with him for years. I started last year with flutters at a couple of bob at a time, and I won quite a bit to give the family a good Christmas. I told Emily it was a Christmas bonus. That was it. I got hooked. I began increasing my bets and my luck changed for the worse. Mr Secombe, I've been borrowing money to make up for what I've been taking out of my wages. I can't pay the church back at the moment. Honest, I can't.'

I put my arm round his shoulders.

'Under those circumstances, let's forget about paying the church the money you have taken, for the time being at any rate. Tony, you are not the first to be trapped like this, nor the last. It's a good thing you've been found out now before you got into very deep waters. All I shall say at the moment is this. If I find that you have continued to dip your hand into other people's money which is intended for the service of God, then I shall have to take drastic action. For the time being I shall tell no one what has happened, not even the Vicar.'

He grasped my hand.

'Believe me, Mr Secombe, it won't happen again. I've learned my lesson. Thank you for being so understanding.'

When I returned to the vestry, Bertie and Charlie were finishing their counting of the collection.

'It's working,' said Bertie Owen. 'Leaving the alms dish on the altar is the answer. You are going to have the best

Whitsun offering we've ever had in St Padarn's. I don't think there's any need to worry any more about pilfering.'

'Neither do I, Bertie. I think we've solved that.'

'I knew once we'd put our heads together, we'd find the answer, Mr Secombe.'

Next day, at our Monday morning meeting in the Vicarage, the Vicar was brimming with vitality after his fortnight's holiday.

'I've been thinking,' he said, as we sat drinking Mrs Lilywhite's diluted coffee, 'that we must do something to attract the men into the church. Do you realize that even in the Middle Ages there was a preponderance of women at worship? I don't think we shall join the Church of England Men's Society – there doesn't seem to be much imagination in our diocesan set up.'

'You can say that again, Vicar,' I commented. 'Apparently

the Society always used to fix their big service at the Cathedral on Cup Final day when most men were sitting at home with their ears glued to the wireless.'

'They have just done it again this year, Fred. It is no wonder their numbers are comparatively small.'

'If I formed a men's group, I would call it a club. There would be a club tie and we'd meet somewhere like The Bull in Tremadoc where we have our Rural Deanery Meetings. That way they could have a pint if they wished instead of being limited to a cup of tepid tea.'

'In Pontywen we shall not be so revolutionary, but you have a point. What do you think, Wentworth-Baxter?'

Charles was aroused from his Monday reverie.

'I beg your pardon, Vicar. What did you say?'

'Really, I sometimes think that your mind is never on anything we discuss. I said that I did not think we should resort to men's meetings in a pub in Pontywen.'

'Which pub were you thinking of, Vicar?' said my bewildered colleague.

Father Whittaker exploded.

'You are the limit. Obviously you have not listened to a word of what has been said. You were brought to Pontywen for training – however, as the old proverb says, you can bring a horse to the water but you can't make him drink. I have never known a more reluctant drinker. Perhaps you ought to go somewhere else for your water!'

'I'm very sorry, Vicar. I have not been sleeping well lately.'

'In that case, I don't want you to make up for it in the Vicarage on Monday mornings. Now where was I? Ah, yes! When you come back from your honeymoon, Fred, I'd like you to sound out your men in St Padarn's about the idea of a men's organization. I shall do the same at the parish church. Is it too much to ask that you do the same at Llanhyfryd, Wentworth-Baxter?'

'Of course, Vicar. Not that there are many, as you know, and what with their farming duties, I doubt if they'd be interested.'

'Just like you, Wentworth-Baxter. Anyway that is another project for the Autumn. We shall have covered all the males in the parish, a cub pack, a boy's club and a men's organization. Do you think Eleanor would be prepared to run something for the young women?'

'I don't think so, Vicar. She is going to be very busy with this new National Health Service, as well as trying to run a home. She is thinking of giving up her activities with the Gilbert & Sullivan Society.'

'Quite so. Quite so. It was just that she would have been the ideal person.'

As we walked down the Vicarage drive, Charles was in low spirits.

'I wish he had stayed in Tenby permanently. He seems to have it in for me at every opportunity.'

'You did ask for it. You were half asleep in church and three-quarters asleep in the Vicarage.'

'To tell the truth, Fred, I'm in love again.'

'Don't tell me you've gone back to Elspeth Evans.'

Elspeth Evans was a precocious sixteen-year-old, at one time a member of our Gilbert & Sullivan chorus. She had led my naïve colleague up the garden path, and as far as he was concerned, almost to the altar. That affair came to an end when he discovered her in the arms of a schoolboy.

'No way!! I've found someone much more sensible. I know she's young. She's eighteen and she attends your church. Her parents don't know of our relationship so far. I asked her not to let them know after the Elspeth fiasco.'

'Perhaps one day you'll find somebody of your own age, Charles. Well, come on. Who is it?'

'Jane Luxton.'

Jane was a pretty dark-haired little girl. She was in the sixth form at Pontywen Grammar School.

'How on earth did you come to be in love with Jane? She is not in the Gilbert & Sullivan Society and she is not in your church.'

'I met her in the library a month ago. She's doing English

for her Higher Certificate. One of the set books is Jane Austen's *Emma*. She was looking in the literature section, for a book called *Jane Austen and her Art*. It wasn't there. I have a copy and offered to lend it to her. That's how it began.'

'Charles you have known her for just a month. How can you possibly say you are in love with her?'

'We spent a day together in Cardiff last Saturday week. She is mature, intelligent and sweet-natured. As the day went on, I realized I was falling in love with her.'

'Is this reciprocal?'

'I haven't said anything about love and neither has she but I can sense that it is reciprocal.'

'Look, Charles. Cool it down. She is still a schoolgirl. You have told her to keep your meetings secret. That is encouraging her to break family trust. Not only that, I have to tell you in confidence that her father is in financial trouble. There will be worry enough for her mother without you compounding her difficulties. I understand Emily Luxton is expecting her daughter to go to university. She will not want you interfering with her career. There's one other thing: if the Vicar found out that you were involved in an association with a schoolgirl, you would be out of Pontywen before you could look round. You should have learned that lesson after the Elspeth Evans episode.'

We walked in silence for a while. My colleague's shoulders were hunched, and his hands were in his pockets. He was a picture of misery. We stopped outside his digs.

'Would you like to come round to my place and have a cup of Mrs Richards's tea?'

'If you don't mind, Fred, I think I'd better go up to my room and think about things.'

'As you please. See you tomorrow morning.'

Coming down Mount Pleasant View I was surprised to see Eleanor's car parked by number 13. We were not supposed to meet until the evening. I hurried my steps and made my way into the house.

Eleanor was standing at the window in my room. When she turned to face me, I could see that something very serious had happened.

'Sit down, love,' she said.

'What's the matter?' I breathed.

'Just sit down in your armchair.'

I did as I was told.

'I was called out an hour ago on an emergency. I'm afraid it's one of your sidesmen.'

'My God! It's Tony Luxton!'

She nodded her head.

'When I arrived at the house it was too late to save him. He had cut his throat. It was very messy. He must have been desperate. Apparently he was working on the two-till-ten shift and had gone up to the bathroom to shave. When he didn't come down after a long time, Mrs Luxton went up to call him. There was no answer and the door was locked. She panicked and went next door to her neighbour, whose husband was working nights. She roused him and he burst open the door. Poor Mrs Luxton is in a terrible state. I have put her under sedation. The police have been there and the police doctor.'

'What about the girls?'

'I have phoned the headmaster and he will call them into his study at the end of the morning session.'

'I think I should be there. It's something I owe them. If I hadn't been so crass, their father would still be alive.'

'Stop that, Fred. You told me last night what you had said to him. I don't think you could have been more understanding. He told you so himself. You haven't taken his life. He took it himself. If you want to go to the girls, do so by all means but for heaven's sake don't feel that you are in any way responsible for what has happened. It must have been an impulse. He had a cut-throat razor in his hand. No way was this a cool and calculated decision.'

'I still feel that it is better that I tell the girls rather than their headmaster.'

'In that case, my dear, I shall drive you to the school and you can have a word with Mr Llewellyn Davies.'

She came to me and kissed me.

'Fred, love, I'm sure you will be much more reassuring than their headmaster. If you wish, I'll wait outside at the school and drive you to their home when you have told them. If Mrs Richards has any of her medicinal brandy left, I think you should have some before we go.'

When my landlady heard about the tragedy, she was more than willing to render first aid to her lodger.

'What a shock for you, Mr Secombe! You must have been bowled an over!'

Fortified by Mrs Richards's brandy and the support of Eleanor, I approached Mr Llewellyn Davies. He was a tall, thin man with a large red nose upon which were reposed a pair of horn-rimmed spectacles. Clad in his graduate's gown, he was an imposing figure.

'Mr Davies, I am the Reverend Fred Secombe, Averil and Jane's Curate. I know the girls very well and I wonder whether you would allow me to tell them about what has happened to their father.'

Mr Llewellyn Davies looked hard and long at me.

'Well, Mr Secombe, I think you are right. They are two delightful girls but my relationship with them is very remote. It is now twenty-past twelve. The school bell will ring at half-past; I have already told their form teachers that I want to see them at that time. I shall vacate my room and my secretary will show them in. It's a very unfortunate business, to say the least. I wonder why the poor man did this terrible thing to himself.'

I thought it better to say nothing.

At half-past twelve a bell rang outside the headmaster's study with a noise that seemed to penetrate the whole of Pontywen as well as the school.

A few minutes later two bewildered girls were ushered into my presence. Averil, who was an extrovert sixteen, and Jane came into the room. As soon as they saw me they realized that something catastrophic had happened. Their faces lost their colour.

'I'm afraid, girls,' I began, 'that I have some bad news for you. Your father has had a tragic accident.

'It's that steelworks!' exclaimed Averil. 'I've always said that one day that furnace would kill him!'

'You're wrong, Averil,' I replied quietly. 'He died at home.'

'A heart attack,' said Jane.

'Not a heart attack,' I said. 'I don't know how to put this ... What has happened is that your father has taken his own life.'

'Dad! Never. He would never do that!'

'I'm sorry, Jane, but it's true. He must have had some tremendous pressure that you know nothing about.'

They burst into tears simultaneously. I wanted to join them but steeled myself. The weeping continued for what seemed an age.

'I know it is a terrible shock for you. What you have to think about now is not yourselves but your mother. She will need every ounce of support that you can give her. Without you she will feel bereft.'

Jane stifled her tears.

'Averil, what Mr Secombe says is quite right. She has to depend on us from now on. Grandpa Luxton is far too old to do anything for her. Her own parents are dead. It's just us.'

Slowly Averil began to control herself.

'Dr Davies is waiting to take us back to your home. She has given your mother some tablets to calm her down. I realize it is a lot to ask of you to be older than your years but if you can show that you are strong enough to face up to what has happened, then your mother will be that much stronger herself.'

The two girls looked at each other and embraced warmly.

'Mr Secombe, I think we'll be able to look after our mother,' said Jane. 'We owe her that anyway.'

After the headmaster had put his arms round the two girls and expressed his sympathy, we left the school and arrived at their home. A neighbour answered the door to us.

'She's fast asleep,' she said.

'I think the best course of action now is for Mr Secombe to stay with you now until your mother wakes up. After that, you can take charge,' said Eleanor. I saw her to the door. She kissed me and left.

A few minutes later there was a knock at the door. It was the girls' grandfather. Unshaven and wearing an old suit, he looked a broken man.

'Will Book and Pencil has told me what has happened,' he said. 'I still can't believe it. Why should our Tony do this when he's got a lovely wife and family?'

'Come and sit down, grandad,' said Jane. We were in the front room. She led him to an armchair, with her arm round his shoulder. In the meanwhile Averil had burst into tears again.

'Averil, come with me and help me make a cup of tea for grandad. You'd like a cup as well, would you, Mr Secombe?'

'Thank you, Jane, I'd love one.'

'I think I'll tell Mrs Evans she can go now and we'll take over until our Mam's awake.'

When they had gone out of the room, old Mr Luxton looked at me blankly, as if in a hypnotic trance.

'Why did he do it?' he intoned. 'Why did he do it?'

This was the second time that question was posed – first by the headmaster and now by Tony's father. It would be asked several times in the days ahead. Since only Eleanor and I knew the answer, I wondered whether I should divulge it to anyone – either to the police or to the coroner. As far as the family were concerned, it was bad enough to know that their father had committed suicide. If they were told that Tony had been stealing from the collection plate, that would rub an intolerable amount of salt into what was already a very deep wound. I decided I would talk it over with Eleanor that evening.

When I left the Luxton house, a deeply shocked Emily was being comforted by her daughters. The old man was still sitting in the armchair in the front room, oblivious of anyone's presence.

Later that day when Eleanor and I were in our house in Bevan's Row, I asked her whether I should inform the police or the coroner or even the Vicar that the suicide had been stealing from the church.

'I think the Luxtons are suffering enough as it is,' she said. 'Probably his borrowing for his gambling debts will be uncovered. It would not be very kind to pull the curtains back any further.'

That was how the curtains remained.

8

Tony Luxton's suicide hung like a pall over my thoughts for several days. I could not escape from the feeling that I was in some way partly responsible. First there was the inquest and then the funeral. All the time I felt as if I were an accessory after the fact. It was Eleanor's support which enabled me to survive the ordeal without permanent damage to my psyche.

By the time the funeral was over, our wedding was only a few days away. It provided a providential release from my guilt complex. There was so much to do, whether it was concerned with badgering the Post Office to see that the telephone was installed or with reminding Mr Roberts the elderly ironmonger that we still awaited the delivery of the tin bath.

Charles was so shocked by what had happened that his burgeoning love was nipped in the bud. The harsh winds of reality had put paid to his Ethel M. Dell romantic notions. He turned his attention instead to his forthcoming duties as best man.

'We must have a stag night,' he said.

'That's going to be awkward,' I replied. 'I am getting married on Monday. There will be the church services to see to on Sunday. I have no wish to appear pie-eyed at the altar for the family communion.'

'In that case, we shall have it tomorrow evening.'

'And, who, may I ask, are going to attend this orgy? It is a wee bit late to invite people the day before.'

'Leave it to me,' Charles tapped the side of his nose with his finger. For such an innocent it was a ludicrous gesture.

When I told Eleanor what my colleague was about to organize, she was highly amused.

'That man would be intoxicated after smelling the barmaid's apron, as they say. It will be interesting to see whom he invites as your drinking companions. If they are all like him, you will be the only one standing at the end of the evening. By the way, I am having a hen party on Saturday evening – just a few of my old college friends for a quiet drink and a cackle. No more.'

'I should have thought of that,' I said. 'The Tony Luxton business drove everything out of my head. A few college friends would be good company.'

'Please forget the suicide, love. Concentrate on the most important event in our lives scheduled for next Monday and get things in perspective. You never know, Charles may surprise you with his party.'

Next morning after Matins, my fellow Curate was in high spirits.

'It's all arranged. Someone will pick you up at Mount Pleasant View at seven o'clock this evening. So don't forget. Collar and tie. Best bib and tucker.'

As the day of my wedding drew nearer, my landlady's spirits sank lower and lower. So it was no surprise when I returned to my digs that she complained about lack of notice in having to wash and iron my one good non-clerical shirt that day.

'It's a lucky thing that it's sunny and blowy. Otherwise you would have had to go in your dog's collar.'

'I'm very sorry, Mrs Richards, but it's all been a last minute arrangement. If you find it is too much, don't worry.'

The old lady softened. The complaint was quite out of character.

'Whatever happens, Mr Secombe, you'll have your shirt ready. You don't want to go to your stag's night in your clergy fit out. I haven't let you down before so I must keep my record in until you leave 13 Mount Pleasant View.'

She seemed near to tears. I put my arm round her shoulders.

'I tell you what,' I said. 'You must be the best landlady any curate could possibly have.'

I kissed her on he cheek. She turned away quickly and went out into the kitchen to hide the tears that were starting.

By six o'clock, not only had she washed and ironed my shirt but she had pressed my suit as well. As I dressed, I wondered who would be my chauffeur and where the rendezvous would be.

Prompt at seven, a car drew up outside. It was a large Wolseley. The last time I had seen it was a year ago when Harry Tench paid me an unexpected visit soon after my arrival at Pontywen. Harry was a tall, thin individual with a large Billy Bunter owlish face on top of his lean body. His horn-rimmed spectacles accentuated his owlishness. He was one of a few eccentrics from my college days. The son of a doctor and well blessed with money, he was not well blessed with intelligence. He had spent five years doing what the normal student would do in three. However, now he was ordained and was a curate in a parish in Cardiff.

Harry came bounding up the steps, his college scarf flung across his neck as if he were still an undergraduate. Before he could knock on the door, I opened it.

'So you are the anonymous chauffeur,' I said. 'Don't tell me, you've pinched your father's car again.'

On his last visit, he had 'borrowed' the car while his father was out with a friend playing golf.

'Not at all, old boy. It's mine – a present to celebrate my ordination.'

'How did you know about this "do"?'

'Mal Evans rang me last night. Your colleague had rung him.'

'So Mal is coming. The demon bowler and the demon

drinker. If that is any indication, it is going to be some party.'

'I shouldn't have told you about Mal and the others. Well, are you ready?'

I said goodbye to Mrs Richards. 'Don't get too indoctrinated,' she warned.

'Where are we going?' I asked as Harry drove off.

'A secret, old boy. You'll see for yourself when we arrive. So you are marrying into the medical profession. My father knows Eleanor's old man. Nice old bozo, he says.'

He spent the whole of the journey, reminiscing about our college days. His freakish voice varying from bass to coloratura soprano would break from one to the other in mid sentence when he became excited. It was unfortunate that he was tone deaf. Otherwise he might have made a fortune as a singer.

Eventually we pulled up at The Collier's Arms, a hostelry further down the valley. There were a number of cars parked outside and a large volume of sound was issuing from the half-opened windows. It was Friday night – pay night.

As we entered the crowded saloon bar, I was greeted by a male-voice choral version of 'The Wedding March' from half a dozen characters in one corner of the room. Through the haze of tobacco smoke I could make out Mal Evans and Charles in the forefront. Then to my great surprise I found that the other four were contemporaries from college days.

Towering above everybody else was 'Verdy' Watkins. He must have been at least six-foot-three. Christened Verdun Kitchener Watkins by his patriotic parents, he was an excellent second-row forward and had been playing for one of the valley teams. Verdy was as gentle as a lamb off the field but a raging lion on it. He made the headlines in the local paper earlier in the year: 'CURATE SENT OFF'. As a result his Vicar banned him from rugby as long as he served in that parish.

Alongside Verdy was Herbert John, a tall, anaemic-looking man; the only one wearing his clerical collar. He was incarcerated in an Anglo-Catholic Vicarage, known as a clergy house. On my last visit to him in his 'cell', he told me he was determined to break out from the tutelage of his autocratic Vicar, Father Willinghurst. That was six months ago. I was amazed to find him in a pub, especially at a stag party. It was a sign of his increasing desperation.

Then there was Tom Griffiths, a diminutive imp, noted in college for his practical jokes. He was in a parish in the neighbouring valley and had charge of a daughter church, which was in the shadow of one of the coal mines. Tom had acquired a fiancée who was six inches taller than himself. He claimed that he had always wanted a partner he could look up to.

The last member of the group was Eddie Rowlands, a fellow performer in the college concert party. He and I provided the comedy with songs and monologues. He had formed a concert party in his parish near Newport and reports of their activities appeared in the local paper from time to time. Eddie was a short, broad-shouldered dynamo; ever-cheerful.

'Pints all round boys. Agreed?' Maldwyn Evans did not wait for an answer. He went to the bar and ordered the round.

'How did you manage to get this gang together at short notice?' I asked Charles.

'It was through Mal. I rang him and asked if he'd contact some of your contemporaries. I don't know them. It was entirely his handiwork.'

'Thank you anyway, Charles, for a very pleasant surprise.'

He flushed with embarrassed pride.

'Go and sit down, Fred,' said Mal. 'We've got that table in the corner. I know the landlord and he reserved it for us.'

'I don't think I can manage a pint,' said Herbert John when I joined him at the table.

'What you can't drink, leave,' I told him.

Soon we were indulging in a flood of recollections.

'Remember our trip with the Dramatic Society to Taly-wern?' began Eddie Rowlands.

Eddie and I had been recruited to provide the comic relief in the society's production of *The Ringer*, Edgar Wallace's thriller. The play had gone well at college. As a result we were invited to perform it in Talywern Village Hall in the heart of a Welsh-speaking district.

It was a bitterly cold February day and snow had been falling before we set out in a small bus hired for the occasion. We were still a few miles away from our destination when the vehicle was trapped in a snow drift. Fortunately the driver was well prepared, with a couple of shovels available.

Verdy Watkins who had come for the ride, did Herculean work that day, first of all with a shovel and then with his muscular power in pushing the stranded machine out of trouble.

When we arrived at the hall the heating had broken down. In a sub-zero temperature we unloaded our props and prepared to perform inside the refrigerator which served as a theatre. We shivered in the dressing rooms and were rescued from hypothermia by thermos flasks of soup provided by one of the college lecturers, Dr Lawson. Like Verdy he was there as a supporter.

What puzzled us was that he seemed to be enjoying the situation. 'It reminds me of Priestley's *The Good Companions*, and all the tribulations they encountered as a travelling company.' I suppose his enthusiasm was derived from the fact that he was a Yorkshireman like the author and, accordingly, was inured to arctic conditions.

There were twenty people in the audience when the curtains went up. They were protected against the cold by their thick overcoats and scarves. Clouds of breath rose from the first two rows of seats. That was the only sign of life. Eddie and I strove in vain to raise a laugh. There was not even a titter. The end of the first two acts was greeted with silence. Came the last act and the conviction among the frozen and dispirited cast that in front of us were overcoated tailor's dummies. The climax of the dramatic action was the shooting of the villain. When the actor raised his gun, it failed to go off.

Suddenly the audience burst into life. They threw up their hands and kicked up their legs. Hysterical laughter filled the air. Evidently this was the funniest incident they had ever seen in Talywern. The startled players went through the motions of the rest of the script. By the final curtain the deathly silence had returned and remained as the actors took their bow before twenty inert figures.

Twice the bus was engulfed in snow on our return journey. Had it not been for Verdy, we might have been marooned throughout the night. The Society never again visited Talywern.

'What about Prof. Williams's daughter Mal,' asked Tom Griffiths.

'You are lucky to be alive after that,' Maldwyn growled.

Tom was a brilliant mimic who could impersonate most of the college staff. He was exceptionally good at 'doing' Prof. Williams, a myopic academic whose sermons were couched in florid verbiage. One of his pulpit gems remains in my memory. 'Some of you gentlemen are lost in the pestiferous miasmas of the swamps of sin.' Prof. Williams had a pretty daughter for whom Mal had developed a deep admiration. Since the young lady was kept in purdah, there was no way he could show his feelings. In any case, it was most unlikely that they would have been reciprocated.

Mal told Tom one day about his longing to meet this girl. Later that evening the phone rang in the grocer's shop where Mal was in digs. His landlady called him. 'Professor Williams for you.' A worried Mal hastened downstairs. Since Professor Williams was College censor in charge of undergraduates' behaviour, he wondered what misdemeanour of his had been discovered.

Instead, to his great delight, he found that he was being invited to tea with the censor and his family at four-thirty the next day. The following afternoon he spent an hour on his toilet preparations, viewing himself in the mirror from various angles. For someone with his reputation as a tough sportsman, it was a most unusual procedure, one which alarmed his landlady. 'Whatever is the matter, Maldwyn?' she asked.

'I'm going to have tea with Prof. Williams.'

'Anybody would think it was tea with King George.'

Promptly at four-thirty he knocked at the door of Professor Williams's house. There was no reply. He knocked harder. Again to no avail. In desperation, he knocked once more.

A bedroom window opened. Mrs Williams thrust her head out and inquired what Maldwyn wanted.

'I've come to tea,' he said.

'You must have the wrong house, young man.'

'Professor Williams rang me last night and invited me.'

'My husband is in Cambridge at a conference. He couldn't possibly have done so. He will not be back until tomorrow.'

'I'm very sorry to trouble you, Mrs Williams. It must have been somebody else.'

'It must have been. Good afternoon.'

The window was slammed shut and Mal was left pondering on the doorstep. As he turned to go back to his digs, he remembered that he had told Tom Griffiths about his regard for the Professor's daughter. He sought him out in the college quadrangle and threw him into the fountain which adorned the centre.

As the recollections continued, I kept a wary eye on the drinks ordered for me. Charles had switched to shandies after the first pint. Herbert had found he had the capacity for two more pints, to the amusement of the others who were imbibing at a considerable rate. The one exception was Harry Tench who was still sipping his first pint.

'I have to see the bridegroom home safely, old boy,' was his answer to anyone who tried to buy him a drink.

By closing time, I was still in possession of all my faculties which was more than could be said for Herbert who was launching into an unmusical rendition of 'Cwm Rhondda'. When he attempted to move away from our table, he collapsed into the arms of Verdy Watkins.

'That's the first time I've seen a drunken vicar,' said one of a group of miners who had spent the whole evening discussing the future nationalization of the mines.

'It's the first and last time for him,' said Verdy, as he held him up.

He drove him back to the clergy house where the front door was locked. After he had rung the doorbell a number of times Father Willinghurst appeared in his dressing gown.

'I'm afraid Herbert is not very well, Father. If you tell me how to get to his room, I'll take him there.'

'You will do no such thing, young man,' snapped the Vicar. 'I'll take him there and I'll deal with him in the morning.'

It signalled the end of Herbert's stay in that parish. Three months later he joined the Missions to Seamen and was sent to Singapore. I never saw him again.

In the meanwhile Charles joined me in Harry's car. He had come down in Verdy's old automobile but decided against the trip to Herbert's clergy house as a prelude to returning to Pontywen.

'I don't fancy Herbert being sick all over me, thank you,' he said.

Harry Tench talked non-stop all the way back to 13 Mount Pleasant View. He had not been able to get a word in edgeways at The Collier's Arms to his great frustration.

'I have enjoyed the journeys there and back, chatting about old times. Are you getting out here, Charles?' he said.

There was no reply. My colleague was fast asleep behind us.

'Perhaps it will be best to drive him back to his digs. It is at Howells the Greengrocers in the square,' I suggested.

'Righto, old boy. I'm afraid I can't make your wedding on Monday. It's our chapter meeting day. Anyway, all the best, Fred. Take care of her – or rather, it's the other way around isn't it, because she's the doctor.'

Squeaking with laughter at this display of wit, he roused Charles from his slumbers.

'Harry wants to know if you are getting out here, Charles?'

'Perhaps I'd better. I think a walk in the fresh air will do me good after all that smoke. I'll come in for a few minutes before I go.'

We said goodbye to Harry and went indoors where Mrs Richards was still waiting up for me.

'I thought I had better not to go bed until you were home. I've got only two more days to look after you. You might have needed some black coffee to stop your head going round like a top. I've bought some.'

'That's very kind of you, Mrs Richards but I have been very careful. Anyway we'd be grateful for two cups of coffee with milk and sugar, wouldn't we, Charles?'

'We certainly would, Mrs Richards, thank you.'

The old lady bustled out into the kitchen pleased that her services were required.

'Thank you, Charles, once again. It has been a most enjoyable stag night. All the more because it was such a surprise.'

Before Charles could reply there was a frantic banging on the door. I rushed from my room to open the door. A distraught Harry Tench stood there, wild-eyed, looking more like an owl than ever.

'The car's conked out at the end of the street. Can you and Charles come and push it to see if it will start again?'

'By all means, Harry,' I replied, 'but if it's anything to do with the battery, you couldn't have started it at The Collier's Arms.'

'We've got to do something. It's too late to phone a garage and I'm not in the AA or the RAC.'

'Harry, if I were you, I shouldn't come to Pontywen again. The last time you did so the car broke down. We

were lucky to find a soldier mechanic up in the hills then
. . . You won't find one at the end of Mount Pleasant View,
I can tell you.'

He did not appreciate my remark. Harry had come to see
me a year ago and had taken me for a ride to show off in
his father's car. When the car broke down, he could not
open the bonnet, let alone examine the inside. Apparently
he was still in the same stage of ignorance.

I told Mrs Richards to delay her preparation of coffee
until we returned from our expedition.

At the end of Mount Pleasant View there was a steep hill.
If it were a flat battery, a good push would be enough to
start the car. Harry got into the car, Charles and I put our
full weight and strength into pushing. Down the hill it
went. Three times he tried to get it going and nothing
happened. There was very little left of the slope, at the
bottom of which was a bridge across a stream.

His fourth attempt to start the Wolseley was equally
fruitless. It came to rest on the middle of the bridge. The
bridge was narrow. Charles and I came puffing down the
hill, ready to move the vehicle. We were too late. Suddenly
a car came round a corner on the opposite side, pulling up
on the bridge but not quickly enough to avoid giving Harry's
automobile a push backwards. It came to rest on a patch of
waste land bordering the stream.

The car pulled alongside Harry. An irate driver jumped
out.

'What the hell do you think you are doing?' he
demanded.

By this time Charles and I had arrived on the scene.

It was Mr Nicholls, Managing Director of the Steelworks,
whose grandchild I had baptized a fortnight previously.

'I can explain, Mr Nicholls,' I said. 'My friend's car is
broken down. We had pushed it down the hill and it came
to rest on the bridge. You see he has to get back to his
parish in Cardiff tonight.'

Mr Nicholls peered into my face in the darkness.

'You're the Curate who did the christenings.'

'That's right. This is my fellow curate in Pontywen. The Reverend Harry Tench, the driver of the car, had kindly run us back to the parish after a meeting. He knows nothing about cars, I'm afraid. It looks as if he will have to leave the car here and come back to my digs until the morning.'

'Hold on,' said the industrial magnate. 'Perhaps I can help. I know a fair amount about cars. I'll get a torch. In the meantime will you lift the bonnet please?'

Harry got out of the car and lifted the bonnet.

'My word, you have improved,' I commented.

'There's no need to be sarcastic,' he replied huffily.

Mr Nicholls returned with his torch.

'Will you get back into the car and use the starter?'

Harry did so and tried the starter a couple of times to no avail.

'All right, that's enough,' said Mr Nicholls. 'Will one of you hold the torch while I have to look at the carburettor?'

I volunteered for service.

'Keep it steady,' he ordered.

A quick examination established that there was dirt in the carburettor. Five minutes later the cleaning had taken place.

'Try the car now,' said the Good Samaritan.

Harry tried the starter again and to his great relief the engine came to life. 'Thank you so much,' he squeaked.

'Remember not to break down on narrow bridges next time,' Mr Nicholls warned.

'Thank you, kind sir,' I said to him. 'You were very quick diagnosing the trouble.'

'When I had my first car,' he replied, 'I had little money and I had to learn to do my own repairs to keep it on the road. I still tinker with my cars now, even with this new Jaguar.' He patted its bonnet as if it were a household pet. 'Good night to you all and a safe journey back to Cardiff.'

After Harry Tench and his rescuer had driven off, I said to Charles, 'To think I said rude things about him and his family – well, about his family mostly. Are you coming back to my digs or going straight to yours?'

'I think I had better make a beeline for the Square,' he replied.

When I arrived at 13 Mount Pleasant View, Mrs Richards was waiting to hear if she had another lodger for the night. She was greatly relieved to see me come back alone.

'What with everything happening this weekend, it would have been that load of straw that broke the old camel's back.'

'Shall we both share a cup of coffee and celebrate our deliverance from a night of Harry Tench?'

'That's a lovely idea, Mr Secombe. Just two more days and I won't be able to sit down with you. So let's make the most of it.'

She disappeared into the kitchen and came back with two coffees some minutes later.

'I think you will like this coffee,' she said.

I took a sip. It was laced with a considerable amount of brandy.

'Mrs Richards, you are trying to make me drunk!'

'Not me, Mr Secombe. It's just that there was a little drop left in Mr Richards's bottle of brandy. I'd rather you have it than anybody else.'

We talked about the past twelve months into the early hours.

When I bade her goodnight, she said, 'I'm so glad that Mr Stench had his car mended. Mind, he can think himself lucky. It's not everybody can have the head of a steelworks for his mechanical.'

9

On Monday morning I awoke to find the sun streaming into the bedroom through a gap in the curtains. I looked at the alarm clock. It was seven o'clock. In five hours' time I would be standing by my bride ready to share a new life. From then on there would be somebody else to consider in everything I did. My responsibilities would be doubled as husband and priest. I was about to surrender my freedom of action.

I sat up. It is too late to think like this, I told myself. In any case, Eleanor's responsibilities would be doubled as well as mine, as parson's wife and doctor. Not only that, she was the most wonderful girl in the world and I was privileged to be her husband.

Whistling the tune from *The Mikado* 'Brightly dawns our wedding day', I jumped out of bed and opened wide the curtains. The sky was cloudless and the sun was brilliant. This was going to be the happiest day of my life.

My brand-new suit, by courtesy of Montague Burton plus clothing coupons, was suspended on a hanger attached to the door of the wardrobe. On the floor, underneath it, was my suitcase, packed with motherly care by Mrs Richards. 'One of the last things I can do for you,' she said.

Half an hour later I was luxuriating in the bath, making the most of the experience. On our return from the honeymoon to Bevan's Row, we would be using the tin bath in the kitchen. Eleanor insisted we did this to avoid asking her mother for permission to use her bathroom.

It was a big breakfast of bacon, egg and fried bread which faced me when I had finished my ablutions.

'This looks delicious, Mrs Richards,' I said.

'Well, it is the last meal I'll be cooking for you. Anyway you must have plenty in your stomach for the big day. It will be a long time till you sit down for your festival in the hotel.'

She was forcing herself to look cheerful but it was a hard battle. I felt that at any minute she would burst into the tears which were hidden behind the façade. The old lady had bought herself a lilac-coloured dress with hat to match from the Emporium in the Square, a great change from the black of her widow's weeds. She was doing her very best to be in tune with the occasion.

At eleven o'clock my parents arrived in a car hired by Eleanor's parents to bring them and my sister, Carol, from Cardiff General Station. The driver had taken them first to my fiancée's house where they had a brief meeting with my in-laws to be, prior to Carol's dressing up for the occasion.

It was the first time that Mrs Richards had met my mother and father. The two women embraced warmly. My mother was more than grateful for the homely atmosphere I had found in 13 Mount Pleasant View.

'Thank you for looking after my boy,' Mam said.

'I've never had a son,' replied my landlady, 'or a daughter, if it comes to that. So I've been very happy to be your subordinate for a year. I must say that he's been the pick in the bunch of all the curates I've had here.'

While my parents were enjoying a cup of tea, Charles came in, looking unusually spruce.

'I think I've got everything in order,' he said nervously. 'Dr Davies is going to propose the toast to you and Eleanor. Then you reply and propose the toast to the bridesmaids. I reply to that on your behalf. No other speeches, except one from the Vicar.'

'Well done, Charles. You must keep it to that.'

Most of the wedding receptions I had attended had been spoilt by numerous embarrassed relatives being called upon to say 'a few words'. Eleanor and I had agreed that the guests should be spared such unnecessary suffering.

'What about the ring, Fred? I'd better have it now. I'll keep it in the box so that I can't lose it.'

I went upstairs to my bedroom and opened the top drawer of the chest of drawers where I had left it for safe keeping. To my horror it was not there. I searched everywhere, through every one of the drawers, the wardrobe, on the mantelpiece, the window sill, under the bed. The ring was not to be found.

Perhaps Mrs Richards had removed it from my safe keeping to her safer keeping. I descended the stairs two at a time. My landlady was halfway into a conversation about my mother's operation.

'The ring,' I shouted. 'Have you put it somewhere?'

The old lady looked startled.

'No, I haven't. I thought it was in your chest of drawers where you said you were going to put it.'

Sweat besprinkled my brow in liberal quantities.

I pulled out my handkerchief from the top pocket of my new suit and out flew a little box. Then I remembered that I had put it there in my semi-alcoholic haze after the stag night.

'Fred, you'll never change,' said my mother.

Charles and I decided to walk to the church. The car was due to come at twenty to twelve to pick up the five of us. I felt a walk in the sunshine would be good for my morale.

At St Mary's there were some early arrivals, mainly guests from Eleanor's family connections and friends. Bertie Owen, Idris the Milk, Charlie Hughes and Moelwyn Howells had volunteered to act as ushers. They were lined up at the back of the church when Charles and I entered. In their best suits with carnation buttonholes provided by Moelwyn, they were a reassuring sight.

'All under control.' said Bertie.

'Famous last words,' added Idris with a wide grin.

Already there were a number of well-wishers occupying some of the rear pews. So far the Swansea contingent of my uncles, aunts and cousins had not arrived. They were coming to Pontywen in a small bus hired for the occasion.

Inside the vestry, the Vicar was sitting at his desk, filling the marriage register. The sun tan he had acquired in Tenby had faded and his sallow complexion had taken over.

He left his seat to greet me as I came through the door.

'What a lovely day you have for your big occasion!' he said as he shook my hand. 'Well, are you nervous?'

'I am petrified. It is one thing to take a wedding. It is another thing to be at the receiving end.

'That's something which has not happened to me as yet, so I have no idea of how it feels. If you don't mind, I'll return to my chore. Perhaps you will check the entry when I have completed it.'

At this point there was a knock on the door and Bertie Owen burst in, breathless with self-importance.

'How many pews did you say you wanted reserved?' he asked.

'Six on either side, Bertie.'

'I thought you said that, but I wasn't quite sure,' he replied and disappeared as swiftly as he had come in.

'That man is incorrigible,' commented the Vicar.

Bertie was his *bête noire*. He had caused more trouble for him than the rest of the Parochial Church Council put together.

Charles was standing in a corner, looking even more nervous than I felt. Every so often his hand would stray to his inside pocket to check that the box containing the ring was there.

Suddenly there was a blast from the organ as Mr Greenfield launched into a murder of Purcell's 'Trumpet Voluntary.'

'I must say that's a change from 'Moonlight and Roses'. I

said to the Vicar. 'I can't say that it is for the better. At least he could play that piece.'

'Perhaps one day he will retire,' said Father Whittaker, 'and then we can employ a real organist. Would you mind checking the register now, please?'

It was a strange feeling to look at this formal record of our marriage. 'Frederick Thomas Secombe, bachelor, aged 27, clergyman,' and 'Eleanor Mary Davies, aged 26, physician.'

'That is quite correct,' I replied.

'Your father is a commercial traveller, I see. What firm does he work for?'

'Crosse and Blackwell. He is very proud of that. Before the war he was employed by a local wholesale grocery company in Swansea.'

'How goes the time?'

'According to me, it is five to twelve, Vicar.'

'Perhaps you had better go out now and sit in the front pew.'

When I opened the door of the vestry, a buzz of conversation met us. By now Mr Greenfield had switched to the tremolo stop and his stock-in-trade, 'Moonlight and Roses'.

Facing me, as I moved with Charles to the front pew, were my mother and father, together with Mrs Richards in her lilac rig-out and behind them my Swansea relations, gazing upon me, rapt in adoration. It reminded me of my first sermon in Swansea when they all turned up to hear it. As I came down from the pulpit, they were singing 'My God, How Wonderful Thou Art' with their eyes trained on me.

We sat down and faced the altar. Charles was so nervous, I could feel his body shaking alongside me. It took some of the tension from me as I tried to calm him down.

'For heaven sake,' I whispered to him, 'try and get a grip on yourself. You are worse than I am.'

Before he could reply, Mr Greenfield pulled out all the stops and crashed out Wagner's 'Wedding March'.

We moved quickly from the pew and stood at the chancel steps. Eleanor had given me strict instructions not to turn around to watch her come down the aisle. I stared steadfastly ahead of me, looking at nothing in particular and waiting until she reached my side.

It seemed an age until the Vicar, who had been leading the bride, walked past me to take up his stand at the top of the chancel steps.

A faint breath of fragrance anointed my nostrils. Then the gentle rustle of a bridal gown announced her arrival at my side. I turned to look at the woman who was to be my partner. It was a moment worth waiting for. She was such a beautiful bride that the sight turned my legs to water. A brunette with big expressive brown eyes, set in an oval face, she wore a floor length bridal gown. It is a picture enshrined in my memory.

'Do I come up to expectations?' she whispered in my ear.

'Five gold stars,' I replied.

'Hymn number 520, "Love Divine All Loves Excelling",' announced the Vicar. He handed us a hymn book to hold.

'Begin by sharing,' he said.

We sang the hymn to the Welsh tune 'Hyfrydol'. The singing was full-throated, with all four vocal parts much in evidence.

The first part of the service passed over my head until I was aware that I was being addressed by the officiant.

'Frederick Thomas, wilt thou have this woman to thy wedded wife?'

'I will,' My voice sounded as if it had come from somewhere else.

'Eleanor Mary?'

'I will,' Her answer was warm and firm.

'Who giveth this woman to this man?'

Eleanor's father stepped forward proudly, took her hand gently and gave it to me. I held it so tightly it must have been painful for her. She showed no sign that it was so but looked at me in such a loving way that my grip slackened as I repeated the marriage vow.

Then it was her turn to make the vow. She held my hand and squeezed it as she said 'to love and to cherish'.

When she had finished her contribution, the Vicar looked at Charles who plunged his hand into his pocket and produced the box. His hands were shaking so badly that when he opened the box the ring dropped out on the floor and rolled towards the heating grating behind me. I made a dive worthy of a Welsh wing scoring the winning try at Twickenham and caught it before it disappeared into the depths.

'Five gold stars', whispered Eleanor as I placed the ring on her finger.

The rest of the service seemed to fly past. Soon we were in the vestry shaking hands with the Vicar. I sat at the desk and signed the register, as both sets of parents followed the bridesmaids and Charles into the inner sanctum. When I arose from the chair, my father and Eleanor's father were in deep conversation. Eleanor's mother was engaged in adjusting the bridal veil to the obvious annoyance of the bride and my mother was chatting to my sister and Heather, Eleanor's friend, who looked stunning in their rose-pink bridesmaids' outfits. Charles was at their side, obviously love-stricken with both but undecided which one should have the priority.

The Vicar called the bride to the desk. My mother embraced me and whispered in my ear that she was proud of me. She was wearing a Marks and Spencer dress with a dignity worthy of the expensive gown adorning the person of Mrs Davies. I shook hands with my father and my new father-in-law. Both working-class lads in origin, they shared a common background and spoke a common language. Then I turned to my mother-in-law who was standing in splendid isolation. I decided that I had better bestow a chaste salute upon her cheeks. There would have been a warmer response from an iceberg.

'Congratulations,' she managed to say.

'Thank you,' I replied, as my mother came to my side.

'I hope you'll both be very happy son,' she said. 'Maybe you have not known each other all that long but from what I can see the omens look good. Don't you agree Mrs Davies?'

'I trust so,' she murmured and walked away to talk to Eleanor's friend.

'That's what you call a happy omen,' I whispered to my mother.

'You are not marrying the mother, love. You are marrying the daughter, thank God,' said Mam.

Eleanor finished her signing of the register and came straight to my mother. She gave her a hug. 'Hello, Mam,' she proclaimed. 'And what do you think of your new daughter.'

'I don't think my son could have chosen a better partner. You look lovely, my dear, and I'm proud of you both.'

My father-in-law came to join us. He embraced his daughter warmly. 'I hope you'll both be very happy, my love. In fact, I'm sure you will be.'

'Dad,' replied my bride. 'You are very perceptive.'

When my father had completed the witnessing of the marriage, the Vicar filled in the certificate and presented it to Eleanor who, in turn, presented it to me.

'Thank you, Mrs Secombe, I said. 'That's a good sign, entrusting it to me.'

'It's not that, husband,' she replied. 'I don't fancy walking down the aisle with a certificate stuck out of my cleavage.'

'Now then, let's get everybody in order for the procession out of the vestry.' The Vicar had become parsonical after addressing everybody in conversational tones for the past ten minutes.

Charles had chosen to escort my sister.

'Would you mind holding on, Vicar,' I said. 'I think I had better get my cousin Freddie out of the congregation as an escort for Heather.'

'You can't go out there now.' My superior sounded shocked.

'I'll go and get him,' volunteered my father.

'This should have been decided long before now,' Mrs Davies snapped.

'Mother, we can't think of everything,' replied Eleanor.

The next minute my father came in with my cousin who was obviously thrilled to receive the call to arms.

Father Whittaker pressed the button which alerted the organist to begin Mendelssohn's 'Wedding March' and we moved out of the vestry to face the world as the Secombes incorporated.

My mother-in-law had ignored the existence of Pontywen's only photographer, Humphries the Snap, and had engaged the services of a well-known Cardiff professional, Edwards the Salon.

It seemed that half of the town's population had gathered outside to witness the photography, much to the annoyance of Mr Edwards who had to shout to make himself heard over the hubbub.

Eventually, after several permutations of the happy couple, 'immediate family', Vicar, best man, bridesmaids, relatives and friends, the session came to a merciful end.

'It's nice to sit down for five minutes,' I said, as we were driven off to the hotel.

'As the first words to your bride now that we are alone, I don't think they will rank among romantic gems,' replied Eleanor.

'Actions speak louder than words,' I proclaimed and took her in my arms. It was a delicious embrace which must have lasted a minute or so.

'I hope the driver has his eyes on the road. Otherwise he will have the wrong idea about parsons,' she murmured.

'Furthermore, I wish to say that you look absolutely wonderful and that I can't wait until tonight to reinforce those words with actions.'

'You daring devil, Frederick, but I second that.'

The Tudor Arms was a Mock Tudor hostelry built in the

late thirties to cater for the more discriminating clientele of the valleys. It lay back some distance from the main road and was shielded from the common gaze by a cordon of fir trees. Mrs Davies had booked the Regency Room for the occasion.

As we drew into the car park, the cars bringing Charles, the bridesmaids and the parents pulled in alongside us. Mrs

Davies was out of the car and into the reception area before any of us had alighted from our vehicles.

'My mother is double or perhaps triple-checking on the arrangements for the meal. Woe betide the 'Tudor Arms' if it does not come up to scratch.' Eleanor took my arm and we walked leisurely into the hotel.

Ten minutes later we were standing in line, with our parents in the Regency Room, greeting the guests as they arrived. No sooner were the ritual handshakings and kisses over than Edwards the Salon invaded the room with his dreaded camera.

Once again there were poses and groupings. Eleanor and I pretended to cut the three-tier wedding cake while several photographs were taken from all angles. In the middle of all this activity Charles was preoccupied with the bridesmaids who were beginning to wilt under the burden of his attentions.

'Charles', I called to him. He came over, to the manifest relief of Carol and Heather. 'Don't you think you should draw everybody's notice to the seating plan? Then you had better check with the manager if the meal is ready. I don't know about you but I am beginning to feel hungry.'

'Right, Fred. I've got some telegrams to read out, by the way. Do I do that first before the speeches?'

'Of course, you chump. That is after you call on us to cut the cake, and don't forget to keep the speeches to the number we agreed.'

'OK, sir, your wish is my command. The other thing is I ask the Vicar to say grace, do I?'

'You do indeed.'

Soon all these preliminaries were over and we were sitting down to the three-course meal. My father – in his black pinstripe suit, fingering his bow-tie from time to time – was in difficulty attempting conversation with Mrs Davies. My mother was enjoying herself with Eleanor's father, doing the bulk of the talking to an attentive listener. Everybody else seemed happy and at ease, except Charles who realized that his hour was about to come. He kept thumbing through a sheaf of telegrams in between courses.

Eventually a waitress arrived with a knife and stood alongside the table on which the cake reposed.

Charles banged on the table with a spoon and announced that he was about to read the telegrams.

'The cake first,' hissed the Vicar who was next but one to him

'Oh, of course. Now the bride and groom will cut the cake.'

Once our combined weight on the knife had broken through the icing and into the cake a feat photographed by numerous guests in the absence of Mr Edwards, it was carried away to be dissected.

My colleague proceeded to read the telegrams which included one from my brother and a number from my 'Stag night' fellow drinkers. 'The first time you have bowled a maiden over' was the message from Mal Hughes, cricketer supreme.

Eleanor's father proposed a warm and witty toast to the bride and groom. He quoted the Reverend Sydney Smith's definition of marriage. 'It resembles a pair of shears, so joined that they cannot be separated, often moving in opposite directions, yet always punishing anyone who comes between them.' This young couple, because of their chosen careers, may move in opposite directions from time to time but woe betide anyone who may try to come between them. I have no doubt that the love they have for each other will stand any pressures from their work.'

I thanked him for his eloquence and my mother-in-law for arranging such an excellent reception. I thanked my parents for all their self-sacrifice on my behalf and Eleanor's parents for producing such a beautiful bride. After I had proposed the toast to the bridesmaids, it was the turn of Charles to make his contribution.

'Speaking for the bridesmaids, I must thank you for your toast. I agree with you that they look really lovely, quite breathtaking really. They certainly have my admiration, I can tell you.

'Thank you, too, Fred for all the support you have given me over the past year. Without your guidance I don't think I could have coped and I now call on the Vicar to say a few words.'

Father Whittaker rose to his feet slowly, glaring at Charles as he did so.

'As requested, my words will be few. In the six months I have know him, I have found the bridgegroom to be a man of integrity, hard-working and possessed of a pleasing personality. The bride, whom I have met only on rare occasions, has impressed me as being equally pleasant and obviously fitted to the noble calling she has chosen. I wish them every happiness.'

'That sounded more like an abbreviated testimonial than a speech.' I whispered to Eleanor.

'Thank goodness for the abbreviation,' she replied.

Charles banged on the table for the last time.

'That is the end of the speeches. Thank you.'

While the guests went to view the wedding presents which were set out on a table, Eleanor was driven back to her parents' house with Carol and Heather to change from her wedding dress into her 'going away' outfit. Her car was parked there with our luggage.

In the absence of the bride, I had an opportunity to have a last word with Mrs Richards who was sitting on a chair, looking forlorn as everybody else was milling around.

'Have you enjoyed the reception?' I asked her.

'Oh yes, it was a lovely meal. I thought Eleanor looked very beauteous.' She caught hold of my hands. 'Don't forget to come and see me when you come back. I know you're going to be very industrial doing your work in the parish and looking after your new wife. If it's only for a few minutes, that's all but just to know you're all right.' She turned away her head to hide the tears.

I went over to my mother and asked her if she would

mind taking her under her wing for the next hour or so. She drew up a chair by my ex-landlady's side and soon the two were engrossed in conversation.

Charles came up to me. 'I've had a wigging from the boss. He said that anybody listening to what I said would have thought you were my Vicar not a fellow Curate.'

'You did ask for that, Charles. Anyhow, thank you for what you said. I hope I can continue to support you until I leave the parish.'

'Don't put it like that. It sounds as if you are going soon.'

'You never know,' I said.

When Eleanor arrived in a lavender-blue twinset with a toque to match, I felt the same reaction as when she appeared at my side in her bridal gown. I could not wait to get to Bristol.

We said our goodbyes in a deluge of confetti and drove off, with the inevitable old shoe tied to the back bumper. It seemed an age before we arrived in the suburbs at the Belvedere Hotel. It was a small family hotel where Eleanor had stayed once when she was a student. We had booked one of the few rooms with *en suite* facilities.

When I signed the register, the receptionist indulged in a faint smile as a few pieces of confetti alighted on the register after falling from my hair.

'Would you like a meal of some kind?' she asked.

'No, thank you,' I replied. 'I think we had better go straight to bed, I mean, to our bedroom. We have a long journey tomorrow.'

The smile broadened.

'Of course, sir. Here are the keys. Room 13 on the first floor. Would you like someone to carry your luggage?'

'No, thank you. We can manage ourselves.'

'Come on, Samson,' said Eleanor. 'Room 13. I don't like the sound of that.'

'Thirteen is my lucky number.'

'Trust you to be different.'

When we opened our cases, we found that Carol and

Heather had managed to insert a liberal amount of confetti which spilled out on the carpet.

'I expect they are quite used to sweeping up confetti. Anyway let's have an early night. I'll go into the bathroom and do my final change for the day and other preparations.'

She disappeared into our *en suite* facility while I undressed and changed into my pyjamas.

Ten minutes later, according to my watch, my bride reappeared in a low-cut white silk nightdress.

'I'm ready for the fray,' she announced.

As I told my love the next morning, it was the happiest fray of my life.

10

'I suppose all good things must come to an end,' sighed a bronzed Eleanor as she packed our suitcases on the last day of our honeymoon in Newquay.

'It's just the beginning, not the end. It has been a fabulous twelve days of sun, sea and love making. Ahead of us stretches a lifetime of happiness.' I put my arms around her and drew her to me.

She raised her eyes and fixed a firm gaze into mine.

'What I mean, my dear, is that when we get back there awaits me a mountain of forms to fill in, an inflated list of patients and a tired old partner who can't cope with the demands of the new Health Service. Add to that the responsibility of being a housewife and these past twelve days of glorious idleness become just a one-off luxury to savour as a memory. I have no doubt that we shall be happy but make no mistake, there will be hiccups in the happiness.'

'All I can say in answer to that is to assure you that I shall do all I can to help in the house, even to the extent of learning to do some cooking.'

'You won't, you know. I like my food. You can lay the table, wash and dry the dishes, make the bed, and perhaps even do a bit of removing Pontywen dust but I think that for the moment you had better leave the cooking to me. There's one other thing. You can heat the water in the boiler for the bath. You have already learned how to wash my back.'

'That is one chore I anticipate with pleasure and the others you mentioned, with modified rapture. In time, my love, I am sure that things will sort themselves out.'

'I wish I had your faith, Fred,' she replied and went on with her packing.

We set out early on the Saturday morning for our return journey. Apart from a leak in the radiator which was cured temporarily in Taunton by the application of a tin of Radweld, the car behaved itself for the whole of the return journey. We arrived at 11 Bevan's Row at four o'clock.

I unloaded the cases as Eleanor advanced on the door, key in hand. She opened up and then stood, looking at me.

'Come on, Romeo,' she said. 'You are supposed to carry me over the threshold.'

'With all the food you have consumed on holiday, it's going to be difficult,' I replied.

'You cheeky husband, get on with your piece of gallantry.'

I picked her up. She was as light as a feather. She put her arms around my neck and kissed me. I advanced down the passage and pushed the half-open door into the middle room with my foot.

'Careful with the newly-painted door,' she warned. 'I think I had better drop off here.'

As she did so, there was a tap on the front door. Standing on the door step and grinning like a Cheshire Cat at our romantic exercise was Bertie Owen who had a bottle of milk in one hand and a loaf of bread in the other.

'Welcome home. I thought perhaps you might have forgotten the staff of life, as it were.'

'That's very kind, Bertie. It will save us going to the shops,' I said.

'Very kind indeed,' echoed my wife.

'Well, here we are.' He handed me the bread and milk. 'I won't stop. You've got plenty to do, I'm sure. Oh, by the way, before I go, Mrs Richards is very ill. She's up in the hospital. I thought you'd better know.'

'When did this happen, Bertie?'

'Not long after you went away, she collapsed in Protheroe the butcher's. Heart, I think.'

'That's a fine welcome home,' I said to Eleanor after he had gone. 'Typical of Bertie. He had to be first with the news, good or bad.'

'It is just as well, love, that he has let you know. I'll run you up to the hospital once we have unpacked and got things shipshape.'

The house still smelt of fresh paint after being shut up for a fortnight.

'Let's open the windows before we do anything else and let some air into the place. Then while I am unpacking, I suggest you ring the Vicar and find out exactly what is wrong with Mrs Richards.'

'Aye! Aye! Sir.' I stood to attention and saluted.

'Sorry to sound so bossy, Fred. It's in my nature and I'm afraid you will have to try and curb it.'

'May I say that I accept your suggestion about ringing the Vicar and that I am not all that good at curbing but I'll try.'

I went into the front room where the brand-new telephone receiver adorned the side table in the far corner. It was the first time that I had used the instrument. I wished it had been for a more congenial purpose. As I stood and waited for the Vicar to answer, I surveyed our parlour with its leather three-piece suite, the china cabinet with Miss Hannah Jones's sherry decanter in pride of place and the mantelpiece with its photographs of Eleanor in cap and gown on one side with me similarly clad on the other. In between the two photographs stood an eight-day clock, a wedding present from our landlord. I was no longer in digs. This was my home. I wallowed in my domestic euphoria until the voice at the other end of the telephone ended the wallow.

'Pontywen Vicarage,' it announced.

'Hello, Vicar, I thought I had better let you know that we are back safely.'

'Good to hear you, Fred. Thank you for your card of Truro Cathedral. I'm afraid I have some bad news for you.'

'If it is about Mrs Richards, Bertie Owen has just been here and told me. How serious is the illness, Vicar?'

'From what I can gather, it is very serious. Apparently her heart is in a bad condition. They hold out little hope for her. It could be a matter of weeks or perhaps even days. She has been asking when you are coming back. She has lost count of the days.'

'Eleanor and I will be at the hospital as soon as we can. See you Monday, Vicar.'

An hour later we drove to the Hospital where the porter greeted my wife as 'Dr Davies' and was put in his place for not knowing the change of name. The Sister in the Princess Royal ward was not so remiss. It was gratifying to be greeted with the deference due to a doctor's husband, especially since a little more than twelve months previously on my first visit to the hospital she had played Mr Bumble to my Oliver Twist.

'Good evening, Dr Secombe, Reverend Secombe. I suppose you have come to see Mrs Richards. She will be very pleased to see you. She's been asking about you, Reverend. I'm afraid she's very ill. Complete heart block, doctor.'

She escorted us down the ward to a bed which was screened off.

'I'll see if she is awake,' said the sister.

As she disappeared behind the screen, she said to Mrs Richards. 'You are awake, then. Visitors to see you. Would you like to put your teeth in?'

'Yes, please,' replied the old lady.

'Let me see to your pillows as well.'

We waited as the sister made the necessary adjustments for the comfort of my erstwhile landlady.

'You go in first,' whispered Eleanor. 'I'll have a word with the Sister while you speak to Mrs Richards.'

When the old lady saw me, her eyes brimmed over with tears and she could not speak. I bent over and kissed her cheek.

'As soon as my back is turned,' I said, 'What happens? You go and get yourself into trouble. I shall have to keep an eye on you from now on, to see that it doesn't happen again.'

'It's lovely to see you,' she murmured, 'and looking so brown. I have missed you. How is Mrs Secombe? I expect you have had a wonderful honeycombe.'

'She's here. She's coming to see you now once she has had a word with Sister to find out how you're getting on.'

'I feel better than when I came in. So I'll be out before long and back in good old Mount Pleasant View before you can say John Robinson.'

As she said this, Eleanor entered and kissed her.

'Hello, Mrs Richards. What have you been doing? I was relying on you for a cup of tea when we came back from Newquay.'

'I only wish I could have done that. You wait, it won't be long before I will be up and out. Then you can come to number 13.'

'No wonder Fred said 13 was his lucky number when our room in the hotel turned out to be that. I had forgotten that it was the number of your house in Mount Pleasant View!'

'Well it was lucky for me, anyway. Look after him, my dear. I can't any more, he's you prodigy now.'

'I'll do that, Mrs Richards. I don't think we should tire you out. We'll come and see you tomorrow.'

We said our goodbyes and left her. As we drove away from the hospital Eleanor told me, 'I'm afraid her end is about to come. With her heart condition it could be next week or next month but it is terminal.'

'In that case, love, all we can do is to make her end as peaceful and untroubled as possible.'

Next morning I was up at seven o'clock, lighting the fire under the boiler and making a cup of tea for us both. By the amount of smoke which invaded the scullery it seemed I had used too much of the *News Chronicle* and the *South Wales Echo* and not enough of the firewood from Owens the Saw mills to ignite the coal. After a second attempt, the coal began to burn and the water to warm.

Once the kettle had boiled on the gas stove, I made the tea and ascended the stairs with a tray bearing two cups.

'Your morning cuppa, Madame,' I announced, 'and your bath water will be ready in about two hours, I hope. In the meanwhile I shall take tea with you before I prepare to remove my beard and my presence for eight o'clock communion.'

'Thank you, Jeeves,' she replied. 'Sorry you will not be here to wash my back.'

'I'm sorry too, my sweet, but business is business.'

When I returned from church, I found the tin bath full of soapy water and minus its occupant who suddenly appeared behind me, clad in her dressing gown.

'It took me about ten minutes at least to fill it via the

bucket,' she said, 'but with your help it will take us half a minute to empty it down the drain outside.'

Between us we manoeuvred the receptacle outside. I tipped up my end too sharply and a deluge poured over the bottom of Eleanor's dressing gown instead of down the drain.

'Secombe, you don't know your own strength. Next time we start to do this, control yourself, please.'

'Humble apologies. I promise to do better next time.'

'You had better do so, chum.'

The glamour of the tin bath had begun to fade after stage one. It would not be too many stages before it vanished altogether and a bathroom would become a *sine qua non* for our future happiness.

Eleanor drove me to St Padarn's for the Family Communion and afterwards to her parents' home where we were to be entertained to Sunday lunch. Our wedding presents had been taken there ready for collection.

'I must say you both look very well and very happy,' said Eleanor's father. 'If the first fortnight of married life is anything to go by, the future is rosy. Let's have a sherry and drink your health. I'll get your mother out of the kitchen to come and join us. I don't think she heard you come in.'

Mrs Davies came into the lounge and embraced Eleanor. 'And how is my daughter?'

'Your daughter is very fit and happy, mother.'

'So you should be after a fortnight in Cornwall. I wish I could have a holiday there and I'd be very fit and happy.'

'Fit, maybe,' commented her husband. 'Don't you think Fred is on a par with Eleanor?'

My mother-in-law turned to me.

'Of course he is,' she replied, 'and why not after a holiday in Newquay and with a daughter like mine.'

She made no attempt to come near me, let alone embrace me.

'Lunch will be ready in half an hour,' she announced.

'Before you get back to the kitchen, woman,' said my father-in-law, 'let's drink a toast to the happy couple.'

He handed her a glass of sherry.

'Welcome home!' He raised his glass in an unsupported toast.

The conversation at the dinner table was three-sided and I was only too happy to make my apologies to have to leave to take Sunday School at St Padarn's. Eleanor dropped me at the church and went on to see what was waiting for her in paper work at the surgery.

At Sunday School there were four teachers missing, leaving Bertie Owen and myself to cope with fifty children. So I decided to do something different.

'We are going to do some acting this afternoon,' I said. There was an excited response from the children.

'This is what I'm good at,' boasted Percy Shoemaker to his rival Tommy Harris. 'I was in the *Pirates of Penzance*.'

'It is not that kind of acting, Percy. I am going to tell you the story of the Good Samaritan. Then you have got to act it in your own words. So sit down quietly everybody and listen carefully.'

I launched into the parable embellishing the story with invented dialogue and extra details not to be found in the Authorized Version.

'Now you are going to act what you have heard. So we want the man who got beaten up, the band of robbers who beat him up, the priest, the Levite, the Good Samaritan, the donkey, and the landlord of the pub where he was taken.'

A forest of hands went up from the boys who all wanted to join the band of robbers hiding up in the hills. 'Sir, Sir! Me, Sir!'

'Hold on, you can't all be robbers. Percy, you said you were good at acting. In that case you had better be the man who gets beaten up and robbed. You've got to be badly injured. It's a difficult part.'

'In that case, Sir, I'll do it.' He slumped forward in his seat, rehearsing his role.

'Sir, can I be the leader of the robbers?' Tommy Harris pleaded.

'All right, Tommy. You've got to plan with your robbers when to come out of the caves and attack the poor old traveller. Four of you boys will be enough.'

I picked the four who started conferring with Tommy about what they were going to do.

'Next, I want the priest and the Levite. That would be like the Vicar and the Churchwarden, two important people from the church. Put your hands up, please.'

Bertie Owen standing at the back, preened himself at this description of his office. His ego trip ended abruptly when not a single hand was raised.

'I think it is about time we had some of the girls in this. Bronwen Williams will you be the Priest and Evelyn Thomas the Levite?'

The two eleven-year-olds blushed and looked at each other. They were bosom friends and had just passed the entrance examination to Pontywen Grammar School. The girls nodded their heads.

'Now then we come to the hero in this wonderful story, the Good Samaritan. For this part I am not going to ask for volunteers. Betty Evans, I am sure you will fill the bill nicely.'

Percy Shoemaker sat up, his face alight with pleasure. Betty was the apple of his eye. To be rescued by her was a fate infinitely more desirable than death. She looked across at him and lowered her eyes.

'Right Mr Secombe,' she said.

'We need a landlord of the pub where the victim was taken by the Good Samaritan and who took good care of him.'

'David Howells can do that, Sir,' suggested Percy. 'His father keeps a pub. He takes good care of his customers.'

David's father was mine host of the Queen Victoria hostelry opposite the Pentecostal Mission, both of whose patrons ignored each other's existence.

'Will you do the part, David?'

He glared at Percy and then nodded his reluctant acceptance.

'There is one other part – the donkey. Who is going to be the kind animal who carried the wounded man to safety?'

Silence reigned supreme at the thought of somebody making an ass of himself.

'Come on, one of you.'

No offer was forthcoming.

'It looks as if it will have to be me,' said Bertie Owen.

Cheers mingled with laughter erupted from the children as they relished the thought of tall Bertie Owen on all fours.

'Quiet, please!' I shouted. 'I don't want him to be a laughing stock. It is very good of Mr Owen to volunteer. It shows that he wants this to be a really good play. We couldn't have done it without the donkey. So let's get ready for action. Boys, I want you to pile up some chairs on that side of the aisle and on the other side. They will be the hills where the robbers hide.'

There was a rush of activity as the chairs were carried and formed into two pyramids.

'Betty. There's a bottle in the vestry. It's empty, but you will have to pretend it is full of wine to pour on wounds. Here's my handkerchief. That is the bandage.' She disappeared into the vestry.

'Mr Owen, could you please give Percy a collection bag which is supposed to be his purse full of money?'

Excitement began to mount, as the stage was set and the props provided. Tommy Harris was issuing orders to his robber band.

'You, Billy and Trev go behind those chairs. Mervyn, Danny and me will stay behind this lot. When I shout "Get 'im!", the five of us rush out.'

'Sir, am I supposed to be tired out, walking?' inquired Percy.

'Yes, you have travelled a long way on foot, but don't forget you are used to walking. So I don't want you staggering around as if you are ready to drop. Just tramp along slowly, whistling or singing, if you like, to keep your spirits up.'

'Sir! Sir! Can we pull his jacket off 'im? You said the robbers stole his clothes.'

'No! All you need do, Tommy, is to catch hold of him and pretend to take his clothes. Take the purse with the money and count it out when you get back to your caves. Now are we all ready? Action!'

Percy started to plod his way down the aisle, singing 'Roll Out the Barrel'. When he was half way down the aisle, Tommy gave the thumbs-up sign, and shouted 'Get 'im!'

The poor victim was hurled to the ground by five enthusiastic actors, giving war whoops like marauding Red Indians.

'Easy, boys,' I shouted. 'Don't overdo it. Take the purse and go off.'

'Tommy Harris, I'll get you for this,' threatened the 'victim'.

'Percy, you are now supposed to be unconscious, not breathing fire and slaughter.'

Tommy and his fellow marauders went back behind the chairs. The chief of the band looked inside the collection bag. 'Twenty-five pounds, thirteen and six,' he shouted. 'We'll be able to go to Barry Island with this. We'll have a go on everything in the fair and have fish and chips after.'

This was greeted with gales of laughter from the audience.

'Calm down, please,' I shouted once more. 'This is not supposed to be a comedy. Let's have the priest on his way down.'

Percy was lying prostrate, his arms outstretched and his eyes closed. Bronwen Williams entered from the vestry wearing a boy's cassock supplied by Bertie Owen and carrying a prayer book which she was studying intently. She was a tall child for her age and walked with a natural dignity.

When she came alongside Percy's inert body, she stopped and looked at him. Then she went back to her prayer book. 'Now where was I?' she said and walked on to the sanctuary.

Next came Evelyn Thomas, short and plump, as the Levite. She carried the Churchwarden's wand of office, again supplied by Bertie Owen. By the time she reached the unconscious victim, she found it easier to drag the pole along the floor. When she reached the unconscious victim, she stopped and had a minute examination of the body. She looked back towards Tommy and his gang.

'I'm not staying here to be beaten up. Anyway if the robbers come after me, I'll hit them with this stick.'

'You try it,' threatened Tommy.

'Shut up,' I told him. 'You are not supposed to say any more in this play.'

After the Levite had disappeared from the scene now came the moment the audience had waited for. Bertie Owen was on his hands and knees ready for his grand entrance. At his side stood Betty Evans, a pretty little blonde with an empty communion wine bottle in one hand and my handkerchief in the other.

'Off we go,' said Bertie.

There was much stifled merriment as the 'donkey' made his way down the aisle.

'Whoa!' ordered the Good Samaritan. 'Look at this poor man. I must help him.'

She bent over Percy and raised his head. 'That looks very nasty,' she said and pretended to pour wine from the bottle into the wound in his scalp. She put the bottle down and then tried to bind the handkerchief around his head.

'The hanky's too small, Sir.'

'That's because he's got a big 'ead,' commented Tommy who was Percy's rival for her hand.

'Tommy Harris, get out. I have had enough of you for one afternoon.' Red-faced he marched out and banged the door behind him.

'Just hold the handkerchief to his forehead and lift him from the floor. Then help him on to the back of the donkey.'

Percy was savouring every second of this attention. She put her arms around him and lifted him up.

'Stand him against the donkey. Now, Percy, get yourself up on the animal's back, sitting sideways or side-saddle. Fine. Come on then, Good Samaritan, help to hold him on and take him to the inn.'

Standing in the chancel was David Howells of the Queen Victoria, ready to receive his guest. Bertie Owen was showing signs of strain. As he attempted to clamber up the chancel steps on all fours, carrying Percy, he was seized with cramp. He let out a cry of agony, raised himself and dumped Percy who fell against Betty, the two of them landing in an ungainly heap on the floor. The children collapsed into hysterical laughter.

'What on earth is going on here?' demanded a voice at the back of the church. 'This is supposed to be the House of God.'

It was the Vicar and standing at his side was the Bishop. There was a deathly silence.

'Chairs back in their places and everyone settle down,' I said.

While this was happening I went down to join the unexpected visitors. 'Good afternoon, my Lord and good afternoon, Vicar. I know this must have looked like a pantomime, when you came in. If you had arrived earlier you would have seen some impressive acting of the parable of the Good Samaritan by the children. Unfortunately the second before you entered, Mr Owen who had volunteered to play the donkey in the story had an attack of cramp quite suddenly which meant that the Good Samaritan, the man attacked on the road to Jericho and the ass ended up in a tangle.'

There was a faint smile on the Bishop's face but the initial scowl remained upon the Vicar's countenance.

'I think there are better ways of teaching the parables than this,' he snapped.

'I don't know about that, Father,' said the Bishop. 'It was unfortunate about the – er – accident but play acting the parables does help them to come alive for the children.

However I have not come here to discuss the presentation of the New Testament. I happened to be passing near Pontywen and decided to make a brief call at the Vicarage where the Vicar informed me that you were married recently. I have come to offer you and Mrs Secombe my felicitations. I must meet her one day.'

'Thank you very much, my Lord,' I replied.

11

I expected a severe reprimand from the Vicar when Charles and I were closeted in his study for the Monday morning briefing session. To my surprise Father Whittaker appeared to be in a jovial mood.

'How has your first weekend in your new home gone, Fred?' he asked as we sipped Mrs Lilywhite's execrable coffee.

'Apart from difficulties with the tin bath, quite well indeed, Vicar,' I replied. 'Neither Eleanor nor I have had to contend with such a contraption before.'

'If ever you need a more relaxing bath, you can bring your towels etc., here,' he said.

'That is very kind of you but Eleanor seems determined to make the best of it at number 11 Bevan's Row.'

'So be it,' he replied, making a triangle of his fingers, his favourite exercise. 'In any case my offer would be for a limited period only. When the Bishop and I returned to the Vicarage after our—er—visit to St Padarn's yesterday afternoon he asked me if I would consider accepting the living of Abergwylfa. As you know, it is a parish in the Anglo-Catholic tradition and more suited to my churchmanship. I had hoped to establish such a bastion here but evidently Pontywen would resist tooth and nail. It is a little less than a year since I came. I realize that and so does the Bishop. However, I had told him I was not happy in my ministry in this parish some months ago. He feels it is better that I leave now rather than to sink into a trough of indifference.'

'Congratulations, Vicar,' I said.

'From me too,' echoed Charles who could not believe his good fortune.

'I shall be phoning the Bishop later this morning to let him know that I accept the living. It will be some months before I go. There are some improvements to be made to the Vicarage there. In the meanwhile I should like to do something to improve the size of our contribution to the Missionary cause. I was going to raise this matter before I knew of the Bishop's offer of a living. It will make a grand swan song if we could double or perhaps treble the amount sent from Pontywen. So I propose we have a garden fête in the Vicarage grounds in late August. That will give us some two months to prepare. What do you think?'

'I think it is an excellent idea in many ways. Not only will it raise money for the work of the Church overseas but it will be useful in bringing the parish together socially. I assume that you will involve St Illtyd's in this as well as Pontywen.'

Charles gave me an unfriendly look at this last remark. It would mean that he would have to be responsible for organizing a few stalls from the little country parish. He was allergic to both responsibility and organization, not to mention work.

'Of course,' said the Vicar. 'I suggest we call a meeting of the PCC representatives from the three churches on Thursday week and get the thing off the ground.'

When I told Eleanor over a lunch of tinned tuna and Howells' tomatoes that Father Whittaker would be departing in three or four months' time she said, 'Wouldn't it be wonderful if you could become Vicar of Pontywen?'

'You must be joking,' I replied. 'I have not been ordained long enough for that.'

'Stranger things can happen. I never believed when I was doing my training that I could become a partner after just twelve months in practice.'

'You must admit that you did have an advantage by

being taken on by an elderly gentlemen at the end of this tether and who was a friend of the family.'

'And I always thought it was because of my brilliance. I tell you something, Frederick, I shall have to be brilliant to cope with a panel of more than two thousand registered customers. You should see the accumulation of paperwork let alone the crowd in the surgery this morning. I'm afraid I have a lot of calls today, so you will have to see Mrs Richards on your own before you go to your clergy meeting.'

The old lady was awake and looked much brighter than she was on Saturday evening.

'I'm sure I'm turning round the corner. Perhaps they'll let me get out of bed tomorrow. Once I get home, I'll come on like a house that's on fire. Home is the place to recoup yourself, that's positive.'

'When they are ready, Mrs Richards, they will let you get up and about. Until then, you will have to be a good girl and do what nurse tells you.'

'I've always been a good girl, Mr Secombe. There's too much trouble when you're not. Mind there have been times when I would have liked to kick off the braces but I never did. How are you and Mrs Secombe settling up in your new home?'

'Very well indeed. There are just two snags. I miss having a bath in your bathroom even if you did stick me to the bath once. The other snag is I miss having you to fuss over me when I come in.'

She glowed with pleasure.

'Your mother thanked me for looking after you at the wedding. I told her that I thought of you as my son. I never had any children and I haven't any nieces or nephews. You are the only one of the curates the Vicar sent who was close to me.'

Her eyes began to fill with tears.

'I've got to go now, Mrs Richards,' I said gently, 'but I tell you what: you are the nearest pin up to my mother in my life, that is apart from Eleanor, of course.'

'Of course,' she replied, 'she is a lovely lady. She will take care of you. Mind, she can't make a fuss over you. She's got all her physical work to do. Are you coming in tomorrow for a few minutes?'

'I'll be here, don't worry.' I kissed her cheek and left her. She was waving goodbye when I turned round at the door of the ward.

By the time I reached the Vicarage, to join Father Whittaker and Charles for our joint visit to the Deanery Chapter meeting, I was ten minutes late. The two men were standing outside by the Vicar's car. My superior was inspecting his pocket watch as I came down the drive.

'Very sorry,' I said. 'I have been to see Mrs Richards and I did not realize how the time had flown.'

He grunted and opened the door for Charles and myself to get into the back of his Morris Oxford.

Twenty minutes later, after some reckless driving we arrived at the Bull, Tremadoc just in time for the meeting.

'Better late than never,' was the greeting from the Rural Dean, the Reverend Daniel Thomas BA, RD as we arrived. 'We have kept three chairs for you.' Seated at his side, was a plump middle-aged lady in a brown jumper and navy-blue skirt, with a string of artificial pearls round her neck. There was the usual collection of elderly clergymen in the back room of the inn, most of them comatose.

'Shall we begin with prayer?' he said once we were seated.

The lady was about to rise to her feet.

'Please stay seated Miss Lloyd Williams. We sit for prayers here like the Quakers.' The Rural Dean indulged in a guffaw at his own remark. He was alone in his laughter. In any case, it was enough for the two clergymen who were in their late eighties to rise to go home let alone stand for prayers.

Our chairman mumbled his way through a couple of prayers and invited us to join in the Lord's Prayer which was punctuated by a couple of snores from the Reverend Llewellyn Hughes, Rector of Penygors who was deep in sleep when we came into the room.

'Before we have the minutes of the last meeting, I must welcome Miss Lloyd Evans to our midst. She is the organizer for the Moral Welfare as you all know and she has come to tell us about her work. Now then the Chapter Clerk will read the minutes.'

The Reverend Herbert Morris, Vicar of Llanafon with Lower Cwmtilio, a tall thin man with a permanently lugubrious countenance, drawled his way through ten minutes of minutiae.

'Now then, we come to the main course, as it were.' Another guffaw at his own attempt at humour. 'Here is Miss Lloyd Evans.'

The organizer for the Diocesan Moral Welfare Society rose to her feet with a sheaf of notes and pamphlets in her hand.

'Thank you, Mr Rural Dean, for your welcome and thank you gentlemen, for your parishes' contributions to my society. I know that some of your congregations are small but you still manage to give something each year. Every little helps. By the way, my name is Lloyd Jenkins.'

'Let me paint you a picture of our work over the past twelve months and then I shall tell you about some existing projects we have for the next twelve months. As you know, we have a home for unmarried mothers, some of them sixteen years old and one only fifteen.'

'Tut tut,' interjected the Rural Dean.

'Somebody has to care for them, Mr Chairman. If it has to be somebody then that should be the Church. Surely it is our duty as Christians to look after these unfortunate children because that is what they are – children, just children.'

'What I meant,' said the embarrassed Rural Dean, 'was that it is terrible for such young persons to be getting into trouble. It's these modern times, what with the wireless and the cinema and everything – so different from the days when I was a child.'

Some of the old men nodded their approval.

'If you don't mind me saying so,' the speaker replied,

'there were unfortunate young girls in your childhood who got into trouble. To return to my report about our work over the past year, we have helped twenty-nine young mothers to cope with their responsibilities. I have spoken to thirty-two branches of the Mothers' Union about the society and we had a very successful one-day seminar in Landulais Church Hall.

'Let me give you an example of our work with unmarried mothers. I shall have to give you details of this case to make you appreciate the plight of this one young girl.'

Charles sat up on the edge of his seat ready to absorb the sordid details.

'Shall we call her Mary. Mary was a sixteen-year-old pupil in one of our Grammar Schools. Her parents were very strict Plymouth Brethren. They had no wireless in the house; no newspapers. The only reading was the Bible. Mary was not allowed friends. An intelligent child, her ambition was to become a schoolteacher.

The five days she was at school were the happiest days of the week. Weekends and holidays were a misery to her, virtually a prisoner in her own home. She struck up a friendship with a boy, shall we call him Bob, in her form. They would stroll around a park near the school during lunch break. As the weeks passed, their friendship became more than platonic, shall we say. They began with kissing each other behind the bushes. Then came the inevitable stage in what had been the highlight of this child's life. They had intercourse.'

She paused after daring to use such a word. Charles was riveted by the story.

'There followed another inevitable stage in the relationship: she became pregnant. The young couple were terrified of the outcome. Soon she was afflicted with morning sickness which she tried to hide from her parents but it was no use. Her mother had become suspicious. Her parents confronted her. She admitted that she was pregnant. Mary was told to pack her bags and leave the house after bringing such disgrace on the family name.'

The Rural Dean shook his head. It was not apparent whether it was at Mary's waywardness or the parents' reaction.

'Fortunately for the young girl she went to the police for help and they directed her to our home. There she was cared for throughout her pregnancy and afterwards with her baby daughter. Both are still there for the time being. She is making up her mind whether she wants the baby adopted or not. The longer she hangs on to the baby, the less likely it will be that she will give the baby to somebody else. In which case we shall have to help her manage on her own.'

'Either way, somebody else will have to pay for her fornication.' This further interruption from the Rural Dean provoked Miss Lloyd Jenkins into an angry outburst.

'Mr Rural Dean you cannot use the word fornication in relation to an innocent and much-wronged young girl who had fallen in love for the first time in her life! She is not a wanton or a whore. If she had been given love and understanding by her parents this would never have happened. She was looking for love and she found it with this young man.'

'Hear! hear!' exclaimed Charles whose face turned red when he realized that he was a lone voice crying in the wilderness.

'If I may proceed,' went on the speaker, 'Mary's case is but one of the many which come to us throughout the year. Each of these unmarried mothers is given love and understanding, the ethos of our society, which should also be the ethos of our churches.'

She looked at the Rural Dean who happened to be looking at the floor at that moment.

'Now, I want to speak about the exciting projects for the latter half of this year and the first half of next year. The first is concerned with helping the clergy to deal with matrimonial problems which may be brought to them at their vicarages and rectories. As you know, with men arriving home after years away in the forces, adjusting to home life can be a tricky business and often there is much unhappiness which could be eliminated if the right sort of guidance were available. So we are arranging to hold a week's course for clergy who are interested. We shall have a panel of psychologists, doctors and other experts to provide advice. There will be sessions when imaginary cases are presented and the clergy present will be asked to say what help they would give. Then the experts will unravel the complexities and pass on their combined wisdom to those on the course.'

'The second and equally valuable, if not more valuable project is a series of lantern-slide lectures on sex education.'

At the mention of the word 'sex' eyebrows shot up. A chastened Rural Dean refrained from comment but registered visual distaste. Charles was agog, anxious to hear more. Father Whittaker wore a cynical expression as if doubting whether lantern-slides were the answer to the sex question.

'I know that just as the Victorians used to cover the legs of their tables to avoid exposing even wooden limbs, so today there is still a hangover from those inhibited days in a reluctance to talk about one of the most elemental forces in life, that is, the sexual function without which mankind would cease to exist.

'How many of us understand our own bodies and the wonderful way in which God has created them to perpetuate our own species? How many of us appreciate the joy which the sexual function can bestow as an expression of love? These lectures will attempt to examine the reproductive process through plant life, animal life and finally human life with all its capacity of mind, spirit and body to give meaning to the sexual act.

'I have brought with me details of the course of lantern-slides which you might like to distribute to your congregations. Details of the course for clergy will be sent to you in the near future. Thank you for listening to me. I shall be more than pleased to answer any questions you put to me.'

The Vicar, Charles and I clapped as she sat down. The Rural Dean and the three others who were still awake abstained, stunned by the mention of the word 'sex'.

'Why did you say in your story of Mary's unfortunate experience, "Then came the inevitable stage. After kissing each other, they had intercourse." Surely it was not inevitable.' This first question came from Father Whittaker.

'To a child from a secure, understanding and loving background it would not have been inevitable. To a lonely, unloved child it was inevitable that she would give herself to the one person who loved her.'

'Thank you,' said my Vicar.

'I think we had better finish now.' The Rural Dean was anxious to bring the session to a close before any more questions could be asked involving sex.

'Well, thank you, Miss Lloyd Thomas for your talk. We shall have our cup of tea now.

As we left the Bull the Vicar said, 'One of the joys of leaving Pontywen is the thought that I shall no longer have to suffer the Deanery chapter meetings. I have never seen anything less like the church militant here on earth.'

Soon after I got back home the telephone rang. It was Eleanor ringing up from a call box. 'I'm afraid I shall be late getting back. I am up to my eyes in work. It means I shall not be able to cook you your first dinner in Bevan's Row tonight. I'll bring some fish and chips on my way home. If you will lay the table, it will be a help. I love you. Ta, ta.'

I sat in one of the armchairs in the front room and switched on the new HMV wireless set which had been given to us as a wedding present by the congregation at St Padarn's. It was *Children's Hour*. Halfway through a bleated sentence of Larry the Lamb, the telephone rang.

This time the Vicar's voice was at the other end. 'Fred, I have just heard from the hospital that Mrs Richards has passed away – heart failure. I thought I had better let you know straight away since you two were very close. Is there anyone I should inform apart from yourself?'

I found it difficult to speak. It was only a few hours ago that she had waved me goodbye and talked about getting up, ready to return to 13 Mount Pleasant View.

'The only person I can think of, Vicar, is Miss Jacobs who was her best friend. She had no relatives as far as I know. If you like I will let her know.'

'Very well then, sorry to have to be the bearer of bad news. We shall have to think about the funeral when we meet tomorrow. See you then. Goodbye.'

When I put the phone down, I began to weep. Perhaps if I had not left her to get married she would still be alive. If I had not approached Trevor Luxton he would still be alive. In the space of a couple of weeks I had been responsible for two people's deaths. Remembering Eleanor's admonishment about my sense of guilt over Trevor Luxton's death, I decided there was nothing to be gained indulging in remorse.

I switched off the set and made my way to Miss Jacobs's house in Hill Terrace just around the corner of Mount Pleasant View. I knocked on the door. The curtains in the front room were moved almost imperceptibly but enough to inspect the identity of the caller. As a backstreet bookmaker, Miss Jacobs could afford to take no chances.

'How nice to see you, Mr Secombe,' she said as she opened the door. 'Come on in.'

She ushered me into the front room, which served as her office. There was a large safe in a recess by the inner wall. A filing cabinet stood at one side of the window and a bureau on the other side.

'Sit down, please. Can I get you a drink? Would you care for a sherry?'

I sat down in an armchair.

'I should love a dry sherry, Miss Jacobs.'

She moved quickly into the middle room and returned with a tray containing a bottle and two sherry glasses. Small, thin, birdlike, she wore a pair of pince-nez on her beaky nose. Miss Jacobs looked even more like a schoolmistress than Miss Hannah Jones. A stalwart at the parish church, she was an unusual backstreet 'bookie'.

'Now then, what can I do for you?' she asked as she poured me a sherry.

'I am afraid I have come to bring you some sad news. Mrs Richards passed away suddenly this afternoon.'

She put down the bottle and handed me the glass of sherry. She poured herself a glass and sat down opposite me. 'Poor old May,' she murmured. 'Well I am not surprised. When I saw her in hospital on Friday, she looked terrible. She was quite a good age, you know. Looking after you kept her going. I think she thought of you as a son – not like the other curates. Drink your sherry. I can see that you are upset.'

As I sipped my drink, she looked at me.

'Now I have some news for you, Mr Secombe. I suppose I should not let you know until after the funeral but I am not a solicitor. She has left the house to you.'

I stared back at her, unable to comprehend.

'Don't look so shocked. She had made a will leaving the house to the church. The old Canon made it out for her and I was the other witness. Then a few months ago when I came round to have tea with her she told me she had changed her mind and she wanted to leave the house to you. She has no relatives and she wanted to show you how happy the past year had been. So we tore up the will I drafted the new one for her. We got Mr and Mrs Williams from next door to witness it and I am the sole executor.'

My head was spinning. Tears welled up once again when I thought of the deep regard the old lady had for me.

'You can see the will when the funeral is over. She has some money in the Post Office savings account. More than enough to pay for her funeral expenses. She will be buried with her husband, of course. I suppose that as executor I must make all the arrangements for the burial and put the announcement in the paper etc.'

She talked in such a calm businesslike manner that it

seemed she was referring to some everyday transaction, and not the disposal of the mortal remains of Mrs Richards. It was typical of the old lady that she had chosen Miss Jacobs as her executor after the death of the Canon, knowing that she would be so competent in that position.

I walked slowly back home, still trying to come to terms with what had happened. I would soon be a house owner. The first thought about the acquisition of 13 Mount Pleasant View was that it would mean an end to the tin bath and that my wife and I would be using the very bath which brought us together.*

As I turned the corner of Bevan's Row I could see Eleanor's car parked outside. I hurried to the house and opened the door to find a somewhat irate wife.

'Where have you been? The fish and chips are getting cold. I put them out on the plate, thinking you were outside in the WC.'

'I'm sorry, love, but so much has happened in the last hour that I don't know whether I am on my head or my feet.'

My expression and my tone of voice were sufficient to dispel the annoyance.

'Would you like me to put the fish and chips in the oven while you tell me all about it?'

'I think that would be a very good idea.'

Ten minutes later, when I finished my recital of the past hour's happenings, she said, 'My apologies for being such a nag. I can see you are upset and bewildered. All I can say is God bless Mrs Richards for her kindness and for bequeathing you the bath which brought us together.'

'It's funny you should say that,' I replied.

*See How Green Was My Curate

12

'For as much as it hath pleased Almighty God of his great mercy to take unto himself the soul of our dear sister here departed . . .'

The Vicar's voice droned on as I stood at the graveside of my late landlady, her chief mourner, with Eleanor and Miss Jacobs at my side. The sun shone down on us and on the fifty or so members of the congregation who had come to pay their last respects to a stalwart of St Mary's Church. From the school playground a few streets away the distant shouts of children composed a descant of life to the solemn tones of death.

I had asked Father Whittaker if I might opt out of taking part in the service to act as chief mourner since the old lady had no relatives. He consented readily to my request knowing how strong had been the bond between Mrs Richards and myself. In accordance with Miss Jacobs's wishes I had not informed him of the will.

As the service drew to its close I wondered what his reaction would be when the will was read at the post-funeral repast which she had arranged at her house. It was a lavish buffet, spiced with an abundance of drinks, worthy of a hospitality tent at Chepstow Racecourse. When everybody had been fed and watered by Miss Jacobs's generous hand, she entered the front room where the mourners were assembled and called for silence.

'Thank you all for coming to show your respect for dear

old May and thank you, Vicar, together with the Reverend Wentworth-Baxter for the lovely service. As the sole executor of her will, it is my duty to read out the details on this occasion.'

She adjusted her pince-nez spectacles and extracted a document from a brown paper envelope.

'This is the last will and testament of me, May Rachel Richards of 13 Mount Pleasant View Terrace, Pontywen and I hereby revoke all former wills and testamentary dispositions made by me.

(1) I appoint Esther Rebecca Jacobs of 3 Hill Terrace, Pontywen, to be the sole executor and trustee of my will.

(2) Subject to the payment of my just debts, taxes, funeral and testamentary expenses I give the residue of my estate, including my house and all its contents to Frederick Thomas Secombe, at present residing at 13 Mount Pleasant View, Pontywen.'

At this juncture there was an audible reaction from the dozen people packed into the front room. Both the Vicar and Charles sat, with mouths agape.

'In witness hereof' continued Miss Jacobs 'I have hereto set my hand this twenty-first day of March one thousand nine hundred and forty six.

Signed by the Testator,
in our presence and by us in her presence.
May Rachel Richards.
Evan Williams, retired,
12 Mountain View Terrace, Pontywen.
Annie Williams, housewife,
12 Mountain View Terrace, Pontywen.

She placed the document back into the envelope and handed it to me, amid the shell-shocked hush which had descended on the small gathering.

'It just shows, Mr Secombe, what she thought of you,' said the sole executor. 'You were much more than a lodger.

You were the son she never had. The only pity is that you came so late into her life. Still, I suppose that was much better than not knowing you at all. I suppose that, apart from her married life, the last twelve months were more fulfilling than at any other time.'

The immediate effect of this explanatory postscript to the will was an outpouring of congratulations to me on my good fortune.

'Evan and me witnessed the will,' said Mrs Richards's next door neighbour, 'but we never said nothing to nobody. She thought a lot of you, she did.'

Father Whittaker came across to me and shook my hand.

'I must say you kept this a secret. When did you know about it?'

'I hadn't the faintest idea until Miss Jacobs told me just before the funeral. She gave me strict instructions not to say anything until she had read the will.'

'Well, what are you going to do with the house now you are its owner?'

'It's too early to say just yet, especially since we have been in Bevan's Row for only a week. One thing is certain.'

'What is that?'

'We shall be coming to Mount Pleasant View for a bath.'

'I thought you might,' he said.

'Any chance of letting out the place to me?' asked Charles when the Vicar moved away.

'Come off it! How on earth would you cope with cooking, washing and ironing? You would be underfed and looking like a tramp in no time. I don't think Mrs Richards would approve of that. What you need is the landlady you have at the moment or perhaps a wife when you grow up a little more.'

'I am trying to find a wife, Fred.'

'Your past two attempts have centred on schoolgirls. You require someone older not younger than yourself. How about Miss Jacobs?'

'I don't think that's funny,' he said.

After the last of the mourners had left I went into the kitchen to join Eleanor and Miss Jacobs who were doing the washing up.

'Thank you for your kind words,' I said to our hostess. 'They certainly helped to cushion the shock to the listeners at the contents of the will.'

'Knowing what people are like,' she replied, 'I thought it was necessary to point out how much she thought of you. It's much better that you have the house rather than St Mary's.'

'Miss Jacobs, you are an angel.' So saying, Eleanor kissed her on the cheek; to the great embarrassment of the book-maker.

The next day, Saturday, was the occasion of the Gilbert & Sullivan Society's first outing. Idris the Milk had hired a forty-seater bus from the Welsh Greyhound Luxury Coaches at Cwmteify to take the company to Porthcawl, which vied with Barry Island for the title the Blackpool of South Wales. We were due to meet at nine-thirty a.m. outside St Padarn's. Eleanor had a Saturday-morning surgery but planned to meet us on the beach after lunch.

By nine-thirty a.m. everybody was present. Only the bus was absent. At nine-forty-five the bus was still missing. Idris decided to go to the callbox in the Square to check with the bus company if the vehicle had left. Bertie Owen chose that moment to proclaim to all and sundry that, had he been in charge of the arrangements, the bus would have been there at nine-fifteen a.m.

'Bertie, if you had been in charge, the bus wouldn't be here at ten-fifteen, let alone nine-fifteen,' said Iorwerth Ellis, first tenor, and aspiring juvenile lead.

A few minutes later Idris returned with the news that the bus had just left Cwmteify and should be with us by ten o'clock. Apparently the driver had been late reporting for duty and had been reprimanded.

'That's handy,' Bertie said. 'He'll take it out on us now. Get ready for a bumpy ride.'

At five past ten the bus pulled up outside St Padarn's. Bertie's forecast proved accurate – the driver's countenance was more suited to a funeral than an outing to the seaside. 'Don't all try to get on at once,' he snarled, as the young girls of the chorus fought each other to get to the back seat first.

'Weren't you young once?' asked Idris, as he tried to control the rush.

'You're talking about ancient history,' Charlie Thomas, one of the wags in the chorus, shouted from the back of the queue.

The driver stood up and pointed a finger at Charlie.

'Any more cracks like that and you'll have to find another driver.'

As we were already half an hour late, there were no more verbal attacks on the obviously disgruntled individual at the wheel.

I am a very poor traveller in the back of a car and anywhere but the front seat of a bus. Unfortunately, by the time Charles and I boarded the vehicle, the front seat was occupied by Mrs Collier, wardrobe mistress and wife of the organist at St Padarn's, together with her husband who had been dragooned into the excursion. 'I always sit in the front seat,' she said.

To make matters worse, the seat my colleague and I occupied was over one of the wheels. Charles sat by the window and opposite me were Idris and his wife, Gwen. Behind us sat Charlie Thomas and Harry Williams both of whom were smoking evil-smelling pipes. I wondered how long it would be before I turned green.

After thundering down the valley roads for half an hour, being driven in anger by a Jehu, I could feel my colour changing as my stomach engaged in several somersaults. It was at this stage that the female chorus began to sing 'Sons of the sea, bobbing up and down like this' with appropriate actions. By now my stomach was almost in my mouth.

Idris looked across at me.

'You look terrible,' he said. 'Shall I stop the bus?'

I could not speak but nodded my head.

He went to the driver and tapped him on the shoulder.

'What do you want?' barked the ill-tempered one.

'The Curate wants to be sick.'

'What?'

'The Curate wants to be sick!!' bellowed Idris.

'Well, he'll have to wait till I can stop somewhere.'

'If you don't stop in the next minute or so you're going to have a mess in your bus and you'll have to mop it up because none of us will.'

The threat worked.

To my great relief, he applied his brakes and pulled in to a roadside, opposite a gate in a field. I made a hasty exit and managed to open the gate to hide behind the hedge before my breakfast and I parted company. I rejoined the bus as white as before I had been green.

'You still look terrible,' said Charles.

'Thank you,' I replied.

Charlie and Harry behind me had extinguished their bonfires and the boisterous revelry had dwindled to a sympathetic murmuring in recognition of their producer's plight. An hour later Porthcawl hove in sight and my ordeal was over.

As the bus arrived in the car park, Idris made his way to the front. 'Now then, let's all keep together. Iorwerth has brought a cricket bat and tennis ball and Rosemary Thomas has got a tennis racquet and ball with her. So we can play cricket and rounders as well as have a swim. The tide is out at the moment but it's on the turn. So we'd better have games first then bathe afterwards. Don't forget to bring everything with you from the bus: your picnic food, bathing costumes, etcetera. The bus is due to leave here at eight o'clock sharp.'

'You can say that again,' came the voice from the driver's seat. 'Anybody not here at eight will have to make their own way back.'

'Thank you, Mr Lovejoy,' said Idris. 'After that, you can't say you haven't been warned. Right, last one out's a sissy.'

That was the signal for a stampede from the girls in the back.

'I think we had better sit still for the time being,' I suggested to Charles. 'Otherwise we might be trodden on in the rush. I don't think I have the stamina to fight my way through at the moment. I hope you don't mind being the sissy.'

'Fred, I gave up childish games long ago,' he said.

'Charles, you amaze me,' I replied.

Porthcawl, situated on a rocky promontory at the end of a long line of sand dunes at the easternmost end of Swansea Bay, was always windswept. On this lovely sunny morning I was grateful for the invigorating breeze, even if it was already laden with the smell of fish and chips in the car park. The fun fair was in full swing in more ways than one. A horde of fun seekers were milling around the various attractions as the chairoplanes swung higher and a steam organ ground out its hurdy gurdy music. Loudspeakers relayed Bing Crosby singing 'Pennies from Heaven', the stallholders' anthem.

Charles and I followed our contingent as they made their way to the beach with the girls leading the expedition to find a patch of sand we could reserve for ourselves. In no time at all they had staked out our territory with a zeal worthy of prospectors in a gold rush.

Bundles of towelled bathing costumes together with shopping bags containing the food and drink necessary for the fiesta formed a large circle in the middle of which some of the girls were besporting themselves already, playing French cricket with a tennis racquet and ball by the time Charles and I arrived.

Very soon the middle-aged male members of the chorus, rediscovering their lost youth, joined them, leaping about like young gazelles. The few who had brought their wives with them busied themselves with settling down by their own mound of belongings, casting envious eyes at the men who had come solo.

Bertie Owen, whose wife was anti-social and never went on outings, had forgotten his chagrin at being ousted by Idris as organizer of the trip and was in the forefront of the activity, diving with gay abandon in an attempt to catch the ball whenever it came his way.

There was a loud blast on a whistle from Idris who had moved into the centre of the circle 'We want everybody in all the games – even if you have a cork leg or bad eyesight.'

'Come on Walter,' commanded Mrs Collier. 'You heard what he said.' Mr Collier heaved a sigh and got to his feet.

'What do you want first?' asked Idris. 'Rounders or cricket?'

'Rounders,' screeched the girls.

'Rounders it is,' said the MC. 'Women against the men. Ladies first. Rosemary you brought the racquet. You are captain of the ladies. Iorwerth you brought the tennis ball. You captain the men.'

'So you bat first, Rosemary,' went on Idris.

Rosemary Thomas was a tall, blonde, muscular seventeen-year-old, evidently a pillar of the sporting life in Pontywen Grammar School. She chose all her contemporaries to lead the batting with the five more mature ladies forming the tail end.

Idris and Iorwerth spaced out the stops with pebbles. The men spread themselves around, with Bertie doing gymnastic exercises to loosen his muscles and impress the females.

Iorwerth tossed up the ball to Rosemary who had put herself at the head of the batting. She launched herself into the attack with a mighty hit which sent the ball soaring into the stratosphere. Charlie Thomas and Harry Williams positioned themselves to receive the ball while Rosemary thudded around the hard sand, like a bat out of hell, urged on by the girls who were jumping up and down. Charlie and Harry with their eyes fixed on the ball had failed to notice a large collie whose eyes were also fixed on the same object. The three of them met as the ball came down. I do not know who was the most surprised, the dog or the two men but it was a most painful collision.

The dog was the first up and yelped away into the distance. Next, Charlie rose to his feet, rubbing his shoulder.

'You can stop running,' Idris shouted. 'Playing is suspended.'

Harry was still prostrate and motionless.

'Bring on the trainer!' bawled Bertie.

'Don't be funny, the man's hurt,' I said. Idris and I went to him. His eyes were closed.

'Put a cold pebble down the back of his shirt. That will bring him round,' advised Bertie.

'For God's sake, Bertie, get away, will you?' Idris hissed.

To our great relief slowly he opened his eyes. As he did so, he began to groan with pain.

'Where's it hurting you, Harry?' I asked.

'It's my shoulder. I think I've broken my collar bone. I had this once before when I was playing rugby.'

There was a St John's Ambulance hut near the fairground. Walter Collier offered his services as an escort, only too pleased to find an excuse to avoid playing rounders. Harry walked slowly with his arm across his middle flanked by the organist and Charlie Thomas who was still shaken by the incident.

'Right. On with the game!' Idris shouted. 'Rosemary, you can only only count one round. I know you went round three times but the ball was dead.'

The game went on, interminably it seemed, with two of the matrons, Gwen Shoemaker and Rhiannon Jenkins, farmer's wife, showing a turn of speed equal to that of the girls. By the time the men had their turn, and had been hopelessly beaten, it was the lunch interval. In the meanwhile there was no sign of Harry and his escorts. Instead there was the welcome sight for me of Eleanor approaching, with a picnic basket and her bathing equipment.

'You should have been here earlier, love,' I said when I met her. 'Harry Williams collided with a dog plus Charlie Thomas and it looks as if he has broken his collar bone.'

'I don't wish to sound callous, Fred, but I am glad I wasn't here. I'm sorry about Harry of course. I've spent most of the morning dealing with the sick and the lame. I am hoping for a pleasant afternoon and evening off duty in this lovely sunshine.'

Before we could sit down, Bertie Owen greeted my wife. 'You should have been here earlier, Mrs Secombe.'

'So I hear,' she replied. 'In any case, poor old Harry would have to go to the hospital to have his collar bone set in plaster. I could not have done that on the beach in Porthcawl.'

'Oh!' said Bertie and took another bite out of his sandwich.

Soon it was changing into bathing costume time. The various contortions involved in this seaside ritual caused shrieks of embarrassment, mingled with giggles, from some of the girls as they struggled to protect their modesty.

However, it was Charles whose manoeuvres caused the greatest hilarity. He had decided to change into his costume, standing up, rather than sitting down. His short legs had enough to do to support his long body when they were both on the ground. Any attempt to imitate the stance of a stork was destined for trouble.

After staggering around with one foot trapped inside his trouser leg, he collapsed. Instead of releasing his foot as he sat on the sand, he tried to stand only to fall down again. This time he learned his lesson and extricated both feet from his trousers. Then he chose to stand again while he strove to pull his underpants down with one hand inside the towel which he was holding insecurely with his other hand. When the underpants had reached his knees he attempted to reach between his legs and pushed them down with one fell swoop. He overbalanced and fell head first, his towel flying and his modesty shattered.

It was at this stage that Eleanor and I moved in to rescue him. After a fortnight of practice at Newquay we had become proficient in the art and were already in our costumes. Eleanor held the towel while I removed his nether garment and put his feet into his bathing trunks.

'All you have to do now, Charles, is pull them up,' I said.

When he had made himself decent and dropped the towel, there was a burst of applause from his hysterical audience.

'Now that the Curate has put himself right, last one in the sea is a sissy,' proclaimed Idris.

Charles had no desire to be branded a sissy for a second time and scampered down to the sea as fast as his little legs could carry him. As soon as his toes came in contact with the cold edges of the Bristol channel he ground to a halt, shivering on the brink.

'Come on, Mr Baxter,' shouted the girls and they splashed him with liberal amounts of icy sea water.

'It takes me a long time to get under,' he said between shudders and then retreated to the safety of the beach.

'Let's get him. You take one side and I get the other,' Eleanor suggested.

We ran out of the sea and performed a pincers movement on the hapless Charles. He was frogmarched into the tide and unceremoniously dumped in a few feet of water. A small wave washed over him. He arose like Triton from the ocean, spitting out Porthcawl effluent and vowing the vengeance of the gods on the pair of us.

'I might have been drowned,' he wailed.

'Don't worry, I would have given you artificial respiration. You would have enjoyed that, Charles,' said Eleanor.

'Now that you're under, you'll be fine,' I told him. 'You won't want to come out I promise you.'

'I don't care what you promise me,' he snorted. 'I've had enough. I had rheumatic fever once when I was a child and I've never been able to stand cold water ever since. I'm off.' He ran out of the sea and made his way back.

'He means water of any kind,' I said to Eleanor.

As we were enjoying ourselves in the sea, Charles joined Mrs Collier who was looking after the bundles of clothing and waiting impatiently for her husband to come back from the hospital with Charlie Thomas and Harry Williams, the victim of the accident.

The sun continued to shine down upon our antics in the sea – ducking each other and attempting to play 'donkey' with a ball which Rosemary had brought with her. In the distance I could see that Charles had changed into his suit and was engaged in conversation with the organist's wife.

When next I looked up, I could see Harry with his arm in a sling accompanied by Charlie Thomas and Walter Collier who was being subjected to a tirade from his wife, judging by the finger wagging involved.

'I think I had better get up there and find out what has happened. It looks interesting. Coming?' My words to my wife had a negative response.

'You go, love, I'll stay here for another half hour or so and get as much sun and ozone as possible – see you later.'

The reason for the tirade became obvious as I approached the quintet. Walter Collier appeared to be somewhat the worse for wear. His eyes were glazed, his speech was slurred and he found it as difficult to stand as my colleague did earlier.

'It'sh not my fault, dear. It'sh Charlie. He can take it. I've, I've only had a few whishkeys.'

'I'm not going drinking with 'im again,' said Charlie. 'We went in the Queen's Arms opposite the Hospital for a stiffener while 'Arry was being seen to. A couple of snifters and 'e was gone.'

'That's the last time you go into the Queen's Arms or anybody's arms, Walter Collier. I'm ashamed of you and on a church outing as well.'

I thought I had better take the heat off Walter. 'Most important of all, how are you, Harry? Is it a bad break?'

'Could be worse, Mr Secombe. The doctor said it will take six weeks and I should be fine by then. Mind, what the wife will say when I go home is a different matter. Having me around the house all that time isn't going to make me very popular.'

'Shall I get you a deck chair dear?' asked Walter with exaggerated solicitude.

'Don't dear me. In any case you couldn't walk as far as the chairs without falling over.' His wife was in no mood to be pacified.

'It's all right, Mrs Collier,' said Charles. 'I'll go and get a couple of chairs. It's not very comfortable sitting on the sand.'

'Thank you very much,' she replied. 'He's not always like this by any means. He very rarely drinks.' As she said this, she glared at Charlie Thomas.

'I'll come with you and get a couple more chairs,' offered Charlie. ''Arry will need one anyway, apart from Walter.'

There were dark clouds building up at the other end of Swansea Bay, an ominous sign.

'I'm going to get dressed,' I said. 'It looks as if those chairs won't be needed for long and if that lot out there aren't careful they will be wetter inside their clothes than they are in the sea.'

As the clouds began to make their way from the west, the bathers realized what was happening and made a concerted rush up the beach. By the time the two Charlies appeared with their chairs, the first drops had made themselves felt. There was a hectic scramble to get dressed as modesty was forgotten and an escape to shelter became a top priority. Mumbles Head at the other side of the bay had disappeared under a grey pall of rain.

'Play is abandoned for the day,' said Idris, in a pathetic impression of John Arlott. 'Every man, woman and child to the lifeboats and row to the fairground.'

'I don't know why we bothered to get these chairs,' moaned Charlie Thomas. 'Money for nothing.'

'Better that than down your throat,' snapped Mrs Collier whose husband was beginning to sober up.

The next couple of hours were spent in the fairground while the rains descended, the floods came and the winds blew and beat upon that place, in the words of the parable in St Matthews's Gospel. Those who, like the wise virgins in another parable from the same Gospel, came prepared with mackintoshes and umbrellas were happy enough while the others stood under awnings and dashed from stall to stall, getting wetter with each foray.

At six o'clock the rain stopped.

'Let's go posh,' suggested Idris, 'and go to the Seabank until it's time to get on the bus.'

The Seabank was the luxury hotel of Porthcawl.

Bertie Owen, whose large nose was put out of joint by the milkman's assumption of command, complained immediately.

'Posh prices too,' he moaned.

'Come on, Bertie, you mean old thing,' said Eleanor. 'You can afford it; after all, it's only you and I who can afford to run a car.'

He was undecided as to whether he should feel insulted or complimented. His ego won the day.

'Of course I can,' he replied. 'I was only thinking of those who couldn't pay the prices.'

'Hands up.' shouted Idris. 'All those who want to come to the Seabank'.

Every hand went up, except Bertie's.

'Carried,' proclaimed the milkman.

Entry into the impressive portals of the hotel muted the exuberance of the young girls in the chorus, who surveyed their surroundings with awesome expressions.

'Lemonade for you,' said Mrs Collier to her husband.

A few minutes later, our contingent surrounded the bar manned by white jacketed barmen with their black bow ties. Voices were hushed as if in church. As time went on and alcohol loosened tongues the mood became more relaxed.

'Watch this!' said Charlie Thomas to a group of the girls. He puffed on his obnoxious pipe and sent a cloud of smoke towards the ceiling. 'The Queen Mary steaming up the channel'.

'I tell you what,' commented Idris, 'if it smelt like that, nobody would sail on it.'

Promptly at a quarter-past seven, we left the hotel and made our way to the car park where the bus was waiting with the driver standing outside, consulting his watch, to the intense annoyance of our organizer.

'The time, driver, is precisely seven twenty-six and what's more we are all here. There's something else. This is the last time we travel on one of your buses, boyo.'

Eleanor and I saw them off.

'Shall we go back to the Seabank for one more sherry?'

'There's only one answer to that,' I said.

At the hotel the barman said. 'They were a nice crowd. Who were they?'

'The Pontywen Church Gilbert and Sullivan Society,' I answered.

'That's a mouthful, isn't it?' he commented.

13

'I don't know about you but I feel like a Peeping Tom,' I said to Eleanor, as I opened a little attaché case which had been secreted under some blankets in the bottom drawer of a tallboy in Mrs Richards's bedroom. We had come to 13 Mount Pleasant View after evening service to survey the property I had been left.

'If she was prepared to leave everything to you, my love, then I am sure the old lady would have no objections to your check on the contents of the house,' she replied.

'Including her very personal correspondence as these seem to be?'

'Look, Fred, if you find the letters too embarrassing then put them back into the case and leave them there.'

They were tied with red ribbon into two bundles, all of them addressed to Miss May Williams, 5 Graig Terrace, Pontywen.

One bundle was composed of green envelopes with the printed heading 'On Active Service'.

'She never mentioned that Mr Richards had been in the First World War,' I remarked.

'Perhaps she found that the enforced parting had been something too painful to recollect. Probably that is why the correspondence is buried in the bottom drawer, out of sight, out of mind. Go on then, open that first envelope,' said my wife impatiently.

On the left hand side was printed a note: 'Correspondence

in this envelope need not be censored regimentally. The contents are liable to examination at the Base. The following certificate must be signed by the writer.

I certify on my honour that the contents of this envelope refer to nothing but private and family matters.'

It was signed in pencil 'William Richards.'

The date stamp on the envelope was 'Field Post Office 3.7.15.'

Inside was a letter written in pencil on yellowing lined sheets headed:

E Coy, 6th Battalion East Lancs, British Expeditionary Force, France, Wednesday.

My Darling May, Thanks very much for your always welcome letter which I received last night. Your letters out here are better than lumps of gold. By gum we will have a good time after this, sweetheart. So buck up and keep smiling for I am all right, love.

Well, old dear, I will give you some idea of our doings. We landed in France about four a.m. on a Sunday morning and had to march three miles away to a rest camp where we stayed until six p.m. in the evening and then marched about four miles to the railway station. We had a great reception on the way being showered with flowers etc. We were put in covered goods vans and travelled until one a.m. in the morning and marched about five miles where we were put up in farms. Ever since then we have been marching on and off behind the firing line all the time. Our big guns are banging away close by us, love, so you can guess the row that is going on but you get used to it and can sleep as easy as if in bed. Part of our company are going in the trenches tonight but it is like being in a house, darling. So don't you worry about anything.

At this stage I stopped reading and put the letter back into the envelope.

'Carry on, spoilsport,' said Eleanor.

'I'm sorry but it is too personal, too sad, and too painful. This desire to reassure his loved one that all was well. Going into the trenches was like being in a house . . . I ask you! As far as I am concerned, these letters are going to keep their secrets as long as they are in my possession. They must have loved each other very much. No wonder she wore her widow's weeds permanently. It was a great tribute to us that she came out of them for our wedding.'

'Not to us, to you, love. God, how they must have wanted a child when he came back from the forces. You arrived on the scene very late in her life, the son she never had. That is why we are here now.'

'And that is why we must move into this house as soon as possible. She would want us to do that. Perhaps we could be living here in a few weeks' time.'

'Hold your horses, Frederick. That cannot happen overnight. For example, I spent many hours making the curtains for Bevan's Row. I much prefer my curtains to Mrs Richards's heavy floral-patterned ones. We have to see if they fit. We have to sort out things from the furniture angle. We shall have to check on the electrical system to see if the wiring needs to be renewed. I must bring my nice new gas stove here. The list is endless. We have all the time in the world to make a move. So don't rush things, there's a dear.'

'But we are going to come here to live?'

'Of course, but in the fullness of time, to borrow one of your phrases.'

Next morning after matins, the vicar asked me if we had made up our minds about 13 Mount Pleasant View.

'We have decided to move there not in the immediate future but once we have got everything shipshape.'

'Very wise. You must also think of your long-term future as a house owner. Perhaps you might consider selling it to the Church when you leave. As you know, a curate's house is a priceless asset to any parish.'

'There's plenty of time to think about that, Vicar. Still, it sounds a good idea and one of which Mrs Richards would approve.'

'To more immediate matters,' said Father Whittaker. 'This garden fête. I take it that you Fred and you Wentworth-Baxter have been sounding out various members of your congregation about stalls etc.'

'There's plenty of interest, Vicar but what is needed now is a meeting to coordinate everything,' I replied.

'That is exactly what I was going to suggest. Next Monday evening at the Vicarage a meeting of the PCC of Pontywen plus that of Llanhyfryd. In the meantime it would be helpful if you two could think up some ideas which we can put to the meeting.'

'We used to have a garden fête at my father's Vicarage.' Charles had come to life. 'A very popular feature was the fortune-telling tent. Miss Popplewell used to dress up in gipsy costume with a veil over her face, call herself Madame Zelda and read the cards. They say in Llanhyfryd that Mrs Mortlock who owns the slaughter house is a witch. Apparently she had a quarrel with Thomas the Village Stores. She told him that before the day was out he would be struck down. Sure enough by half-past six that evening he collapsed with a heart attack. What about asking her to have a tent? After all, she is a real fortune-teller not a fake like Miss Popplewell.'

The Vicar looked at him with open-mouthed incredulity.

'Charles,' I said. 'Mrs Mortlock has had three husbands all of whom died suddenly and left her a widow. They say she has a room full of dolls ready for pin sticking. To invite her to operate at a church fête would be the equivalent of asking Count Dracula to a blood donor session.'

'It was just an idea,' he murmured, looking peeved that this suggestion had not met with approval.

'Wentworth-Baxter, if that is the best idea you can offer, you had better keep silent for the rest of this discussion,' growled the Vicar.

Charles slumped into his armchair and attempted to

imitate Christopher Robin who curled up small so that nobody knew he was there at all.

'With so many babies about why not a baby show? I am sure Eleanor would willingly be one of the judges.'

'Good idea, Fred. It would certainly attract a lot of young families.'

By the time the Vicar and I pooled our ideas we had a long list to put before the meeting.

'One other thing,' said Father Whittaker. 'We had better approach all the tradesmen in Pontywen to see if they will contribute items or money for the various stalls and competitions. I think it is best if you would do that Fred (my heart sank). These next weeks are going to be very busy for me preparing for my move. Wentworth-Baxter, you are in touch with the Group Scoutmaster. See if we can borrow some tents for the occasion.'

'In touch with the Group Scoutmaster!' moaned Charles as we walked up the Vicarage drive. 'I've only met him once when I was ordered to find out how to run a pack of wolf cubs.'

'You have the easy job, as usual. What about me calling on all the tradesmen in Pontywen for donations!! I did not think when I put on a clerical collar that I would be given the job of commercial traveller like my father. I am beginning to wish that I had never heard of this Church fête.'

When I arrived back at Bevan's Row that wish was intensified when I told Eleanor that I had suggested she might willingly be one of the judges in the baby show.

'Thank you very much indeed,' she said. 'Have you ever been to a baby show? I shall be like Daniel in the lionesses' den. Each mother is convinced that her baby is the most beautiful specimen ever produced. I shall be lucky to escape alive after the judging.'

'And to think that the Missionaries in Central Africa imagine that theirs is a dangerous occupation,' I replied.

'That's enough sarcasm for today, Frederick.'

'I am not being sarcastic. My lord and master has commanded me to call on all the tradesmen in Pontywen, begging for donations either in kind or money. If my father's experiences with the retail trade are anything to go by, I would rather be in your lionesses' den. At least it is just an hour or so's ordeal and it's over. I shall face any number of dragons all this week in single combat sessions and any self-respecting bookie would lay short odds on them winning the encounter.'

'There is one slight difference between our situations. Your dragon fights are part of your job. I am under no obligation to cope with thirty or forty angry mothers. I know that in prewar days the parson's wife was expected to be a parsoness. Times have changed, Fred. Please don't take me for granted. I will be a judge at this baby show but not willingly. Next time it would be more gracious if you consulted me first before volunteering my services.'

'My apologies, love. Point taken. Rest assured it will not happen again.'

'You dare,' she said and kissed me.

After lunch I decided to face the first of my dragons, Lewis the Grocer whose shop was just a stone's thrown from 11 Bevan's Row. He was a short, thin, elderly man with a grey moustache, waxed at the ends. His premises were a survival from the twenties. Sawdust covered the floor and Peek Frean biscuit tins formed a wide colonade to the counter. I assumed they were empty. Rationing had put an end to a surfeit of biscuits long ago.

'Ah, Reverend Secombe.' He shook my hand. 'How nice to see you. The last time you came here, if you remember, was to call for an ambulance for Miss Bradshaw. I don't expect you ever thought that you would be living in that hovel with your lady wife.'

'It's no longer a hovel, Mr Lewis.'

'I'm sure not, with professional people like yourselves. Now what can I get for you?'

'More to the point, Mr Lewis. What can I get from you?'

'What do you mean, Reverend?'

His eyes narrowed and the lines on his forehead deepened. Suddenly I was aware that his neatly parted grey hair was a wig, a discovery which triggered an irrational urge to break into laughter. I controlled myself.

'The Vicar has asked me to call on you to see if you would be willing to contribute something to the church fête we are having in a few weeks' time to raise money for the overseas missionary work of the church.'

'Overseas!' he exclaimed. 'I would have thought that after five years of sacrifice to save the world from the Nazis, we need all the money we can get to rebuild our own country.'

At this stage in the conversation, a little lady whose sparse ginger hair was in curlers, irrupted into the shop, obviously in distress.

'Mr Lewis, you 'aven't seen our ape by any chance?'

'I saw her outside a few minutes ago. She can't be far away. I wouldn't worry if I were you.' She left looking more assured.

He looked at the astonishment on my face.

'It's all right, Reverend. When she said "ape" she meant April, her daughter – a pretty little child, not at all like an ape.'

'So you are not prepared to give anything to our fête, Mr Lewis.'

'I'm afraid not. Charity begins at home, as it says in the Bible.'

'The Bible says nothing of the sort. You are quoting the Bible of the selfish. In fact the scriptures say the opposite. They tell you that the whole world is your neighbour whom you have to love. If there is someone badly in need of help in Central Africa he is just as much in need of your help as that lady who came in then and asked if you had seen her ape.'

His tight-lipped mouth began to curl up at the ends. There was a glimmer of a twinkle in his eye.

'You are very persuasive, Reverend. It must be your theatrical ability. I saw your *Pirates of Penzance*. Very good it was. I am something of a Thespian myself – not in the field of light opera but in straight drama. I once played Sweeney Todd in the Welfare Hall, 1936, it was. They say it was one of the best productions ever in that theatre. Plenty of scope for acting in that part. That's what I like – full-blooded melodrama.'

'I must say, Mr Lewis, you couldn't have found a more full-blooded part than Sweeney Todd. You must have been knee deep in it.'

He began to laugh uproariously. It was a strange laugh, like the bray of a donkey. The top set of his dentures began to slip and his wig went slightly askew.

'Very funny, Reverend Secombe,' he said after his guffaws had ceased. 'I can see you have a keen sense of humour, a man after my own heart. Now if I had grass skirts to sell, I would have given you some for your Africans. As it is, would a tin of biscuits do all right? I have had them some time but the tin is sealed and airtight. So they should be fine.'

'That is most kind, Mr Lewis. Perhaps I could pick up the tin the day before the fête.'

'By all means. They won't run away. They are like me, a fixture. Do you know I haven't had a day's holiday since before the war? Ever since my wife died in 1938, I haven't had any inclination to go. Mind you, I'm thinking of retiring before long. All this coupon business. I'm seventy-two now and I'm getting too old to have all the bother. Perhaps I'll go away for a real holiday then. I fancy a cruise in the Mediterranean and might just be able to afford it. I might even pick up a rich widow in the process.'

He began to bray again.

'You never know your luck, Mr Lewis,' I said. 'Well, I had better be on my way to the next shop. Thank you very much for your generosity.'

'Call in any time for a chat or even for a purchase. You'll always be welcome.' He saw me to the door and stood twirling the ends of his moustache as I made my way down the steps of his shop and off to the town square.

Next stop, I thought, should be Moelwyn and Myfanwy Howells's greengrocer shop. Since they harboured my colleague, I felt sure that they would be sympathetic at least to a plea for a donation to the fête. I was correct in my assumption.

'Certainly,' said the greengrocer. 'We'll make a donation of three pounds.'

'That is extremely generous, Moelwyn,' I replied.

'I tell you what, I would give a lot more if we could get Charles off our hands.'

'What do you mean?'

'As you know, we only took him on as a favour to you in the first place, and we did all we could to make him feel at home. Myfanwy mothered him, still does, but he's impossible. He leaves his bedroom in a mess and he treats our living room as if it's a pig sty. I've never known anyone take other people for granted as much as he does. I'm telling you all this because Myfanwy is not here. She would put up with it for ever. I won't. It's not fair to her and unless he changes his ways, I'll ask him to find accommodation somewhere else.'

'Do you think it would be any use if I had a word with him?'

'Well, it wouldn't do any harm that's for sure.'

'OK, I'll do that. Don't say anything to the Vicar.'

'Don't worry. I'd see you before I did anything.'

'Thanks, Moelwyn.'

I went next door, to Davies the Newsagent. Emrys Davies was a tall, well built man who had an artificial leg. Mrs Richards, a mine of information about local people, had told me that he used to be a fine rugby player until he was involved in an accident with a colliery engine. Apparently he slipped while trying to cross the line at a siding and fell in the path of the engine.

'Thought you've had your paper, Mr Secombe,' he said.

'I have, Emrys. I'm here on a different errand. The Vicar is organizing a church fête to raise money for the missionary work of the church. He wants to know if you would make a donation and give something to raffle, perhaps.'

'Well, I'll give something but I would give more if it was for something nearer home like Dr Barnado's or the Salvation Army. Anyway I'll go and sort out what I can find in the stock room. Would you care to come behind? I'll get the missis to make a cup of tea, if you would like one.'

'Thank you. I should love a cup of tea.'

He led me into the middle room behind the shop and called out to his wife as we came.

'A visitor, Bronwen.'

Bronwen Davies bustled into the room, wiping her hands on her apron. A lock of grey hair straggled over her forehead. She was a little bright-eyed pixie, with a ready smile.

'Nice to see you, Mr Secombe. Sit down by there and I'll get you a cup of tea. Milk and sugar?'

'Very little milk and two spoonfuls of sugar, thank you.'

'Like me, you are then.' She flitted out into the kitchen.

'Excuse me while I see what I can find,' said Emrys and hobbled his way down the passage.

On the mantelpiece was a colour photograph of him as a schoolboy, proudly wearing a Welsh jersey and his red cap.

A few minutes later he was back with a blonde doll in a party dress.

'You can have this for the raffle – part of our stock from last Christmas. I'll get a box for it while you're having your cup of tea.'

'Thank you very much. I didn't know you were a schoolboy international Emrys.'

'Played second row for Pontywen Grammar and then for Pontywen. I was going to have a trial for Cardiff when I had my accident. Never bothered about rugby since. I'm a player, not a watcher.'

Bronwen came into the room on the end of the conversation.

'I wish he would be a watcher, Mr Secombe. He never goes anywhere. It would be a nice break on a Saturday afternoon. There's not much doing in the shop then.'

Emrys exploded.

'I've told you, woman. I never want to see a rugby ball again. Never. Sorry, Mr Secombe, but the very mention of rugby rubs me up the wrong way. I'll get that box.'

It was evident that when the engine wheel ran over his leg the iron entered into his soul.

When he had gone his wife said. 'I often wish we had two boys instead of two girls, much as I love them. He could have relived his rugby through them.'

'Perhaps when they start courting they will find rugby players as their boy friends and the same process could begin,' I suggested.

'I hope so,' she replied without an atom of conviction. 'Try some of these Garibaldi biscuits. They're lovely.'

As I was coming out from the newsagent's shop, I met Charles who was on his way back to his digs.'

'The very man I want to see.' I caught hold of his arm and steered him in the opposite direction.

'What's going on?' He looked at me with a mixture of suspicion and apprehension.

'Would you care for a cup of tea at my humble abode?'

'It's not just a cup of tea, is it?'

'To be truthful, no, but come all the same.'

'What's it all about?'

'I'll tell you over the cup of tea.'

We walked in silence to 11 Bevan's Row where I ushered him into the front room and into one of the leather armchairs. I gave him my copy of *The Times* to read.

Five minutes later when I brought in the tea and biscuits, he was staring at the window, with the newspaper unread on the table at his side.

'What have I done now, Fred?' He presented a picture of injured innocence.

'While you drink your cup of tea, I'll tell you what you have done. I have been on my rounds this afternoon, getting promises from shopkeepers for donations to the fête. One of the shops was your landlord's. I can assure you, Charles, that Moelwyn is absolutely livid about your lifestyle in their house. According to him, your bedroom is a permanent mess and you give their living room the same treatment. Myfanwy has enough to do helping in the shop and looking after a lodger at the same time, without clearing up for ever after a lazy, ungracious person.'

'Come off it! I'm not as bad as that, Fred.'

'I'm afraid, you must be. What's more unless you mend your ways, Moelwyn is determined to have you out of his place. In a way I feel responsible for all this. If I hadn't persuaded the Howellses to take you on, you would have been out of Pontywen long ago and in limbo, as far as I can see. You have a marvellous landlady in Myfanwy. Can't you appreciate that? I tell you what. If they do evict you, you really will be in limbo and it will be goodbye Pontywen. Possibly, goodbye to your prospects in the Church. To put it crudely, if Father Whittaker is still here and you get notice from Moelwyn, he will have your guts for garters. It will be curtains for you.'

There was another period of silence.

It was broken by the sound of Eleanor's car pulling up outside the front door.

'Saved by the bell,' I said. 'I could have launched into a list of all your narrow escapes from expulsion in the short time you have been here. For God's sake, Charles, grow up and behave like a responsible adult.'

He rose to his feet, looking like a chastened schoolboy.

'OK, Fred. I know that you have got me off the hook on a number of occasions. I promise you I shall do my utmost to keep my room tidy and check my bad habits generally. I didn't realize how much I have got up Moelwyn's nose.'

I saw him to the door as Eleanor was about to open it.

'It's up to you, remember,' I said.

'What's up to him?' asked my wife when he had gone.

'The usual story. He has been blotting his copy book again, this time by his pigsty habits in his digs. Moelwyn told me this afternoon that unless he changes his ways, he will be shown the door.'

'Oh! dear,' she replied. 'If he's not a good boy, it's ta-ta, is it? Now let me give you a piece of good news. I was talking to Nurse Thomas the Midwife this afternoon. She has been responsible for bringing half of Pontywen into the world, including me. I mentioned the baby show and she said she would be only too pleased to be a judge. None of the mothers will dare to criticize her choice. So I have been saved from a fate worse than death.'

'Let's hope the same thing happens to Charles,' I murmured.

'Nurse Thomas will be no use to him, love. It's only Charles who can save Charles, plus the grace of God, of course.'

'In that case, the grace of God will have to be working overtime when the new man arrives.'

14

'Fine before seven, rain by eleven,' said my wife as she pulled aside the bedroom curtains. It was the morning of the fête. The sunlight streamed through the window.

I sat up in bed. 'You should have been christened Cassandra not Eleanor. I would prefer that other chestnut, "The sun always shines on the righteous".'

'In that case, Frederick, we are due for a heavy downpour.'

She beat a hasty retreat as I chased her to the bedroom door.

'Any violence on your part,' she shouted from the foot of the stairs, 'and you will not have your cup of tea.'

So far all had gone well with the preparations for Father Whittaker's missionary swan song. The three churches had cooperated without a sign of acrimony and the various stalls had been allocated at the Parochial Church Council. As it was the first big church social function since before the war, much effort had gone into obtaining donations and making contributions for the fête.

Minty the Coal's lorry had delivered the contents which Charles had managed to borrow from the Group Scoutmaster in a desperate desire to please his superior. Since my warning shot across his bows my colleague had become a temporary paragon of virtue, both in his digs and his ministry. This morning the lorry was to be decorated to provide a suitable setting for the Carnival Queen of Pontywen and her attendants to grace the proceedings.

Hours of feverish activity lay ahead. The tents had to be erected, the stalls set up. Chairs had to be collected from the Church hall to seat the Pontywen Silver Band who were to play throughout the afternoon. Bertie Owen had promised to supply the public address system. Charles had to accompany the Vicar in his car to pick up the drum to contain the raffle tickets for the big prize draw. Eleanor and I had to deliver the prizes I had managed to extort from the tradesmen in the town.

The vicar had arranged for matins to be held at eight a.m. instead of nine a.m. 'It's vital that we begin the day with prayer,' he said. 'As we are told, all our doings without thy favour are nothing worth.' Evidently this saying had so implanted itself in the mind of my colleague that he had gone already to service by the time I called for him. 'I can't get over the change in him,' said Myfanwy Howells when she opened the door to me.

'Long may it continue,' I replied.

Charles was sitting in his stall, looking like a Cheshire cat, when I joined him. 'Sorry I wasn't there when you called. I thought I'd give you a big surprise,' he whispered.

'"Big" is too small a word to use. "Gigantic" would be better.'

'Keep your voice down, Fred, here comes the Vicar.'

Father Whittaker entered from the vestry, the tips of his fingers meeting together to form a spiritual triangle with his thumbs. He wore the fixed smile on his countenance that indicated he was about to be in communication with the Almighty.

We had a spate of prayers for the missionary work of the Church and he ended with a home-made intercession for God's blessing on 'our endeavours in Pontywen to further the work of Thy Kingdom this afternoon and evening'.

As we left the vestry after service he said, 'Let's have an all out effort from you both. I'm sure I'll have it from you, Fred, and it looks as if I might have it from you, Charles, too.'

'Did you hear that?' exclaimed my colleague when we came down the church path. 'He called me Charles for the first time. I can't believe it.'

'Make the most of it,' I replied. 'One swallow doesn't make a summer.'

When Eleanor and I had finished our breakfast, we went first to the church hall, a small building at the bottom of the road from St Mary's. There we unloaded the scales, and various health posters for the Baby Show. It had been decided that the Vicarage lawn was no suitable place for such an event.

As we came through the Vicarage, it seemed as if the whole population of Pontywen was involved in preparing for the fête. Half a dozen cars were parked around the Vicarage, with the coal lorry at the side of the house swarming with decorators, armed with crêpe paper and bunting.

On the lawn, trestle tables were being set up and scouts were erecting the two tents in an orgy of self-importance, under the direction of a scoutmaster whose knees would have won him first prize in a holiday camp competition. In the middle of the chaos was Bertie Owen attempting to carry a standard microphone, trailing a lead over which several people tripped as he made his way to the centre of the lawn.

There was just enough room for Eleanor's Morris Minor to squeeze into a corner.

'Any car from now will have to park outside,' she said.

'The Vicar will be pleased,' I replied 'Here he comes now, looking like grim death.'

Seated in the back of the car and holding on to a large ticket drum was Charles whose Cheshire Cat smirk had given way to one of his injured innocent's looks.

'There's been trouble,' I murmured to my wife.

As the shiny, clean Morris Oxford pulled up halfway down the drive, the Vicar flung open the front door and then the back door.

'Out you get Wentworth-Baxter,' he commanded.

'I'm afraid you'll have to help me, Vicar. We'll have to get this thing out together.'

Father Whittaker snorted.

'Just hold on to the stand at your end and I'll hold the drum. Stand up then! Don't sit down!'

'There's no room to stand, Vicar.'

'Make room!'

My colleague stood up sharply and banged his head against the roof of the car.

'Now you're on your feet, bend down and lift the stand your end. Right, now tip it forward and I'll manoeuvre the drum out of the car.'

Charles pushed rather than tipped. The drum catapulted and bowled over the Vicar who lay on his back in the middle of the drive with the contrivance on top of him.

Eleanor and I ran to remove it. We helped him to his feet and dusted him down.

'What a start to the day!' he stormed. 'That idiot was supposed to help me reverse the car out of the Welfare Hall car park and only succeeded in jamming the back between a boulder and the concrete gate post.'

He pointed to a buckled wing and a badly dented boot.

'Sorry, Vicar,' said my colleague as he emerged from the car.

'So am I,' said his superior. 'I'm very sorry I inherited you from my predecessor but I'm very glad I'm leaving you behind. The next unfortunate incumbent will be equally sorry when he finds out what he has taken on. Go and make yourself useful, if that is possible.'

Charles sloped off to one of the Llanhyfryd stalls where the helpers were laying out home-made cakes, jams and pickles. It was obvious from his reception that they felt they could do without his help. Instead he turned his attention to the second-hand bookstall which Ivor the Milk was setting up, as part of the St Padarn contribution. He picked up a book and began to read it.

'He's there for the day,' I said to Eleanor. 'My grandfather used to do that.'

'Do what?'

'When he retired from his work as a tally man on the docks he would go down to the second-hand book stall in the Swansea market and begin to read through a book which took his fancy. After spending the morning there, he would leave a piece of paper to mark where his quota for the day had ended and then come back next morning to resume his reading. The man who ran the stall used to present him with the book when he arrived. They became great friends.'

'I don't think Charles will become great friends with Ivor if he stops there for the rest of the day,' she said. 'I'd better be off to the church hall and organize things there.'

By now Bertie Owen had set up the microphone stand and had recited nursery rhymes of an expurgated kind suitable for a church fête to make sure that the apparatus was in working order. I joined him as he made his way to the bottle stall which was another of St Padarn's efforts.

'The secret of this stall,' he told me, 'is to have a bottle of whisky as your big attraction but you don't put its equivalent ticket number into the box until you have raised a fair amount of money.'

Each bottle on the stall had a cloakroom ticket pasted on it and for threepence a time participants would be invited to dip their hand into a box containing a jumble of tickets. If the colour and number tallied with that on the bottle, then it was theirs. Bottles of sauce, mineral water, shampoo, etc., surrounded the centrepiece, whisky supplied by the landlord of the White Hart.

'That's immoral, Bertie,' I said. 'People will be spending money on getting the whisky when the tickets they are drawing are worthless.'

'It's not immoral, it's for the missionaries,' he replied. I've got the big ticket here in my pocket and it's going to stay there for quite a while.'

'In that case, I hope you don't get lynched if they find out what you have done.'

As we were talking a battered old Rover came down the drive towing a trailer in which was a fat piglet. 'Bowling for a pig' was to be one of the big money spinners for the afternoon. The car was driven by Evan Meredith, a rosy-cheeked chirpy sparrow of a man who owned a piggery in Llanhyfryd. In view of the strict meat rationing, the prize of a pig, however small, was bound to be a main attraction. The skittles and balls were unloaded from the car. The trailer was uncoupled and towed by two hefty farmers to a place under the beech tree at the side of the lawn where the animal could enjoy the shade and, more importantly, where the smell would be less obtrusive.

As the morning merged into the afternoon, the temperature rose well into the seventies, bringing with it a corresponding rise in temper among some of the gathering over the use of a tent. One tent housed an exhibition of the work of the Missionary Society with photographs of African kraals as well as a display of knobkerries, shields, masks and other paraphernalia. The other contained some crates of beer and was intended as a refuge for the male helpers and the band.

The ladies of the Llanhyfryd home-produce stall, led by Blodwen Bowen, a farmers's wife of Amazonian proportions, insisted that unless they could remove their wares out of the intense heat of the sun into the shelter of the refuge tent they would pack up and go back to their homestead. They were confronted by the male contingent led by Charlie Thomas – of the prodigious thirst – who threatened to go on strike if they lost their oasis.

Even Solomon in all his glory would have been hard pressed to bring his judgement to bear on this contention and Father Whittaker was no Solomon. When faced by the two protagonists he told them to settle it among themselves. Blodwen and Charlie strode off to their waiting supporters with the news of the Vicar's non judgement. A heated argument ensued. Blodwen looked so enraged that it would not have surprised anyone if she had planted one of her custard tarts in the middle of Charlie's face.

It was at that moment that an unexpected dove of peace arrived in the form of Charles Wentworth-Baxter. 'There's another tent behind the garage,' he said. 'Mr Willoughby, the group scoutmaster, sent three by mistake when the Vicar had only asked for two. The only trouble is the scouts have gone.'

'We don't need the scouts to put the tent up.' Bertie Owen had come from the loudspeaker van, eager to be involved in the dispute as usual. 'I've put up hundreds when I was a scout, I'll supervise its erection.'

'No, you don't, Bertie,' said Charlie. 'You get back to your van. We'll put this one up ourselves, thank you. All right, ladies, you can move into our tent.' He made a grotesque attempt at a bow. Blodwen sniffed and ordered her helpers to hurry before the sun did any more damage to their wares.

In no time at all the third tent was erected and the erectors were celebrating with the help of the crates of local brew. Peace returned to the lawn.

The fete was due to be opened at two-thirty p.m. by Sir David Jones-Williams Bart, squire of the neighbourhood. At two twenty-five p.m., his antiquated Bentley (late twenties vintage) squeezed its way through the Vicarage gates causing considerable peril to the populace of Pontywen who were making their way into the grounds. It pulled up, halfway down the drive and stayed there effectively blocking any further traffic movement. Sir David considered that all roads, lanes and drives in his bailiwick were subject to his priority.

'Sorry my wife can't come,' he said to the Vicar who had hurried to greet him. 'Touch of the sun, after gardening this morning. Now where do I go for this opening.'

'The microphone is just there, Sir David.'

'Oh, one of those blasted things. Can't stand them. Can't I just shout a few words and get the jamboree started?'

'Well, if you like, Sir David, but if you don't mind we shall have to go to the microphone so that I can introduce you. I trust Lady Jones-Williams will soon recover.'

'Probably be as right as rain as soon as I get back. Her own fault. She should have worn a sun bonnet.'

As they reached the focal point, Bertie Owen arrived on the scene and did a final check by tapping on the microphone.

'There you are Sir David, it's alive and in good shape.'

'So am I and that means I don't need the bloody thing.' Father Whittaker moved swiftly to take possession of the microphone.

'How encouraging to see so many present here on such a beautiful afternoon to support this very worthy cause.'

In his anxiety to shield the ears of his listeners from Sir David's language he spoke with his face so close to the microphone that it looked as if he were about to eat it and caused the apparatus to whistle.

'And now I call upon Sir David Jones-Williams whose name is a household word in Pontywen and who therefore needs no more introduction, to open our fête.'

The Vicar moved the standard away from the vicinity of the Squire and began to clap. Few of the crowd felt moved to follow his example.

Undaunted, Sir David began to bellow his few words.

'Well, here you are. Do what you can to help these missionaries in their work with the natives. I declare this fête open.'

There were even fewer claps.

Once again the Vicar took possession of the microphone.

'Thank you, Sir David. You heard what Sir David said. Do all you can to help our missionaries. The band will be playing in a few moments. Our thanks are due to them and their bandmaster Llewellyn Hopkins. So carry on and enjoy yourselves.'

Sir David spent five minutes on a quick tour of the lawn, presented the Vicar with a cheque for ten pounds and proceeded to reverse his Bentley erratically back up the drive as incomers scattered in panic. After narrowly missing the left-hand gatepost, he headed the car in the direction of his mountain fortress and disappeared in a cloud of exhaust.

The Pontywen Silver Band in their navy blue uniforms, white shirts and black bow ties were seated in front of the Vicarage drawing-room window. Already they were sweating as the sun beat down upon them.

As Llew Hopkins raised his baton to lead his players in a performance of 'Colonel Bogey', Tommy Harris and a few of his friends from Sunday school appeared on the scene sucking oranges.

After twenty bars or so of the martial music, one by one the players opted out, glaring at the schoolboys.

'Stop,' shouted the bandmaster. 'Now, then, you kids move away from here, sucking those oranges. They can't play if you do that. Go somewhere else.'

Tommy was grinning from ear to ear. 'There you are, what did I tell you? My dad said he used to do that when he was a boy. It'll stop them sucking and blowing on those trumpet things every time. You three owe me threepence each for the bet. I paid for the oranges from Howellses anyway.'

'That only leaves me ninepence to spend,' complained Billy Evans.

'A bet's a bet,' replied Tommy and collected his money.

My main task was organizing the selling of raffle tickets for the prize draw. I had recruited some of the girls from the Gilbert & Sullivan chorus to help me. They were very persuasive, especially with the menfolk among the large crowd thronging the lawn.

When the Vicar came to inquire how the tickets were going, I was able to tell him that six books of cloakroom tickets had already been used up.

'Excellent!' he said. 'My one worry at the moment is to avoid those farmers' wives from Llanhyfryd. I am sorry now that I allowed myself to be drawn into 'Guessing the weight of the Vicar'. They keep coming up to me prodding and pinching, viewing me from the front, the side and the back as if I were an exhibit in a cattle show. Speaking of that, I understand that there are a large number of entries in the baby show.'

'In that case, I expect Eleanor will be doing more than her share in prodding and viewing. I know one thing, she is only too pleased to have Nurse Thomas with her for protection when the results of the judging are announced.'

'I'm afraid my knowledge of babies is confined to christenings and that is not always of the happiest kind. I have had to fight with quite a few.'

'It is easier to fight with babies than irate mothers, Vicar.'

As I spoke there was a distant clap of thunder. Creeping into the blue sky from the east was a menacing blue black accumulation of cloud. The afternoon was hot, sticky and airless.

'Let's hope that storm passes us by,' said Father Whittaker prayerfully.

On the bottle stall which was heavily patronized, the number of bottles had diminished rapidly and the bottle of whisky was beginning to look lonely. What was more, the buyers of tickets were beginning to look sceptical.

I went to the microphone where Bertie Owen was acting as MC and who had just announced that the Carnival Queen and her attendants were on their way.

'Bertie, you are going to be torn apart limb from limb if you don't put that ticket into the draw,' I warned him.

'It's OK Mr Secombe, I'm on my way.'

He fished into his pocket for the missing ticket. His face paled even in the heat of the sun. Deeper into his pocket dived his hand, to no avail. He stared at me, wide eyed and speechless.

'Where did you get the tickets?' I asked, as calmly as I could.

'The newsagents in the square.'

'You had better get down there as quickly as you can and hope that they have another book of green tickets.'

Before I could finish speaking he trotted through the gates watched by bewildered spectators.

By now there was a long queue of miners, steelworkers,

farmers and farmers' hands, waiting to bowl for the pig. A skittle score was being kept meticulously by Evan Meredith. Already there had been two complete clearances of the pins.

In the meanwhile the inky clouds encroached further and a clap of thunder echoed around the valley. The band finished off the first half of their repertoire with a selection of music from 'The Arcadians', including Dooley the jockey's song, which contains the saying, 'Every cloud has a silver lining'. There was no silver in that black bank of trouble threatening us.

The Vicar became agitated. 'What are we going to do if there's a downpour?'

'It might be a good idea if we announced that teas and refreshments are being served in the church hall. That will get rid of some of the crowd.'

'Good idea, Fred. Ask Bertie to announce that.'

'I'm afraid he's gone to get some cloakroom tickets but don't worry I'll take charge until he comes back.'

The Vicar looked puzzled. 'It's not like him to leave the microphone.'

'There is a very valid and urgent reason I'm afraid. I'll tell you later.'

I went to the microphone and announced that the ladies in the Church Hall were eager and waiting to serve their excellent refreshments.

Some of the crowd began moving towards the gates but there were still numbers of people moving around the lawn. The band had disappeared into their refreshment tent as a third clap of thunder shook the ground underneath our feet. A fork of lightning stabbed its way into the valley.

The next minute the heavens opened and emptied themselves copiously upon the earth beneath. The hapless crowd fought for cover in the three tents which had a capacity to shelter twenty people at most. Some made for the Vicar's garage. In the meanwhile Father Whittaker ran to his Vicarage and opened the front door to allow others to escape the elements. I joined them in the drawing room, all of us

189

uncomfortably wet. Through the window I could see the Carnival Queen and her attendants perched on the back of Minty's lorry about to enter the drive – as they drew near we could see that they were drenched to the skin with the sodden bunting dripping dye on their faces.

Then through the gate came the lone figure of Bertie Owen accompanied by a flash of lightning, staggering along, like the last exhausted survivor of a marathon race about to collapse at the tape. I went to the door to open it for him while the Vicar had gone to the back door to receive the Carnival Queen and her Court.

'I've got it, thank God,' he breathed as he stumbled into the hall.

'That's not the only thing you'll have, Bertie. You might have pneumonia as well, the state you're in. I'll ask the Vicar if you can go up to the bathroom and dry yourself.'

As I spoke Mrs Lilywhite, the Vicar's housekeeper, emerged from the kitchen, leading the five girls upstairs. Streaks of blue and red dye decorated their faces, their hair straggled in untidy strands, plastered to their skin by the rain, while their dresses clung to their bodies in an immodest embrace. It was small wonder that the Vicar wished to remove them from the sight of their indoor audience.

'I'm afraid you'll have to wait, Bertie,' I said.

'Certainly,' he replied. 'I can see their need is greater than mine.'

It was half an hour before the storm moved away to plague fêtes and cricket matches in other valleys. As the sun blazed down once again, the Vicarage disgorged its sheltered fugitives on to the lawn where the heat began to dry their clothes in a faint aura of steam. The bulging tents bulged no longer and the occupants of the Vicar's garage spread the smell of petrol wherever they went.

After drying himself in the bathroom, Bertie Owen donned his wet clothes and hurried to the bottle stall to place No. 71 green ticket into the box of unsold tickets,

more concerned with saving his neck than with the discomfort he felt. Meanwhile the Carnival Queen and her attendants were incarcerated in Mrs Lilywhite's bedroom while their dresses were drying by the range in the kitchen.

The rest of the day went without incident: Charles kept out of harm's way 'helping' Idris the Milk with the secondhand bookstall where the Zane Grey Westerns had become a pulpy mess but the hardbacks had been rescued and stored in the missionary tent where the two had sheltered from the rain. Long after the prize draw had been made and the stalls dismantled, the battle for the piglet continued until it was won by Ianto Lewis, Penylan Farm, much to the disgust of the miners and the steelworkers. 'Why does he need a pig?' they said – or words to that effect.

As far as the Vicar was concerned, he was quite happy that the fête had raised ninety-eight pounds, eleven shillings and ninepence for the missionary society. 'I'll put in the rest to make it a cheque for a hundred pounds,' he said. 'That's the highest donation they will ever have from this parish.'

When I went to meet Eleanor in the church hall, she was sitting exhausted in the kitchen drinking a cup of tea in splendid isolation. 'I don't think I ever want to go through that again,' she complained. 'It was bedlam and mayhem to the 'nth degree. Nurse Thomas has gone home in high dudgeon. Not only did we have a crowd of proud parents and their offspring, each convinced their child was the best on display, but we had that influx of wet spectators fleeing from the rain. It has been pandemonium. Mother, is it worth it?'

'The Vicar thinks so. Apparently the fête has raised a hundred pounds.'

'At the high price of blood, sweat and tears – especially tears.'

'Never mind love,' I said. 'Let's go to 13 Mountain View and get the boiler going for a bath à la Mrs Richards. I tell you what, she would have loved to hear an account of today's happenings. It never rains except when it's pouring down, she would have said.'

15

'I had a man called Thomas in the surgery this morning,' said Eleanor when she came in for a lunchtime snack.

'That's an unusual name in Wales,' I replied.

'Very funny. I mention him because he told me you had christened his son not so long ago.'

'Sorry, love, for being flippant. Yes, I know him, Tom Thomas, ex prisoner-of-war in a Japanese camp. A delightful man who has been through hell.'

'I'm afraid he is destined for heaven before very long. I have arranged for an x-ray but I'm positive that he has cancer of the stomach. In an advanced stage, I would think. He was obviously in severe pain and should have been in bed, not in the surgery.'

For a few seconds I could not speak.

'Oh! That's not fair, Eleanor. To have survived all that torment to come home to a loving wife, who for a year or so had been hoping against hope that he was still alive. To find that hope fulfilled and now just after twelve months together to have him taken from her. It's not fair.

'You are the parson, Fred. I'm simply the doctor. It's you who has to justify God's ways to man. In defence of God might I suggest that at least he has given her a child who will be a great comfort to her in the years ahead.'

'Is there any chance that your diagnosis may be wrong?'

'From what he has told me about the symptoms of his illness and from what I can gather from my examination, I should be very surprised if I am wrong. He is going to hospital for an x-ray tomorrow. After that we shall know for certain. If it proves positive, they will keep him in hospital for surgery.'

'How on earth are they going to tell that poor woman that her husband is going to die? Or will they keep it from her?'

'That is the surgeon's problem. I suppose that he will have to judge by conversation with her whether she has sufficient resilience to take the shock of the news.'

'Elspeth Thomas is a strong character as far as I can see but whether she can face up to this atomic bomb in her life, I shouldn't like to say. I feel like going along to see them this afternoon on my way back from the Mothers' Union meeting.'

'Don't do that, love. Knowing that you are my husband they may smell a rat, if you'll pardon the phrase. I should leave any visit until he is in hospital. That is when you can be most useful.'

'And what about Tom himself? After all, he is the person who is going to die and who will have to make his peace with God.'

'Fred. That man has looked death in the face month after month in the loneliest of circumstances. At least he will be surrounded by love and his hand will be held by his dearest one. I'm quite sure he will cope. It's his wife who will need all the support she can get.'

Some weeks had passed since the church fête and Father Whittaker's mind was concentrated on Abergwylfa, his parish-to-be, rather than on Pontywen. Consequently all the donkey work became a burden, on my shoulders, while Charles Wentworth-Baxter took avoiding action on every possible occasion. This afternoon was no exception. It was supposed to be my day off and Charles was due to take the service at the Mothers' Union meeting in the church hall. A manufactured migraine confined him to his digs for the day. This was the third headache which had coincided with a parish duty in a fortnight. As Eleanor observed, a single-minded Vicar could have cured him much more rapidly than a neurologist.

'Help us to be faithful wives and loving mothers,' prayed Miss Jessie Philips (a retired schoolteacher), the enrolling member of the Mothers' Union branch, together with the thirty elderly ladies present. Miss Philips was the daughter of a Vicar, a tall, thin white-haired lady with piercing dark brown eyes which must have put the fear of God into every one of her pupils. It was evident that she regarded the members of the Pontywen branch of the MU as being in the category of Form 1 and liable for the same discipline.

My presence at the afternoon's proceedings was superfluous. All I had to do was to read a few prayers from the special service book and to give the blessing at the end. The President, who was a female Pooh-Bah, did everything else. She played the piano for the hymns, collected the money for the Christmas Club, read the lesson, introduced the speaker, thanked the speaker, organized the cup of tea and a biscuit, as well as supervising the washing up, not to mention the locking up.

'The King of Love my Shepherd is' was going too slowly for the pianist who banged on the instrument at an accelerated pace which left the congregation at least two bars behind and in breathless confusion. As I looked, at her, bent over the keys, the large bun of her white hair, bristling with fearsome looking hairpins, she appeared to be more like Katisha than Pooh-Bah.

When the hymn had raced to its conclusion, she moved quickly from the piano and introduced the speaker to her exhausted audience. 'I am sure you will all remember Mrs Butler who gave us such an interesting talk last year on the Women in the Bible. This afternoon she is going to talk about flower arranging in Church with special reference to wild flowers.'

The speaker was a large rosy-cheeked lady in tweeds, obviously as much a product of the countryside as the wild flowers which lay on the table beside some vases which had been borrowed from St Mary's.

'Good afternoon, ladies. How nice to be with you once again. This time something quite different from my last visit. Not the women in the Bible but the flowers of the field in the church. Here is a collection of wild flowers which can adorn the sanctuary as effectively as those from a florist. On the table are bladder campion, black horehound, herb robert, greater stitchwort, rosebay willow herb, ragwort, buttercup, ivy and of course, traveller's joy.'

By the time the lady finished her list, the MU members were beginning to look forward to their cup of tea. For the next half hour she indulged in several permutations of her specimens in the vases in front of increasingly restive spectators who looked as if they would have been glad if the flowers had been left in the fields.

'Finally, ladies, just as you can save money by using wild flowers for decoration, here are a few household tips to help in these days of austerity. First: dirty electric light bulbs. You know how unsightly they can be. If you want to stop flies dirtying your bulbs, smear them with camphorated oil.'

Her concluding suggestion caused me to stifle a guffaw by blowing my nose loudly. 'Now we all like to have our clothes smelling nice and sweet don't we? So don't discard any of your empty perfume bottles. Just take off the stoppers and put them in your drawers. You would be surprised to find what a difference that makes. I can vouch for that.'

Miss Philips rose to her feet immediately.

'Thank you, Mrs Butler for your helpful talk. We all now know what to do with our old scent bottles and how to use wild flowers to the glory of God. We shall finish with 'Now thank we all our God'.

This was sung with enthusiasm by the thirsty ladies excited at the prospect of the long awaited cup of tea.

'And now, I shall ask Mr Secombe to give us the blessing.'

Before the 'Amen' had time to die away, the President was into her stride once again. 'Mrs Harris and Mrs Williams will you please go to the kitchen? I shall be with you in two ticks. Thank you Mr Secombe, are you staying for the cup of tea?'

'My apologies, Miss Phillips. I have some visits to make before I go home.'

She looked at me as if I were a pupil who had fabricated an excuse to avoid a turgid lesson.

'We forgive you this time. Next time you must stay. I'm sure the members would love to have a chat with you.'

'I promise you, Miss Philips, that next time I shall stay, come what may. Oh, that rhymes doesn't it?' I said with a sickly smile.

'It does, doesn't it?' she replied with a deadpan face and went off into the kitchen.

When I came out from the claustrophobic atmosphere of the church hall into the sunshine of the late summer afternoon I was greeted by a shout from behind me. 'Hold on Fred, don't walk so fast. Anybody would think you were glad to escape.'

I turned round to behold the Reverend Godfrey Thomas, BA, BD Minister of Moriah Congregational Church. He was a short, plump, bespectacled man with the jam jar-bottomed variety of glasses. Jovial and verbose, Godfrey had been friendly to me ever since I had come to Pontywen. He had a keen sense of humour which had become apparent on my first meeting with him.

'What do you call yourself?' he had asked, 'Frederick or Fred?'

'Fred, of course,' I replied. 'To call myself Frederick would be to make a pompous ass of myself.'

'There's no danger in that for you but can you imagine what it means for me? My wife shortens my name, like most Welsh women. A couple called the other day about a wedding. I was upstairs getting my sermon ready in my study. Rhiannon shouted, lifting her eyes up to heaven,

'God, there's a couple here who want to get married!' The pair of them were out of the door and down the steps before you could say Jack Robinson.'

'Well, I gather your Vicar will be off before long,' he said. 'If he keeps on like this, it's a caravan he'll be needing not a Vicarage.'

'I'm afraid he misjudged Pontywen. He thought that Canon Llewellyn was an Anglo-Catholic instead of a central churchman. He'll settle in his new parish.'

'That's all gobbledegook to me, Fred. Dressing up and burning incense seems a strange way to be in touch with the Almighty. Still, there's no accounting for tastes.'

The Manse was only a few streets away from the church hall. 'How about a cup of tea before you get back home?' he asked.

'Thank you, Godfrey. I have a half hour or so to spare before my wife will be home.'

I was invited into the front room while Rhiannon Thomas was making the tea.

'You know, Fred. Sometimes I envy your lot,' he said, slumped in his armchair.

'In which way?'

'Well, you don't have to deal with the deacons. They run the chapel, I don't. They crack the whip and I have to jump to it. Some of them are good, wise men but there are a few who would find fault with any of the saints and dare I say it, even with Our Saviour Himself. Their knowledge of the scriptures is minimal but they think they know it all.'

'What Father Whittaker would call the arrogance of ignorance.'

'For once, I would agree with him. All I can do is to bite my tongue if I want to keep my job. It must have more bites in it than a toffee apple. There are times when I feel like coming over to your crowd but then I think if I could get a call to some other chapel I might be quite happy. Anyway there's one thing, Rhiannon is happy in Pontywen. She likes the place very much. We have been there ten years now and since we are in our fifties perhaps it is best to ignore the few and to enjoy the company of the others.'

'As a Curate, Godfrey, I know how you must feel. I have no say over what happens in this parish. However, the time will come when I shall be boss in my own parish. At least I hope so. My present Vicar found out that he could not do as he pleased in Pontywen. That's why he is going. So it may be that it's just as well that you put up with things as they are in Bethel.'

'You'd say Amen to that,' said Godfrey as his wife came into the room with a tray of tea and cakes.

'Fred says that it's just as well that we stay put in Bethel.'

'Of course,' replied Rhiannon. 'I think Pontywen people are very friendly. There are a handful who think they are God's gift to the universe but everybody else knows them for what they are. They may be deacons, but thank God, they are not in the majority. If they were we'd have left Bethel long ago.'

'Isn't she a wise woman? Not only that, she's a good cook as well. Try one of her Welsh cakes,' invited the Minister.

Rhiannon Thomas was considerably taller than her husband and even plumper. Her ample bosom gave her that comfortable look, appropriate to a Welsh grandmother but singularly inappropriate to her because the Thomases were childless.

'Fresh-made this morning,' she said as she offered me her produce. 'Godfrey was eating them hot off the bakestone, the greedy thing.'

'I used to do that when my mother was baking them. Come to think of it, I must get a bakestone to induce Eleanor to make Welsh cakes.

'With Mrs Secombe being a doctor, I don't suppose she gets a chance to do much cooking, poor soul.'

'That's very true but when she does cook, she is excellent – what you might call a good all-rounder.'

'Rhiannon is good all round,' said her husband, carving wide acres of space with his hands.

'If I were you, Godfrey Thomas,' she replied, 'I should refrain from making comments about people's shapes. At least I don't look like an overfed midget.'

'And I always thought you loved me,' the Minister remarked.

'But I do, my dear. It's surprising what you can do if you put your mind to it.' So saying she left the front room for the kitchen where the appetizing smell of the preparation for an evening meal was beginning to emerge from beyond its four walls.

'I understand the induction of Father Whittaker is next Monday week. Any news of the new appointment to Pontywen?' asked Godfrey.

'Not a dicky bird. It's the Bishop's turn to appoint. In that case you never hear of the probable runners in the Vicarage stakes. I should imagine that he will make a move some time next week.'

'All I can say is that I hope he will be easier to get on with than his predecessor. Whittaker gave me the impression that Nonconformity had no right to exist, that we were intruders on his cabbage patch. Perhaps this next one will be more friendly.'

'We shall soon know. One thing is certain. I'm positive the Bishop will not appoint another Anglo-Catholic. It is not fair to the parish or the priest. However, I must say that the present Vicar dug his own grave in Pontywen. He was very anxious to come here because he thought he could introduce vestments and ritual at once without opposition. It didn't take him long to learn that he was mistaken. In this parish it's the carrot that is needed not the bulldozer.

He raised his cup of tea. 'Here's to the cooperative carrot this time.'

'I drink to that,' I said and swallowed a mouthful of Rhiannon's strong brew.

'How did the Mothers' Union meeting go?' asked Eleanor when she arrived home.

'They were treated to a half-hour lecture on wild-flower arranging for the sanctuary followed up by a few household tips. The first required catching flies and smearing them with camphorated oil to protect electric light bulbs and the last involved placing stoppers of empty scent bottles in their drawers to sweeten them.'

'Highly original, not to say uncomfortable,' said my wife. 'However, I think you must have misunderstood what was said, deliberately, no doubt. By the way, I met Miss Jacobs when I was on my rounds. She is coming here at eight o'clock. Probate has been granted and she has settled up what little business was involved in her job as executor. So you'll know this evening whether you are a millionaire or not.'

It was typical of Annie Jacobs that she was knocking at our door at eight o'clock precisely, carrying a briefcase.

'I trust you have finished your evening meal,' she said when I opened the door to her.

'Some time ago, thank you Miss Jacobs. Would you come into the front room, please?'

She looked round with approval at the furnishings.

'I must say you have done wonders with this room. When you think what it was like when Miss Bradshaw lived in the house.'

'Here is the lady responsible for this.' Eleanor had entered the room with a tray containing a bottle of dry sherry, Miss Jacobs's favourite tipple, and three glasses.

'That is one reason why I am in no hurry to leave it. Fred would be off to Mount Pleasant View tomorrow but I feel I should enjoy the fruits of my labours for a little while at least, despite the lack of amenities.'

'And so you should, my dear.' The bookmaker sat down in an armchair with the briefcase on her lap.

'Would you care for a sherry?' asked my wife.

'Very much so. However, if you don't mind, I shan't indulge until I have finished what I have come here to do.'

'In that case I'll pour it out later.' Eleanor put the tray on the coffee table and sat beside me on the settee.

Miss Jacobs adjusted her spectacles and opened the brief-case. 'I have settled the few bills that May had not paid. The funeral expenses have been seen to. You can see the accounts now in a minute. Her savings were in the Post Office Savings Bank. I have filled in all the various forms and the result is that I can tell you that you will have one hundred and ninety-five pounds, three shillings and six-pence, in addition to the house. I have brought the money with me.'

To someone whose monthly cheque amounted to twenty-two pounds, the bequest sounded enormous. I whistled my astonishment.

'That's a lot of money, Miss Jacobs.'

'To a Curate, yes. To a bookmaker, no. I'm sure you will use the money wisely.'

'The first thing to do, Fred, is to open a bank account,' said Eleanor. 'I've had one for years.'

'Your parents saw to that, I expect,' I replied. 'Mine have never had enough money to indulge in such a luxury. What little money came in to our house was from my father's weekly wage. It was amazing how my mother coped with bringing up three children on less than three pounds a week. Yes, I shall open a bank account tomorrow. In the meanwhile let's drink a toast to the memory of Mrs Richards coupled with gratitude to you, Miss Jacobs for all your kindness.'

'I shall drink to that,' Eleanor proclaimed.

We drank to the memory of Mrs Richards. Eleanor and I drank a toast to Miss Jacobs. As we were drinking our third glass of Dry Fly sherry, the telephone rang. My wife answered it. The happiness in her face evaporated in an instant. 'Don't worry, Mrs Thomas, I'll be with you in a few minutes.' She put the receiver down.

'My apologies, Miss Jacobs, an urgent call. It's Tom Thomas, Fred. Apparently he is in agony. I'll phone the hospital to get a bed ready and an ambulance on the way.'

After she had done so, she hurried from the room and was gone.

'You have a splendid wife, Mr Secombe,' said our visitor. 'Well, I shall finish my glass and make my way home. Before that I had better give you your money.'

She produced a bundle of notes and proceeded to count out one hundred and ninety-five pounds. Then she handed me a small bag of silver containing three shillings and sixpence.

I looked at my unexpected wealth and said. 'Elspeth Thomas would be willing to forgo all of this and a lot more beside if she could have her husband restored to health.'

'Yes,' said Mrs Jacobs, 'health is much more important than wealth. Even a bookmaker recognizes the truth of that.'

She raised her glass and said. 'Here's to the recovery of Mr Thomas.

'It seems there is very little hope indeed,' I replied.

'You never know. Where's there's life there's hope,' she stood up, closed her briefcase and shook my hand. 'If there is to be no recovery then you will have to take over where your wife has left off. I don't envy you your job but I must say, you seem to cope with it very well.'

'Thank you, Miss Jacobs. I try to do my best.'

After she had left, I sat staring at the notes beside me on the settee. Years ago that money would have been much more than one year's wages for my father. I felt humbled and unworthy. After all, I had been with Mrs Richards for little more than twelve months, yet she had given me her life savings.

When Eleanor returned, I was still sitting glumly on the settee, looking more like someone who had lost a fortune rather than gained one.

'I've given him a pain killer injection,' she said. 'I expect they will do an exploratory operation first thing in the morning. All that will do will be to accelerate his end, which will be a mercy for him.'

'How is Elspeth? Is she aware that the end is near?'

'Her main concern at the moment is that his pain should be eased. She has gone with him to the hospital. I should imagine they will send her home and tell her to come in after the operation is over. At that stage the Surgeon will probably tell her the bad news. As you say she is a strong character who will not dissolve into hysterics but I think she will need you badly tomorrow afternoon.'

We prayed for Tom and Elspeth Thomas next morning at matins where Charles was present having made a full recovery from his 'migraine'. Father Whittaker informed us that he would be absent from parish duties for the rest of the week, but of course would be present for his last Sunday in Pontywen. I spent the morning giving Holy Communion to house-bound members of the congregation while Charles was scheduled to spend the day visiting in Llanhyfryd.

Eleanor came in at lunchtime with news that the operation had revealed extensive cancer originating from the stomach.

'The Surgeon has told Mrs Thomas what they have discovered. He said that she was very brave. She is at his bedside now. This is where you come in, Fred.'

Later that afternoon, I made my way slowly to the hospital, steeling myself for the encounter ahead of me. Tom Thomas had been put in a side ward where Elspeth sat holding the hand of her unconscious husband. She looked up and attempted a smile when I entered.

'I expect you know the circumstances, Mr Secombe.'

I nodded.

'He has been in pain for some time but wouldn't go to the doctor. He said he had been through a lot worse in the Prisoner of War Camp. All I hope is that he will not suffer for much longer. Tom has had more than his fair share of that.'

'That's very true. We said prayers for you both in church this morning.'

'Thank you. We'll need all the prayers we can get and so will our baby. I shall have to be father and mother to him, poor little boy.'

I sat alongside her in silence for some time. She was dry eyed and focussed all her attention on her husband's face, as if examining every detail of his features.

'Would you like me to say prayers with you?'

'Oh yes, please.'

I prayed for Tom, for her and her baby. Then we said the Lord's Prayer. Through all this, she never broke down. Her strength of will was incredible.

'I'll be in again tomorrow to have a word with Tom. If you need me at any time, don't hesitate to let me know.

'That's very kind of you, Mr Secombe. I appreciate that.'

As I was coming down the hill from the hospital, I met Full-Back Jones, the gravedigger, who was wearing a decent suit and sporting a collar and tie. To my amazement he had even shaved, but he had not gone so far as to insert his dentures.

'Where on earth are you going, all dressed up?' I asked.

Cardiff, for the boxing. You ought to come and see it one day. Do you good, boss. See life in the raw for a change.'

16

'Well, Vicar, it's almost a case of "hello and goodbye", as you might say.' David Vaughan Jenkins, People's Warden, was presiding at a presentation ceremony in St Mary's Church Hall after Father Whittaker's last service in Pontywen. There were more empty chairs than people.

'I know we have not seen eye to eye on many occasions, that's very true. All I can say is that I am sure you will be happier in your new parish than you have been here. It's more your cup of tea, as it were, with its High Church ways.

'One thing about you, Vicar, is that you are an honest man and always speak your mind. Another thing is the care you have shown for the sick. These things are important in a priest. Abergwylfa will be all the better for them.'

'We wish you every happiness in your new parish and would like you to accept this cheque as a token of our esteem.'

The cheque amounted to twenty-five pounds, collected from the few people who were prepared to give and including ten pounds from Sir David Jones Williams as a thank-offering for his departure.

John Whittaker looked around the almost empty hall.

'Thank you, Mr Vaughan Jenkins for your words and thank you all for this cheque. Yes, my stay has been a very brief one indeed but I have learnt much in that time and I hope I shall be a better priest as a result. The Bishop thinks that I shall have more to offer Abergwylfa than Pontywen. One thing I ask is that you will give my two colleagues every support until my successor arrives in the parish. Thank you, once again.'

He sat down amid applause which was polite rather than hearty and the brief ceremony was over.

Charles came back to Bevan's Row with Eleanor and myself, for a cup of coffee and a chat. He had heard a rumour that Elias Jenkins, an ecclesiastical martinet, was interested in coming to Pontywen.

'He may be interested but there's nothing he can do about it,' I said. 'It is the Bishop's turn to appoint and he would not take kindly to Elias putting his oar in. In any case he is the last type of incumbent to place in this parish. So sleep soundly, Charles. The bogey man won't get you.'

'Anyway, I wish his lordship would hurry up and put us out of our misery,' sighed my colleague.

'By the end of this week we shall know who it is. Not that I am in any kind of misery and I can see no reason why you should be. Unless, of course, you are fearful that you might have to work harder.'

'That's not fair, Fred.'

'Only playing, Charles. I know how you like hard work. So would you mind taking the sick communion this week. Here's the list. I'll do the hospital visiting. Oh, and there's a funeral on Wednesday at three o'clock. The name is Bevan – Agnes Bevan – an old lady who was living with her daughter at 14 Balaclava Street. So would you call to see Mrs Smith, the daughter, tomorrow afternoon?'

'Poor old Charles,' said Eleanor, 'and he only came in for a chat!'

Next evening there were almost as many empty seats on the bus, booked for Fathers Whittaker's induction, as there were in the hall for the presentation. Eleanor and I waved off the handful of parishioners plus Charles who was sitting glumly in the front seat. Then we were away in her car to St Peters, Abergwylfa, overtaking the parish contingent on the outskirts of Pontywen. After the Porthcawl outing I could not face another bus trip.

The Parish Church of Abergwylfa was on the side of a hill in a mining village and had been affected by subsidence. I was told of a wedding which had taken place there on a wet Saturday morning. The rain was coming through the roof and splashed into buckets, strategically arranged in the chancel. After the service the Vicar apologized to the bride and groom for the state of his church. 'Don't worry, Vicar,' said the bridegroom, 'this rain is just what we need to beat England this afternoon in Cardiff Arms Park.' Fortunately the induction had been blessed with a fine autumn evening.

As we entered St Peter's our nostrils were assailed by the stale smell of incense. Eight tall candles adorned the high altar, while numerous little votive candles were burning at the foot of a statue of the Virgin Mary in a corner of the nave. On the walls were garish representations of the stations of the Cross. 'This is what St Mary's Pontywen would have looked like ultimately, if Father Whittaker had had his way,' I whispered to Eleanor.

'In that case,' she replied, 'we would have been its sole occupants.'

She sat in a pew at the back of the church. Some thirty or so of the congregation had already taken their places, staking a claim to their own preserves. I walked down the aisle into the vestry which was at the south end of the chancel. John Whittaker came to greet me. He had been talking to a group of clergy whose thirty-nine buttoned cassocks indicated their churchmanship.

'Welcome to St Peter's, Fred. Where is Wentworth-Baxter?' he asked.

'He is coming on the bus with the Pontywen crowd,' I replied. 'I could not face another journey on a Welsh Greyhound coach.'

'Wise man. Let me introduce you to some of my friends.'

As he did so there was an influx of local clergy whose loud voices contrasted with the hushed tones of conversation, prior to their entry.

'Hasn't his Lordship arrived yet?' demanded Dan Williams the Rural Dean, Vicar of Treleddyn, a neighbouring parish. 'We'll have to give him his cards.' The Anglo-Catholic group looked at him as if he were something the cat had brought in, to quote a favourite phrase of my mother.

'His Lordship' arrived a few minutes later, followed by his chaplain who was carrying the case containing the Bishop's robes. Soon it was time to begin the service and there was still no sign of Charles. The Vestry prayer was said and we moved out in procession with the choir and servers into the church.

Halfway through the Bishop's address after the induction had been completed there was an incursion at the back of the church. The Pontywen party had arrived, led by Charles who was carrying his case and who looked considerably flustered. He stood in the aisle apparently undecided as to whether he should sit in a pew with the congregation or make his way into the vestry. Since the service was almost over, there was no point in his robing in time to sing the last hymn. However, common sense and Charles were strangers to each other. Ignoring the presence of the Bishop in the pulpit, my colleague marched down the aisle and disappeared into the vestry. By the time his Lordship was ending his sermon with an ascription of praise to the Almighty, he made his entry into the chancel with his surplice and stole awry, squeezing himself into a small space at the end of a choirstall, to the consternation of his neighbour and the amusement of the choir.

The newly inducted incumbent gave out the notices for the week, announcing that mass would be said daily and that next Sunday there would be low mass at eight o'clock and high mass at eleven o'clock with benediction at six o'clock. Then he invited us all to come for light refreshments in the church hall after service.

As soon as the final prayer was said in the vestry, Charles made a bee line for me. 'That stupid bus broke down not long after we left Pontywen. The driver had to phone for another bus to come and pick us up. It took absolutely ages to arrive and an old boneshaker it was.'

'Why on earth did you dress up just for the last hymn? Not only that, you came pounding down the centre aisle while the Bishop was preaching. It's a good thing for you that he always appears to be oblivious of anything or anyone, including the congregation. Another Bishop would have stopped in his tracks and glared at you, following up with a lecture in the vestry afterwards.'

'It's all right for you, Fred. I expect you were well in time for the induction. I wanted to be part of what was happening even if it was only for the last hymn.'

When I went to shake hands with Father Whittaker, he said. 'I see we had a typical Wentworth-Baxter episode in the service. I feel sorry with all my heart for the new man inheriting such a millstone round his neck.'

As I was unrobing, the Bishop came across to me. 'Mr Secombe, I should like to see you at my residence on Friday at eleven o'clock. There is something I should like to discuss with you. Is the day and time convenient?'

'Certainly, my Lord.'

'Good. I look forward to seeing you then.'

The congregation of St Peter's Church had spared no effort to make their light refreshments more like a meal. Home-made cakes were supplemented by sandwiches of various kinds. Contrasting starkly with the presentation ceremony in Pontywen which was devoid of even a cup of tea and a biscuit. It was obvious that Father Whittaker had come into a goodly heritage and that he was enjoying every minute of it, including being 'Fathered' by his new flock.

Throughout the refreshments my mind kept wandering to the unexpected appointment with the Bishop and what it could mean. 'Perhaps he is going to offer you Pontywen,' suggested Eleanor.

'Hardly, my love. After the short time I have been in holy orders. No way. It is probably he wants to give me the task of looking after the parish until the new man comes, as he did last year. Knowing what Charles is like, he will want to give me full power to take charge of him.'

When we went to see off the Pontywen crowd – all twenty-five of them – they had forgotten the disappointment of missing the service in the enjoyment of the splendid repast provided by Abergwylfa. 'We'll have to do something like this when we have our new Vicar inducted,' said Bertie Owen. 'Mind, I'm glad I don't have to worship in a church like that. I wouldn't go there anyway. I'd find somewhere else without pictures on the wall and where they didn't worship the Virgin Mary with candles.'

On Wednesday afternoon at four o'clock, Eleanor and I were sitting in the middle room drinking a cup of tea, prior to her stint at the surgery. There was a knock at the front door. It was Charles, clad in his cassock and carrying his surplice and scarf over his arm. His robes were discoloured with mud, it seemed. His face was grey.

'Is Eleanor in?' His voice was shaky.

'Yes, come on in, Charles. What on earth is the matter?'

I led him into the middle room.

'It looks as if you have a patient, love!' I took his surplice and scarf from him and then put a chair under his bottom. He winced as he sat down.

'Pour him a cup of tea, Fred,' said my wife. 'Now then, Charles, tell the doctor what has happened.'

'Well, I was taking that funeral service this afternoon – you know, the Agnes Bevan one – and I was walking in front of the coffin, reading the sentences from the Prayer Book. 'In the midst of life we are in death,' I said, and the next minute I was inside the grave. I had my head down, buried in the book as it were. I hadn't realized I was so near the end of the grave. Fortunately it wasn't a full-size grave. It was a second burial so I only went down a few feet. They soon pulled me out but I've bruised myself and I think I may have done something to my shoulder.'

'Let's have your cassock and your shirt off,' said Eleanor. She examined him thoroughly.

'You haven't broken any bones, Charles, you'll be pleased to know. I expect you will find plenty of bruises tomorrow but that's all.'

'All I can say,' I remarked, 'is that you are lucky it was Full-Back Jones who dug the grave. It could have been a lot deeper. What's more, you will become a legend in Pontywen. It was bad enough when I slid into a grave with two bearers, because one of Full-Back Jones's planks broke, but at least we were saved from falling into the bottom by those who supported us. That was a talking point in the town for some time. You have gone solo, head-first down to the bottom. That really is something.'

'It's not funny, Fred.'

'I didn't say it was. You are very lucky that you haven't broken any bones. On this occasion Full-Back won't have to take the blame, anyway. The fault lies with the Prayer Book which enticed you into the pit.'

'Shut up, Frederick,' said my spouse, 'and let the young man drink his tea.'

Charles sat in his chair, groaning and emptying his cup while Eleanor prepared to go to the surgery.

'Here you are,' she said to him when she came back to the room. 'Take these tablets and they will deaden any pain you may have. You will feel a different man in the morning. I'll give you a lift back to your digs once you have made yourself decent.'

'Don't bother to come to service tomorrow morning, Charles. Stay in bed and get over your ordeal,' I suggested as he left with Eleanor. The suggestion was sufficient to put some of the colour back in his cheeks.

My colleague stayed in bed for the whole of Thursday, and was not visible in church on Friday morning either. I called at his digs after service. Myfanwy Howells answered the door.

'He's making a meal of this,' she said, 'a four-course one, to say the least. I think you had better have a word with him.'

I went up to his room, knocked and entered without

waiting for an answer. He was sitting up in bed and reading a thriller with a breakfast tray containing two emptied plates and a cup and saucer on the table beside him.

'Charles, you look one of the healthiest invalids I have seen for a long time.'

'Looks are deceptive, Fred. I have been in a lot of pain.'

'Eleanor tells me that there is no reason at all now why you should not be up and about. I am on my way to the Bishop's palace in half an hour's time. So you are in charge of the parish for this morning and you can't take that responsibility if you are lying in bed. You had better obey doctor's orders and get up, ready for any emergency that may happen. You never know. You can read that thriller downstairs in any case. Come on, get cracking.'

He pulled back the bedclothes and manufactured a couple of groans as he moved his pyjama legs into the daylight.

'I'll do my best, Fred.' He stood up and limped towards his dressing gown which hung on the back of the door. 'Let me know what the Bishop has said, won't you?'

'I shall indeed, when I return this afternoon to find you back on your feet downstairs, washed and shaved, fully operational.'

The Bishop's palace was sheltered from the main road by a screen of tall trees. A long drive wound its way from the entrance gates past well kept hedges into the forecourt. It was a Georgian Mansion overlooking a large lawn bordered with Cypress trees.

As I made my way down the drive, I remembered the last time I had done so, an apprehensive young man with three college friends *en route* for the great moment in our young lives, our ordination. We had laughed and joked as we carried our suitcases, pretending that we had not a care in the world but with enough butterflies in our stomachs to supply Kew Gardens.

Today, apart from distant bird songs, the only sound to break the silence was the crunch of my feet on the gravelled forecourt. My heart began to beat faster as I pressed the doorbell button. The melodious tone echoed around the hall. A figure appeared from a side room. It was the slim form of the Bishop's secretary, a trim, middle-aged lady wearing rimles spectacles.

'Mr Secombe?' she asked.

'I am,' I said.

'The Bishop is on the telephone at the moment. If you would care to wait in the hall, I will come and collect you when he has finished his conversation. Please take a seat.'

A grandfather clock ticked slowly standing in a corner near the foot of the wide, carpeted stairs. Facing me was an oil painting of a former bishop, suspended over the ornate empty fireplace. The clock and the benign bishop had a soothing effect upon my pulse rate, which decelerated to normality by the time I was ushered into his Lordship's presence.

'Mr Secombe, my Lord,' announced the secretary.

The Bishop rose to his feet and left his desk to shake hands with me.

'Good morning, Mr Secombe. Good to see you again. Would you care for a coffee.'

'I'd love one, my lord.'

'Miss James would you bring us some coffee, please?'

'Milk and sugar?' inquired the secretary.

'Both, please.'

'Sit down, will you?' He indicated an armchair near the French windows which overlooked the lawn.

A long, lean, silver-haired, fresh-complexioned academic, the Bishop was a shy man with whom conversation was a difficult exercise. I sat down in the comfortable armchair while he resumed his seat behind his desk. A silence ensued. In the few interviews I had experienced with him, most of the time was occupied with periods of silence rather than words.

I waited for him to stop looking out through the window and to turn his attention indoors.

'Pontywen,' he said, suddenly, addressing a large blotting

pad in front of him. 'Pontywen,' he repeated, this time examining the ceiling.

'Not an easy parish.' He was looking out through the window once again. 'Canon Llewellyn had done wonders with it in his long incumbency but I am afraid that much was undone in a short time by Father Whittaker. Not, intentionally, of course. As far as he was concerned, with the best of motives.'

He returned his attention to the blotting pad.

'To repair the damage requires another long incumbency to restore trust between priest and people. I have given the situation much thought and prayer since the gift of the living is in my hands. Father Whittaker, as you are aware, was appointed by the Diocesan Board of Patronage. Now it is my sole responsibility to choose his successor.'

Another interminable silence, as he mused on the scene outside, his fingers toying with the pen on his desk.

'Sometimes in life one has to take what is known as a calculated risk. I feel the parish needs someone who knows it and its problems but one who is young and fresh enough to bring a new and lively approach in these postwar years. That is why, Mr Secombe,' swivelling his head around and looking me full in the face, 'I am offering the living of Pontywen to you.'

There was a knock on the door.

'Come in, Miss James,' called the Bishop.

The secretary placed my cup of coffee on a table beside the armchair. Had she put it in my hand, it would have been impossible for me to hold it. When she left the room the Bishop continued where he left off, anxious to get his decision off his chest. Decisions must have been painful to a man who had been cloistered in a college all his adult life until the Lord called him to high office.

'I know it must come as a shock to you as a young man with just four or five years in orders. However, I noticed how well you coped in the interregnum before Father Whittaker's induction. He tells me that you were also a great help to him during his short incumbency. Then, too, it was quite refreshing to see you acting out a parable with the children in Sunday School, even though your Vicar thought it unseemly.'

Silence number three arrived while we drank our coffee; my right hand had difficulty holding my cup and required the assistance of my left hand.

'There is one thing which has to be mentioned,' went on the Bishop, looking at his cup and saucer, 'and that is the problem of your colleague Mr Wentworth-Baxter. I know that he is somewhat inept and, worse still, lazy in the extreme. You have the advantage of knowing him very well. On the other hand, he may take the opportunity to presume upon your good nature. If you accept the living, you may be well assured that you have my full backing in anything you may do as far as he is concerned, even to the extent of giving him notice.'

He paused briefly this time.

'I think that's all. You do not have to give your answer now. You may wish to let me know after you have consulted your wife.'

'If you don't mind, my Lord,' I said, swallowing deeply, 'I can give you my answer now and that is I accept your offer of the living. It is a challenge I am prepared to take on. I know the people of Pontywen very well by now and I like them greatly. All I hope is that I can live up to the trust you have placed in me.'

He stood up smiling and held out his hand.

'Thank you Mr Secombe. I shall be in touch with you about the date of the induction later on. In the meanwhile perhaps you will contact the Board of Dilapidations and arrange with the Diocesan Architect to meet you at the Vicarage to consider anything that needs doing.'

I walked back down the drive in a daze. Before very long I would be a Vicar. It only seemed yesterday that I had walked down the drive as a young ordinand.

Travelling back to Pontywen in the train, I remembered

my journey to the station on my first day in the parish. Today there was no Canon Llewellyn to greet me and no Mrs Richards to receive me at my digs. Instead I was the new Canon Llewellyn and my dear wife had taken the place of my old landlady.

It was past one o'clock when I arrived at 11 Bevan's Row. Eleanor's car was outside. Instead of opening the front door with my key, I knocked. My wife's footsteps pattered down the hall. 'Lost your key again, have you?' she said.

'Not at all,' I replied. 'May I introduce the new Vicar of Pontywen?'

She flung her arms around my neck and kissed me until I was breathless. 'I told you so, but you wouldn't believe me.'

As we sat down to our lunch of tuna and tomatoes, supplemented by fresh bread from Evans the Baker, Eleanor was irrepressible.

'What an important person you are now, Frederick. Vicar-to-be and man of property. It's a good thing we did not start moving into Mount Pleasant View. Otherwise there would have been two moves in a few months.'

'Only one thing worries me, love and that is the problem of Charles. If I had a real curate with me, we could make our mark in Pontywen, but with Charles?'

'Dare I suggest the answer?'

'Go on, suggest it. You will do it anyway.'

'It's goodbye Curate for you now. If he doesn't behave, then it's goodbye Curate for him.'